KISSING IN MISTY HARBOR

Matt moved an inch closer to Sierra. "There is one good thing about all those tourists and sightseers flowing in and out of town."

"What's that?" She could tell by the warmth of Matt's smile she was going to like his answer.

"It brought you and me together." Matt leaned in and lightly kissed her.

She felt the warmth of his lips and wanted more. Matt's gaze was screaming heat. She wanted that heat. For days she had been thinking about their first kiss. It was inevitable that they were going to kiss. She had known that since sitting across from him at the Methodist church eating spaghetti. They had been surrounded by his family and half a dozen kids, and all she could think about was kissing Matt. She had almost gotten that kiss in his mother's kitchen early this evening. Matt had been a breath away from taking her into his arms when Ned had ruined the moment.

"Is that how they kiss in Maine?"

Matt slowly shook his head and smiled. "No, I didn't want to frighten you off."

"I'm not running, Matt."

Just to prove her point, she slid the tip of her tongue over her lower lip . . .

Books by Marcia Evanick

Catch of the Day

Christmas on Conrad Street

Blueberry Hill

A Berry Merry Christmas

Harbor Nights

A Misty Harbor Wedding

Published by Zebra Books

A Misty Harbor Wedding

Marcia Evanick

ZEBRA BOOKS
Kensington Publishing Corp.
www.kensingtonbooks.com

ZEBRA BOOKS are published by

Kensington Publishing Corp.
850 Third Avenue
New York, NY 10022

All Kensington titles, imprints, and distributed lines are available
at special quantity discounts for bulk purchases for sales promo-
tion, premiums, fund-raising, educational, or institutional use.

Special book excerpts or customized printings can also be cre-
ated to fit specific needs. For details, write or phone the office
of the Kensington Special Sales Manager: Attn. Special Sales
Department. Kensington Publishing Corp., 850 Third Avenue,
New York, NY 10022. Phone: 1-800-221-2647.

Zebra and the Z logo Reg. U.S. Pat. & TM Off.

First Printing: December 2006
10 9 8 7 6 5 4 3 2 1

Printed in the United States of America

Chapter One

The gravel road that wound its way up to the old light-house was in dire need of a grading job. The heavy storm that had blown through the town two days ago had washed major ruts into the road, and the early morning darkness was making driving difficult. Matthew Porter shifted the truck into a lower gear and tried not to spill his hot coffee all down the front of him. He wanted the caffeine in his stomach, not poured all over the crotch of his jeans.

Matt knew this particular road like his own driveway. He had traveled it while riding anything from a broken-down old bike when he was eight to a Honda motorcy-cle he had driven for two years back when he had been in his early twenties. He had spent many an hour sitting up on Carrie's Hill watching the sun come up and drink-ing his first cup of coffee. There was nothing more beau-tiful or spectacular than a Maine sunrise. It helped put the world into a perspective he could understand.

In the predawn light he steered his truck over the last rise in the road and frowned. A fancy red SUV was parked in front of Misty Harbor's lighthouse. He never ran into anyone at the lighthouse at dawn, except once in a while one of the deputies patroling the area or catching a catnap. This morning was different.

Nothing different ever happened in Misty Harbor, especially to him. His life was as predictable as the sun rising in the east.

Matt parked his truck and glanced across the mist-shrouded grass to the small rise that was known by the locals as Carrie's Hill. In the ever-increasing light he saw a woman sitting on a blanket cradling a cup between her hands and looking back at him. A child was asleep next to her on the blanket. The woman didn't appear to be lost.

For one fanciful moment he wondered if she was waiting for him. All his dreams were spread out before him, being lightened by the rising sun. It was as if he had stepped into an alternative reality and he had been granted his every wish: the lighthouse, the beautiful woman, and even the child.

Matt shook his head to clear away those uncharacteristic whimsical thoughts and returned to reality. He was about as fanciful as an NFL linebacker. He blamed his active imagination on the lack of coffee. It was payback for leaving his place without the first cup of caffeine flowing through his blood stream. But he had been in a hurry to watch the sun crest the horizon.

He held his still-filled cup of coffee in one hand, reached for the Thermos with the other, and got out of the truck. He could either go find another peaceful, quiet spot to enjoy the sunrise, or he could go make nice with the tourist. The woman wasn't from around there. He knew every female within ten miles between the ages of twenty and forty.

People who got up before the crack of dawn just to see the sunrise interested him. All three of his brothers usually got up while it was still dark out, but not a one of them made time to appreciate the beauty of the new day's arrival. His brothers were always too busy getting ready for work and to start their day.

He was curious as to what had made the woman and child leave their beds and head for Carrie's Hill, and who had told them this was the best spot in town to watch the sun rise above the horizon. It wasn't like the lighthouse was the town's hot spot.

Misty Harbor didn't have a hot spot, just a couple of warm ones, depending on who you were and what you were looking to do. The Catch of the Day restaurant was the place to go if you were in the mood for a great meal that wasn't served with french fries or in a bag. Tourists flocked to Lawrence Blake's Whale Watching Boat Tours like lemmings off a cliff, paying a nice chunk of change to hopefully spot one of the many whales that fed off the Maine coast during the warm summer months. For those of less discernable taste there was the One-Eyed Squid north of town. There, one could always find a cold beer, a challenging game of pool, or a bar-room brawl, depending on one's mood.

While all the town's brochures mentioned the light-house and its 180-year history, none of them raved about the beauty of the sunrise. The tourists flocked to Cadillac Mountain on Mount Desert Island to catch the first glimpse of the rising sun, not Carrie's Hill. Carrie's Hill was his secret.

So who's been spreading his secret to the summer migration? He headed for the woman huddled in her pale pink hooded sweatshirt.

He was a couple feet away from the quilt when he saw the wariness in her expression. For the first time he realized her vulnerable position. She was a lone woman, with a small child on a deserted cliff overlooking the Atlantic Ocean with a strange man approaching. He watched as one of her slender hands slipped into the front pocket of the sweatshirt.

He stopped. "Part of me is hoping you're smart enough to be carrying a can of pepper spray or something that would help you out if you were in trouble." He gave her what he hoped was a reassuring smile. "The other part of me is praying you're not one of those people who shoots first and asks questions later."

She kept her hand in the pocket. "I'd be stupid to comment on what exactly is in my pocket, wouldn't I?"

"Someone taught you right." Matt smiled at the touch of humor lightening her words. He could see her stunning face and the smile twitching at the corner of her mouth. It probably had been her husband, and the father of the child laying beside her, who had given her a can of mace and safety tips. With a yellow blanket tucked up to the child's chin, he couldn't tell if it was a boy, or a girl with really short hair.

He gave her another nonthreatening smile but didn't step closer. "Matthew Porter, born and raised in Misty Harbor. Anyone in town can vouch for me."

"Sierra Morley, and the town's still tucked in their beds. It would be kind of hard to ask them."

"So why aren't you?" He chuckled at the child. "Someone obviously is still visiting with Mr. Sandman."

"My son, Austin." Sierra placed the empty cup on the blanket next to her and then reached over to brush a lock of brown hair off her son's brow. "Half an hour ago he was wide awake and pleading to see the sunrise."

Matt glanced over his shoulder at the pinkish-orange light filling the distant horizon. "Well, you might want to wake him up, then. The show is about to start." He had never shared a sunrise with anyone before. "Want some company?"

Sierra looked hesitant. He didn't blame her. He couldn't imagine what her husband was thinking, allowing her to leave their bed without him. Some men didn't use the sense they were born with.

"Who's that, Mommy?" Austin sat up, rubbed his eyes, and stared up at him.

"Matt Porter." He squatted so his height wouldn't look so intimidating to the small child. Six feet three inches was a long way for a child to look up. "I come here all the time to see the sunrise."

Austin's eyes grew wider. "You do? Why?"

"Because it's the best part of the day." Matt couldn't help but grin at the boy. Austin had a severe case of bed head. "Why did you want to see the sun come up?"

"Because my mommy said it looks like it rises right out of the ocean."

"That it does." Austin looked a little too young to grasp the concept of orbits and planetary movements. Matt pointed out to the horizon. "Keep your eye on that spot right there."

"Where?" Austin pushed aside the blanket and stood up. "I don't see it."

"That's because it's not up yet." Matt positioned the boy in front of him and pointed again. "See where all the pink and orange is? Right where the ocean meets the sky."

Austin squinted. "How come all the clouds are pink? The sun's yellow and clouds are post-to-be white."

Sierra chuckled and stood up to stand next to her son. "That's his father coming out of him. Jake would question the devil himself."

So much for that fantasy that Austin's father wasn't in the picture. The lighter it got, the more beautiful Sierra became. Her eyes were sea-tossed gray and she had a pair of legs on her that went halfway to heaven. Sierra Morley was five feet ten inches of willowy curves and an impossibly long blond ponytail.

Matt pulled his gaze off of Sierra's face and smiled at her son. "There's nothing wrong with having a good curiosity. Keep watching where all the pink and orange is. That's where the sun will rise." He made sure the boy was looking in the right direction. "The clouds are all pink and orange because of the way the light is hitting them."

"Why?" Austin didn't take his eyes off the distant horizon.

"Something about particles in the atmosphere." Matt wasn't sure if that was exactly right. Tenth-grade science had been many years in his past, and he had been more interested in football and girls than in what the teacher had been lecturing.

Before Austin could question him further, the top of the sun rose above the misty horizon. With the light reflecting off the mist and the water, it did appear as if the sun was rising magically from the depths of the ocean.

"I see it, Mom!" Austin started to jump up and down and pointed out toward the sea. "Do you see it, Mom? Do you?"

"Yes, I see it." Sierra was laughing at the sight of her son's excitement.

Matt hadn't seen a kid this excited since Christmas morning at his brother's place. His five-year-old nephew, Tyler, nearly wet himself when he saw all the presents Santa had left under their tree. "Easy there, Austin. The sun comes up this way every morning."

"Four-year-olds get excited easily." Sierra was still laughing with her son.

"I have two nephews and two nieces. I've seen excitement before."

"Oh, no children of your own?" Sierra grabbed the back of Austin's sweatshirt when he started to head down the hill toward the cliffs. "Austin, I told you before, you must stay up here with me. It's too dangerous near the edge."

"Your mother's right, Austin. It's not safe." He glanced at Sierra's left hand but didn't see a wedding band or an engagement ring. She was wearing a silver and turquoise ring on one of her other fingers, though. Interesting, but it didn't mean anything.

"I'm not married, so no children." He wasn't about to tell her that his mother would wipe the floor with his sorry butt if he had gotten a woman pregnant and not married her. Peggy Porter was a force to be reckoned with when things didn't go her way. All four of her sons, and husband, made sure things went Peggy's way.

"It's getting bigger! It's getting bigger!" shouted Austin, almost breaking free of his mother's grip.

"Hey, take it easy. The sun's not going anywhere." He glanced at the quilt still spread out on the ground. "Why don't we sit down on Carrie's Hill and watch it come all the way up?"

"Carrie's Hill?" Sierra looked intrigued, while her son still looked like he wanted to join the sun out in the middle of the ocean. Sierra gently guided her son to the blanket and made him sit next to her.

Matt sat on the edge of the faded quilt. There was no sense in getting the seat of his jeans damp. "We're sitting on it. This little rise is known by the locals as Carrie's Hill."

"Who's Carrie?" Sierra asked.

"Who *was* Carrie." Matt looked at Austin, but the boy wasn't paying him the least bit of attention. He was still fascinated by the fiery ball rising from the sea. The sun appeared to have molten gold dripping off of it and back into the ocean. "Carrie Porter was my great, great, I think another great is in there, grandmother. She was married to the first Horatio Porter."

"How many Horatio Porters were there?" Sierra looked amused but was polite enough not to laugh at the name.

"Four." He was still extremely thankful that his grandfather, Horatio the fourth, hated the name and had refused to carry on the family tradition of naming one of his sons Horatio. With a name like Horatio he would have had to learn how to fight at a lot younger age.

"Carrie's Horatio was a captain of a ship that transported lumber down the coast to the major cities, like Boston and New York. When his ship was due back she used to come up here so she would be the first to spot his ship. Even after the kids started to come, she used to haul them all up here to look for their dad.

"Rain, snow, or heat of summer—it didn't matter. Carrie had promised her husband she would be the first to spot his ship, and Horatio had promised to always return. Family legend has it that one of her mad buckboard dashes down to the harbor to greet his ship put her into early labor. By the time Horatio docked and was able to leave the ship, he had a new baby daughter waiting for him in the harbormaster's office. Since Carrie wouldn't break her promise, dear old great-great-Grandpop had to time his trips better after that. It had been a hard life back then."

"Is this the part where you tell me she died here waiting for his ship, which was lost at sea, to return?" Sierra's expression said it all. She was waiting for a typical dismal Hollywood ending.

"Nope." He grinned. "Carrie and Horatio had seven children and lived a good life well into their eighties."

Sierra looked like she either wanted to hit him or laugh. "You did that on purpose, didn't you?"

He couldn't help but chuckle. "Did what?"

"Look, Mom," cried Austin. "It's almost out."

Sierra dutifully looked where her son was pointing. "It sure is, sweetie." Seeing the excitement on Austin's face as the sun rose from the ocean made the cross-country trip to Maine worth it. The jet lag didn't bother her, but Austin's internal clock was all messed up. Nothing but her son could get her out of bed at this ungodly hour.

She glanced over at Matt Porter and thought about all the things that might get her *into* a bed. The handsomely rugged jean-clad man just might rank very high on that list. Usually it was total exhaustion that had her thinking about a nice soft mattress and a down comforter. This morning her hormones had decided to leave common sense behind when they went on their flight of fancy. Either that or there was something in Misty Harbor's water supply.

She must be more tired than she had thought. Never before had she had indecent thoughts about a total stranger. She shook her head to dislodge those unsettling images and muttered, "I must need more caffeine."

Matt held up a gray Thermos. "It's black with no sugar, but I'm willing to share."

Everyone knew you didn't take candy from a stranger, but she wasn't sure if the same applied to coffee. She watched as he poured some into his own cup and took a sip. In today's world you couldn't be too careful, but if he was drinking the coffee, it had to be safe. She held out her empty cup. "Thanks."

"My pleasure." Matt filled her cup with the remaining coffee and recapped the Thermos. "It's not every morning I get to share the sunrise with such enchanting company." Matt's gaze was on her son.

"Mom, are the whales awake yet?" Austin was squinting and gazing out at the ocean. "I don't see them yet."

She heard Matt chuckle as she followed her son's gaze. "I don't think we'll be able to see them from here, hon. We're too far away."

She was surprised to see quite a number of boats making their way out of the harbor and into the open waters. Obviously no one in Misty Harbor liked to sleep. "Look at all the boats, Austin. Can you count them all?"

Her son started to count and she knew exactly where he was going to mess up: fourteen. For some reason her son skipped from fourteen to twenty every time. If she prompted him by saying fifteen, he would repeat it after her and then skip to twenty.

Without her prompting, Austin continued to count as his finger pointed out each boat, ". . . twelve, thirteen, fourteen, twenty!"

Matt chuckled into his cup and hurriedly took a sip.

"Very good, Austin." She gave him a big squeeze. "Maybe, if you ask nicely, Mr. Porter would tell you what kind of boats they are." Surely anyone born and raised on the coast of Maine knew something about boats. She knew the difference between a tug boat and a canoe, but that was about as far as she would trust her nautical knowledge.

"Call me Matt, and you don't even have to ask, Austin." Matt pointed to a small dark green and white boat that was the closest to the shoreline. "That little one is a lobster boat."

Austin frowned. "Is not."

She glanced at her son in surprise. Austin wasn't the argumentative type. He might ask questions until she was ready to pull her hair out, but he didn't sass back. "Austin, why isn't it a lobster boat?"

"Lobsters are red with little eyes and big claws." Austin held out his hands and made pinching motions with his fingers. "You ate one last night, and it tasted yucky."

"You had a lobster on the coast of Maine, and it tasted yucky?" Matt sounded like he couldn't believe it.

"The lobster had been delicious and worth flying three thousand miles for. Austin took one bite of my dinner and declared it *yucky*. He preferred his fish sticks and macaroni and cheese."

She turned back to her son, who still looked bewildered. "The boat down there catches the lobsters and brings them to the restaurant, where people eat them for dinner."

"Do lobsters eat worms like fishes?" Austin was watching the small boat carefully.

"No, lobsters are caught in traps that lay on the bottom of the ocean." Matt squatted next to Austin and pointed near the boat. "See those yellow, red, and blue things floating on the water? They are buoys, and attached to them is a real long piece of rope that is also tied to the trap. Each lobster fisherman has his own colors so he'll know which traps are his."

"Mom, can we go get a lobster?" Austin stood back up so he could get a better look.

"I'm afraid not, hon. We don't have a boat." She had taken Austin fishing once before, on Lake Tahoe in Nevada. The entire morning had been a disaster. She couldn't bring herself to bait the hooks with live worms, and the fish hadn't been particularly fond of bologna sandwiches. There was no way she was handling a live lobster or throwing one into a pot of boiling water.

"If you're staying in town for a while I'm sure you can find someone to take you out for a couple hours. Just ask around down at the docks." Matt looked pleased with himself for coming up with that solution.

She knew there was a look of horror on her face, but she didn't care. Austin started to tug on the sleeve of her sweatshirt and beg, "Please, please, please. Can we, Mom?"

"Umm . . . then again, maybe you won't." Matt must have noticed her expression. "What about your dad, Austin? Maybe he can find a boat and take you out."

"Daddy isn't here." Austin released her sleeve. "He lives in Texas."

"Oh, he couldn't come on vacation with you?" Matt was looking at her, not her son.

"We're divorced." She pretended to ignore the smile tugging at the corner of Matt's mouth.

"How long are you both in town for?" Matt's short dark blond hair was gently tossed by the morning breeze, while his light blue eyes danced with interest.

She looked like hell from lack of sleep, while he looked like an L. L. Bean model selling sex on a stick. "The entire month of August and up until Labor Day weekend." Six glorious weeks nestled in a small fishing village on the coast of Maine. Who could ask for anything more? When the opportunity had come up, she had jumped at the chance.

"Where are you staying? Not at the local Motor Inn, are you?"

"No, I've rented a house on Hamilton Street." She had spotted the Motor Inn while exploring the town yesterday afternoon. It wasn't the kind of place she would willingly stay in for six days, let alone six weeks.

"Whose? My parents live one street over on Pepperell."

"Kathy and Kurt Albert. They left for Colorado yesterday, about two hours after we arrived. They're visiting their daughter and grandchildren out there."

"Jennifer? I heard she just had twin girls."

"You heard right. Kathy had to show me about a dozen photos she printed off the computer before she left." She smiled at the image of the refrigerator back at the house. The entire front of it was covered with baby photos and crayon drawings. Kathy and Kurt now had eight grandchildren. The Alberts' home was warm, inviting, and totally comfortable. It was the perfect home to vacation in.

"Mom, what's that boat?" Austin was pointing to a large fishing boat leaving the harbor.

"That's a tuna boat." Matt grinned, stood up, and waved. "Listen, Austin."

In the distance there was a loud mournful cry of a boat horn. Austin's eyes grew wide. "They see us?" He jumped up and down and started to wave wildly.

"They sure do." Matt swooped Austin up and placed him on his shoulders.

"They can see us all the way up here?" She shaded her eyes from the rising sun and tried to see the people on the boat. The horn sounded again as she spotted what might have been a man in the wheelhouse. He was the size of an ant. "How can they see us?"

"They know where to look." Matt lowered Austin back onto his feet as the tuna boat throttled up its engine and headed out to sea. "That was my parents. They always look up here when they head out."

"Both of your parents are fishermen?" Having a dad as a fisherman was one thing, but his mother?

"Yep, mainly tuna." Matt chuckled at Austin, who was wildly waving to another boat.

"Your dad's the captain, and what . . . your mom is the

first mate?" It sounded kind of sweet to her. With all the kids grown and out of the house, mom went fishing with her husband to keep him company. Not a bad way to spend your day.

Whatever she said must have been funny. Matt started to laugh hysterically. "What's so funny?" Sierra felt her lips twitching. Matt had a wonderful, strong laugh. She wanted to laugh with him, but she didn't get the punch line. Austin didn't seem to have her problem. Her son stopped waving at boats and joined Matt in laughing.

"Don't ever let my mom hear you call her the first mate." Matt laughed again at the thought.

"Why?" Maybe it was an inside joke that only people who lived on the coast understood. Thirty-one years of moving about the country had taught her one thing. Different regions of America had different ways of looking at things.

"She's the one who taught my dad the ropes in the business. They own the boat together and are cocaptains, because my father is just as stubborn. Neither would settle for being first mate."

She stared at Matt and wondered what kind of woman had raised him. The mothers in her world were on boards of charities and volunteered at their children's private schools. The women she knew might order tuna in a five-star restaurant but wouldn't know the first thing about catching one. "Your mother sounds like a very interesting woman."

"That she is. You should meet her sometime." Matt squatted down next to Austin and pointed out one of the ships still docked. "See that shiny white and black boat down there?"

"Yes," answered Austin.

"That's Lawrence Blake's whale-watching boat. He handles the boat and about twenty passengers at a time.

His nephew is a great guide. You get your money's worth, and you just might see a whale or two."

"Really?"

"Really." Matt stood back up and looked at her. "If you get seasick I would recommend taking something for that before you get on the boat. Lawrence has one speed, full throttle, and the best place to spot a whale is their feeding grounds, about twenty, thirty miles off the coast."

"Can we go, Mom?" asked Austin.

"I think we can manage that while we're in town." She didn't get seasick and Austin would love the adventure. "Any other suggestions, Mr. Porter?"

"Call me Matt, please. This coming weekend is the annual Maine Wild Blueberry Festival. You can't miss that."

"What do you all do? Sit around and eat muffins?" How did one have a festival about a fruit? A small purplish-blue fruit at that.

"The day starts off with a parade down Main Street." Matt looked amused.

"A parade?"

"Marching band and all. The theme of course is blueberries. There are a couple floats sponsored by the various growers and agricultural agencies. Parents get into it by making costumes and competing for prizes, and the spectators cheer wildly for the cutest muffin or cobbler."

"You're serious, aren't you?" No one could make that up on the spur of the moment. "How does one dress a child as cobbler?" The thought boggled her mind.

"With great difficulty and flair." Matt chuckled. "It's hard to explain, but it's something you don't want to miss. After the parade it's on to the town square, where there'll be tables set up selling everything from pottery to preserves."

"All blueberry, of course." She was starting to look forward to the coming weekend and counting the different things one could do with a berry.

"It's their special day." Matt seemed tolerantly amused by the whole thing. "Later that night there will be live music at the gazebo in the park and the Methodist church has a spaghetti dinner fund-raiser."

"Let me guess, with blueberry pie for dessert?" She could picture it now.

Matt's smile could melt polar icecaps. It was doing one heck of a job on her knees. "Ah . . . no. By dinnertime everyone is kind of sick of blueberries. The Women's Guild usually gives you a choice between chocolate cake or orange Jell-O."

She tried not to laugh. "Why orange Jell-O? Why not cherry or lime?"

"They did a survey a couple years back. Seems orange is the overwhelming favorite flavor of Jell-O." Matt glanced at her son, who was now busy waving to every boat leaving the harbor. "Austin, what flavor Jell-O do you like, red, orange, or green?"

"Orange." Austin looked around like he expected someone to hand him a bowl and a spoon. His look of excitement faded when no bowl of Jell-O was forthcoming. "How come no one is blowing their horn at me?"

"They aren't looking up here, hon." She ruffled her son's hair. "All the people on those boats going out are doing their jobs. They're busy getting ready to catch all kinds of fish for us to eat."

"Why don't they just fish there?" Austin pointed to the dock area.

"That's the harbor, Austin." Matt squatted next to the

boy. "All the docks and the surrounding water is known as a harbor. It's protected on three sides by land, and it's really deep." Matt's fingers pointed toward the sun. "That's the Atlantic Ocean. That's where the whales live."

Austin glanced from the harbor to the horizon and then back again. "Boats live there"—he pointed to the docks—"and whales live out there." He motioned to the horizon. "What lives there?" Austin waved to the body of water on their right.

She looked where her son was pointing. It was a huge area of water, but off in the distance she thought she picked out a small island or two. The lighthouse was sitting on a high point that jutted out into the sea. Below them, she could hear the sound of waves crashing against the rocks.

"That, my new friend, is Mermaid Bay." Matt looked serious.

"Do mermaids live there?" Austin shielded his eyes with his hand as he looked out over the bay.

"Legend has it that they do." Matt gave her a quick wink. "That's how the bay got its name."

"Have you seen one?" Austin looked thrilled with the idea.

"Not a one, and believe me, I've looked for years." Matt stood up to his full height and stretched. "I've got to be heading off to work, Austin. I'm sure if your mom asks around down at the docks, someone can take you out mermaid watching." Matt looked at her. "Or, if you're not in a hurry and can wait until Sunday, I can do the honors."

"Really? You have a boat?" Austin's words were tripping over each other in his excitement.

"No, but I know where I can borrow one." Matt's gaze

met hers. "Don't hound your mom, Austin. Let her decide which would be best."

She wasn't positive, but she thought she just had been asked out on a date. A family date. One that included her son. Now that was a change. Most men preferred her undivided attention and privacy. "Thank you, Matt. I'm sure we'll run into you during the blueberry celebration." She wasn't sure if she was going to accept his generous offer to take them mermaid watching or not. "I'll give you our answer then."

"Great." Matt gave Austin a pat on the shoulder. "Nice meeting you, Austin."

"You too, Mr. Porter."

Matt shook his head. "The name's Matt." Matt gave her a long look before slowly smiling. "I'll see you on Saturday."

She stood there watching Matt walk away and hid her smile behind her cup. Matt's coffee tasted horrible, but what he lacked in culinary skills, he more than made up for in the physique department. What Matt did for the back end of a pair of jeans should be classified as the eighth wonder of the world.

Chapter Two

Sierra took one look at her son's mouth and tried not to cringe. It was going to take a week for his purple lips and tongue to fade back to normal. Who knew blueberries had such staining power? She glanced around the park and shrugged. Every kid there had the same purple lips and none of the other mothers looked overly concerned. Maybe they all dipped their kids into a vat of bleach before tossing them into the tub at night.

So far Austin had consumed a blueberry snow cone, two muffins, and three cups of blueberry punch. He was now eyeing a vendor selling peanut butter and blueberry jam sandwiches. It was lunch time, but one had to wonder how many more blueberries he could fit into his little tummy.

"I don't know, hon. Are you sure you want a peanut butter and jelly sandwich? They have hot dogs and hamburgers over there." She pointed to a stand set up by the local Lions Club. Half a dozen men were gathered around a fire pit that was billowing smoke, flipping burgers and slapping hot dogs onto buns. They appeared to be doing a brisk business. Experience had taught her that if all the locals were lined up at that stand, that was where she wanted to eat.

"We are post-to-be eating blueberries, Mom." Austin tugged his baseball cap, embroidered with MAINE and a humpback whale underneath. The cap was a souvenir from the whale-watching adventure they had gone on Thursday.

Ever since Austin had spotted a finback whale, he hadn't stopped talking about whales, boats, and all the other wonders the ocean might hold, real or imaginary—especially mermaids and a talking fish named Nemo. This eventually led the conversation to Matt Porter and his promise to take them out on a boat looking for mermaids. Her son had been looking for the handsome stranger they had met at the lighthouse all morning long. So far, Matt was a no-show.

She didn't know who was more disappointed, her or her son.

"Tell you what, hon. How about I buy you a hot dog and a bag of chips with a blueberry lemonade?" She eyed the burgers and watched as they were slapped onto thick buns with slices of tomato, cheese, onions, and lettuce. Not a blueberry in sight. Her stomach rumbled with delight.

It took Austin all of two seconds to make up his mind, "Okay."

They walked over to the Lions Club stand and took their place at the end of the line. The first week of August in Maine was gorgeous. The sun was shining and a light cool breeze was blowing in off the water. Perfect shorts and tank top weather. By this evening, when the sun went down, she would have to change into jeans and a sweatshirt.

The Alberts' home didn't have air conditioning, and at first she had thought that might be a problem in August.

The past couple of nights she had slept with the windows wide open and buried under the blankets. It was the best sleep she'd had in ages, and she particularly loved waking up in the morning to the cries of the gulls as they went about their morning business.

"You want ketchup on your hot dog?" she asked. Sometimes Austin liked mustard, but usually it was plain ketchup.

She was startled and quickly spun around when a deep, familiar voice behind her said, "I'm a mustard and relish man, myself."

"Matt!" shouted Austin with delight as he turned with her. "You came."

"Sure did." Matt nodded down to the small boy at his side. "Austin, I would like you to meet my nephew, Tyler. He's five years old. I figured you two might have a lot in common."

"Hi," said Austin as he moved closer to his mom's leg. "I'm four."

"Do you live here?" asked Tyler.

"No, we're visiting." Austin reached for her hand.

Her son was always shy around other kids. Austin didn't make friends easily, because they usually didn't stay in one place long enough. It was the main drawback of the family business. The intense traveling and moving was the reason she employed Rosemary Thatcher as Austin's nanny. That and the fact she would be lost without Rosemary.

When she had been seven and her mother had passed away, Rosemary Thatcher had become her nanny, friend, and surrogate mother. Sierra could barely remember her own mother, but she could describe in detail all the lectures Rosemary had given her over the years. She also remembered all the warm praise, huge bear hugs, and the love. She wanted her son raised with the same memories.

Rosemary was sixty-one and, even though she would never admit it, getting a little bit slow to be running after a very active four-year-old. When Sierra and Austin headed for Maine, Rosemary flew to Toledo, Ohio, for a long-overdue visit with her family. She missed Rosemary's company, but she was thrilled to have this time alone with her son. Austin was growing up so fast.

"Hi, Tyler. I'm Sierra, Austin's mom." She could see the family resemblance between Tyler and his Uncle Matt. Both were on the tall side and had dark blond hair and the most amazing light blue eyes. The square, stubborn-looking jaw had to be a Porter trait.

"Hi. Who are you visiting?" asked Tyler.

"We don't know anyone here. We're just visiting your town and the surrounding area for a couple weeks." She smiled down at the boy. "It's a wonderful place to call home, Tyler."

"We went out on a really fast boat and saw a whale," added Austin, trying to gain back Tyler's attention.

"What kind?" Tyler's face lit up with excitement.

"Finback," answered Austin, who seemed very proud of the fact that he remembered what kind of whale it had been.

"No, what kind of boat?"

"If it was real fast, I'm betting it was Lawrence Blake's." Matt ruffled the top of his nephew's head until dark blond hair was standing up in all directions. "Tyler's the boat fanatic of the family. The faster it goes, the better he likes it."

"Don't you like whales?" Austin seemed confused as to why Tyler wouldn't be excited about the whale he had spotted.

"Whales are okay, but boats are cooler. You can't ride a whale." Tyler glanced up at his uncle. "Can I have a hot dog too?"

"Sure thing." Matt gave Sierra a crooked apologetic smile. "He's seen quite a few whales, so they've lost their ability to fascinate."

She tried to ignore the hot slide of desire Matt's smile had caused. The man was lethal, but he didn't seem to be aware of that fact. Amazing. She glanced down the hill, toward the docks. From her limited vantage point, she could still see more than a dozen boats were bobbing in the harbor. "Tyler's never seen or been on a boat before? How did he see all those whales?"

Matt's gaze followed hers and he chuckled. "My nephew has wheedled and begged his way onto just about every boat down there. My brother John swears Tyler was born going thirty knots. My sister-in-law disagrees, claiming ten hours of labor doesn't constitute a speed demon."

She couldn't help but agree with that logic. "Well, he would have loved our whale-watching adventure. Your friend Lawrence and Tyler have one thing in common: the need for speed." She had had such a firm grip on Austin for the entire ride that her hand had ached for the rest of the day. But at least her son hadn't been flung overboard during the hair-raising ride. Lawrence should have his captain's license taken away from him for what he put those poor engines through. If she closed her eyes, she could still hear all that horsepower screaming.

"There was a bathroom on the boat," Austin said, trying to impress Tyler and regain his attention and admiration. When that didn't seem to work, he played what any four or five-year-old would consider his trump card.

"Two ladies and a guy threw up over the side of the boat. It was gross."

Tyler's eyes lit up with excitement. "Cool! What did it look like? Did they gag like this?" Matt's nephew then proceeded to execute a stunning display of gagging and hacking. Three people who had the misfortune of standing nearby, moved back a couple of steps, out of the splatter zone.

She shivered as a shudder went through her, and she hoped her complexion hadn't turned as green as she felt. Tyler was so convincing that she had to wonder if Misty Harbor's nursery school offered drama lessons. Or had he been born with that natural talent? She gently grabbed the back of Austin's shirt and pulled him farther away from the future Academy Award winner just in case he wasn't acting.

Matt rolled his eyes and groaned at his nephew's acting ability. "Hey, Sport, why don't you and Austin go over there"—he pointed in the direction of some wooden picnic tables that had been set up for the occasion—"and save us a seat. Sierra and I will pick up lunch."

Her son looked up at her. "Can we, Mom?"

"Sure." The tables were only a few yards away under the leafy canopy of some maple trees. Austin and Tyler wouldn't be out of their sight for a moment. "Pick the first empty one you come to, sit down, and stay there." Austin had obviously taken a liking to Tyler.

Matt grinned at his nephew. "You heard the lady, get."

Both boys hurried off with a squeal of delight.

She watched as they settled themselves at the first empty table. Austin was talking about something and gesturing wildly with his hands. By his movements, she didn't want to know what the topic of conversation was. Her queasy stomach already knew that answer. "Amazing.

That is the same little boy who won't touch brussels sprouts and claims cauliflower will make him puke."

"Can't blame Austin. I won't touch brussels sprouts either." Matt crossed his eyes and made a gagging sound that rivaled Tyler's earlier attempt. "Do you know what those things taste like?"

She chuckled at his antics. "I now see where Tyler gets his acting ability. The talent must run on the Porter side of his family."

Matt's sexy grin curled her toes. "You think?"

"Yeah, I think." What she was thinking had nothing to do with his acting accomplishments and everything to do with the way his light blue eyes lit up with his smile. Here she had thought a woman could drown only in men's eyes that were deep, dark, and brown. At thirty-one years old and divorced, she still was learning a thing or two about the male population. With warm liquid desire tugging at her gut, she had only two words to say to that: *Thank heavens!*

Life was too short to think she had seen and experienced all it had to offer. To top that, she loved surprises. Matt Porter looked like he could be full of surprises.

Her smile matched Matt's, but she was thankful for the dark lens of her sunglasses hiding her eyes from his scrutiny. Everyone had always told her that her eyes were windows into her soul, that her every emotion sparkled in her gray eyes. She didn't want Matt to see whatever feeling she was experiencing. The delicious sense of longing was too new and different. She didn't fully trust it, but she was curious enough to see where it might lead.

She was in Misty Harbor on a working vacation. There was nothing preventing her from enjoying the vacation part of the next six weeks. "So, Matthew Porter, do you attend the Blueberry Festival every year?"

"Only when there's something interesting going on." The glint in his gaze told her exactly what he was interested in, and it had nothing to do with blueberries or the surrounding activities.

Her vacation was certainly looking up. "So what has you so interested? The hot dogs or the hamburgers?"

Matt was saved from answering, as an older man with a combed-over bald spot and a grease-splattered apron approached the folding table that was set up as a makeshift counter. "Well, Sierra, I see you already met one of the town's most eligible bachelors." Lenny Holmes had big brown eyes, a gut so big the apron barely covered it, and one of the warmest smiles she had ever seen.

"You did warn me, Lenny, that they would be falling out of the trees and lying thick on the ground." She grinned at the memory of meeting Lenny on her third day in town. He had shown up at the Alberts' house ready to mow the lawn bright and early one morning. The grass hadn't really needed cutting, so he pulled a few weeds, entertained Austin with wild tales of shipwrecks and pirates, and stayed for breakfast.

So far Matt was the only bachelor she had met, if one didn't count the annoying Wendell Kirby, who had cornered her one evening while she and Austin had been enjoying double-scoop cones at Bailey's Ice Cream Parlor and Emporium. Wendell had given her the creeps with his slicked-back thinning hair, fake smile, and pushy ways.

"I take it you two know each other." Matt seemed both amused and embarrassed about being labeled an eligible bachelor.

"Sierra makes a western omelet so hot and spicy that

you will think you've died and all your sins have caught up with you." Lenny chuckled at his own description.

"I thought you liked it." She had warned Lenny the omelet was going to be spicy, and he had assured her the hotter, the better. Maybe she had spent too much time in the southwest and had become accustomed to the Mexican influence in her cooking.

"I didn't like it. I loved it." Lenny gave her a big grin. "I've been trying to get my gal, Evelyn, to make one just like it, but so far it's just not the same. Is there a secret ingredient or something you forgot to tell me when you gave me the recipe?"

"You stood there and watched me make it, Lenny. There was no secret ingredient." She chuckled at the sweet thought of sixty-one-year-old Lenny having a girlfriend. One who made him breakfast, no less. "Maybe your Evelyn can come over one morning and I'll show her how I do it."

"Evelyn Ruffles wins the Misty Harbor Bake-Off every year with a German chocolate cake that is out of this world." Matt closed his eyes and sighed at some dreamy distant memory.

She tried not to laugh. The men of Misty Harbor sure liked their food.

"That's my Evelyn." Pride deepened Lenny's voice. "How about if I can get her to make you one of her prized cakes, and you can teach her how to make that western omelet?"

"Sounds like I'll be getting the better end of that deal." She loved chocolate in any form and it would be the perfect excuse to invite Matt over one evening. "How about you talk it over with Evelyn and then let me know?"

"Deal." Lenny glanced at the customers waiting not so patiently behind them before turning his attention back to them. The time for small talk was up. "What can I get you two?"

Matt felt like a teenager on his first date. This evening's meal wasn't really a date. It was an all-you-can-eat spaghetti dinner at the Methodist church. Adults were nine dollars, kids under twelve were five, and anyone three and under got to eat free. He had eaten there a couple times over the years, but he wasn't very fond of slightly overcooked spaghetti noodles with meat sauce. He was a steak and potato kind of guy, but what did one expect for nine bucks? Plus it came with dessert.

It was going to be a totally ho-hum meal that didn't require him to change his shirt for the third time. So why was he standing in his bedroom trying to decide between the blue plaid button-down shirt or the designer polo shirt he had gotten last Christmas? He decided on comfort and went with his first choice, the blue plaid.

Sierra and Austin seemed anxious to experience all that Misty Harbor had to offer. Who was he to disappoint them? Besides, his brother John and his wife, Kay, were having a great time teasing him about hijacking their son, Tyler, to get a date. With his brother Ned's upcoming wedding, he'd be the last unattached Porter, the butt of their jokes and matchmaking attempts. He loved his sisters-in-law greatly, but they had lousy taste in women.

He preferred to find his own dates.

Even though technically this wasn't a date. He and Tyler were going to meet them outside the Methodist church in half an hour. This way Sierra would know someone there, and Austin would get to spend some more time with his new friend. A totally harmless evening. So why did he just misbutton his shirt?

With a curse of self-disgust, he rebuttoned the shirt and finished getting ready. It was time for him to get going.

Twenty minutes later he was standing on the edge of the town's park, directly across the street from the Methodist church. His brother John, his wife, Kay, and the kids were running late, as usual. His three-year-old niece, Morgan, could make a Rolex watch run late.

"Hey, Matt. How's it going?" asked a deep, softly spoken voice.

Matt knew it was Gordon Hanley by the smell of his pipe. "Fine, Gordon. How's it going with you?" Gordon owned the local bookstore and tobacco shop on Main Street, the Pen and Ink. It was a strange combination for a store. Tobacco products were in a decline, even with the strange phenomenon a couple years back with everyone thinking they were cool by smoking cigars. Gordon's love was his pipe. He had never seen the man without one. Hence the problem with his store. Every book, magazine, and stationery supply smelled like Prince Albert or whatever tobacco Gordon was currently smoking.

"Can't complain." Gordon puffed on his pipe. "Expecting a shipment of books on Tuesday. Want me to put aside the Koontz, Fairstein, and Lescroart?"

"Of course." He watched as a wreath of smoke circled Gordon's head. "Our usual deal?" Gordon sealed Matt's books in a Ziploc bag to prevent them from absorbing the smell and smoke of the shop. The last time he bought a book at Gordon's that had been sitting out on the shelf, he'd had to leave it sitting on the windowsill for days trying to air it out. He never could get rid of the stench.

"Won't dream of changing it." Gordon puffed on the stem of his pipe and another billow of smoke filled the air. "If you took up the pipe, you wouldn't notice it."

Matt had to chuckle at the thought. When he had been twelve years old, a friend had dared him to smoke a stogie. He had never been so sick, or green, in his life. He wouldn't touch a tobacco product if Catherine Zeta-Jones handed it to him herself. "You just want another smoking buddy to sit in your back room and play chess all day." Everyone in town knew that Gordon was an excellent chess player. Gordon was always on the lookout for a challenge.

"Can't blame a guy for trying." Gordon took the pipe out of his mouth and held it out for inspection. "Look at this beauty. Treated myself to an early birthday present." The pipe had a clear amber-colored stem and a beautifully carved figure head as the bowl. "It's a Meerschaum. It's called Swashbuckler."

The carved face was that of an old man with a beard and a big old-fashioned hat with a feather sticking out of it. It took guts to walk around town smoking the unusual pipe, but he'd seen Gordon puff on stranger-looking things. "He kind of looks like Shakespeare to me."

Gordon chuckled. "I thought so too. That's why I got him." Gordon stuck the stem between his lips and puffed away. "The Bard had a Vandyke, though, not a full beard."

"If you say so." Gordon was a Shakespeare nut. The man could probably recite entire scenes in his sleep.

Gordon closed his eyes and drew in a deep breath. "I'm trying a new brand of tobacco tonight, Captain Black Royal. I must say that I like the aroma, but it is awfully expensive."

"Smells like any other pipe you smoke." He couldn't smell a difference. Tobacco was tobacco to him.

Gordon almost matched Matt's six foot three inch height. Gordon missed it by an inch, but Matt had a good thirty or forty pounds on the older man. With an unusually pale complexion, startling hazel eyes, rail-thin build, and an angular face, Gordon had long been rumored to be a vampire. The interior of the Pen and Ink was always dark, dreary, and stunk of cigars, cigarettes, and pipes, which only added to the allure.

School-age boys started to place dares on who would be brave enough to walk into the shop and buy the latest comic book. Gordon went along with the gag and started stocking more comic books and being more mysterious to the young customers. He was Misty Harbor's vampire, and he loved it.

Matt figured he was just lonely.

"Aren't you afraid to be seen out in the daylight?" He tried to keep the laughter out of his voice when he noticed two boys, around ten, hiding behind a nearby tree listening to their every word.

Gordon must have sensed the boys were there. "These special sunglasses protect my eyes, and it's after six. The sun really isn't that strong." Gordon's thin, pale fingers raked through his long black hair, which was liberally streaked with gray. For the benefit of their young audience, he added, "Besides, I'm feeling awfully hungry."

He coughed to cover up his laugh, as both boys sprinted across the park without once looking back. "Gordon, that wasn't very nice of you."

Gordon's lips curved around the stem of his pipe. "Ah, it will give them something to talk about tonight with all their friends." Gordon chuckled. "I wonder what they'll say if they see me enjoying a plate of spaghetti and meat sauce?"

"Probably the same thing we used to say when we caught you out in sunlight or eating real food." He could still remember the dares and the spine-tingling excitement of entering Gordon's store when he had been around nine years old. Gordon Hanley used to scare the starch right out of his shorts. "That you were only doing it so the adults wouldn't suspect what you really were"— he lowered his voice and whispered dramatically—"one of the walking dead."

Gordon roared with laughter.

"What's so funny?" asked Matt's brother John as he joined them on the sidewalk. Three-year-old Morgan was perched on his shoulders. She was wearing a pink tutu, fairy wings, and a silver tiara. She also was waving a sparkling silver wand at everyone.

"Just reminiscing about the good old days." At thirty years old, he thought it seemed strange having old days, good or bad. "You're late. What happened?" Matt glanced down the walkway to where Kay was busily combing Tyler's hair and straightening out his shirt. His nephew looked like he had just crawled out from underneath some bushes. Either that or he was being raised by wolves.

"Tyler was supposed to bring Cletus into the house while I belted Morgan into her car seat."

Cletus was John and Kay's two-year-old, sixty-five-pound black Labrador that was as obedient as a kitten. "Let me guess, a chipmunk?"

"Close, a squirrel. Before I could stop him, Cletus was across the yard and in the undergrowth with Tyler right on his tail." John had a couple of fresh scrapes on his arm and one nasty-looking one running the length of his jaw. "I honestly don't know which one is worse—my son or the dog. Took me fifteen minutes to fish them both out of the thistles."

"Ah," Gordon said. "Did they catch the critter?"

"No, it ran under a bush." John reached for Morgan's wand after it whacked him on the head for the third time.

"Morgan, sweetie, how many times have I asked you not to hit people with that wand. It hurts."

Morgan stuck out her lower lip and pouted. "One, two, three, four, five."

"That's about right." John stuck the end of the wand into the back pocket of his jeans. "After dinner, if you're a good girl, I'll let you have it back."

Morgan's lower lip started to tremble, and if he wasn't mistaken a sheen of tears glistened in her eyes. The waterworks were about to begin. "Now, Daddy."

Matt looked down at his shoes and tried not to laugh. It only encouraged his niece more. Morgan was a handful and had her daddy wrapped around her little finger. At the first sight of tears, John would give her back the wand. It wouldn't matter if she bashed his head in with it. John, all six feet five inches of him, was a sucker for tears.

Then again, Matt would give her back the wand too, just so he wouldn't have to hear the fit his niece was about to throw. If Sierra thought Tyler had inherited the drama gene, wait until she got a load of Morgan at full volume.

"My, Matt, who do we have here?" asked Sierra as she was gazing up at Morgan. Speak of the devil—Sierra and Austin had come down the sidewalk to join them, and he hadn't even noticed. Sierra smiled up at Morgan. "Are you a fairy or a princess? Maybe a princess fairy?"

Morgan's pout turned into a grin. "Hi."

"Hi yourself." Sierra smiled at John. "You must be a Porter."

"How can you tell? The height?" John smiled back at Sierra, apparently enjoying the view.

"No, the stubborn-looking jaw." Sierra glanced at him and winked.

Matt felt the concrete beneath his feet shift. He had thought Sierra's eyes were the color of a wind-tossed sea, a beautiful turbulent gray. The glint of laughter in her eyes appeared to be more green than gray. He wondered if Sierra had eyes that slightly changed color with her every mood. He'd heard about eyes like that but had never actually seen them. An intriguing thought occurred to him as Tyler ran up to Austin and his nephew pulled something from his pocket. What color would Sierra's eyes turn if he kissed her?

His sister-in-law Kay joined the group. "If you think John's jaw is stubborn, try arguing with him. I've known rocks that are more flexible."

Sierra's soft laugh caused his stomach to clench with desire. "Kay, I would like you to meet Sierra Morley and her son, Austin." He looked at the woman who had suddenly made life a lot more interesting. "Sierra, this is my sister-in-law Kay and my brother John." He reached up and swept his niece off of John's shoulder. "This little fairy princess is Morgan."

Sierra placed her hand on Austin's shoulder. "Glad to meet you all, and this is my son, Austin."

"We heard all about Austin and his very, let's say, bumpy boat ride," said Kay. John laughed, while Kay just shook her head. "All men have a twisted sense of what's important in life."

"Hey, I have to take exception to that." Gordon had joined the conversation.

"Oh, sorry, Gordon." Matt had completely forgotten about the man standing next to him. With Sierra looking so darn beautiful he would be lucky to remember his own name. "Sierra, I would like you to meet Gordon Hanley. He owns the bookstore, the Pen and Ink, on Main Street."

"I've already met Mr. Hanley. He was kind enough to assist me in locating a couple books I was looking for."

"It's Gordon, remember." Gordon gave her a warm smile. "Sierra doesn't mind the smell of my shop. In fact, if her son, Austin, hadn't been bored by the selection of books, I might have been able to talk Sierra into a game of chess."

"Next time I'll bring something along to keep Austin amused for a couple minutes."

"A couple minutes?" Gordon raised a brow at that boast. "You think you're that good?"

Sierra's smile bordered on being wicked. "My father taught me to play." She nodded at his pipe. "My father also smokes a pipe, and I find the smell of pipe tobacco quite comforting. I know enough about pipes to know that's a Meerschaum."

"'This is the very ecstasy of love,'" quoted Gordon.

"Shakespeare?" Sierra looked intrigued.

Gordon's expression turned to one of pure devotion. "'She's beautiful and therefore to be woo'd, She is a woman, therefore to be won.'"

Matt heard his brother and sister-in-law groan. "Don't get him started, Sierra. Gordon will quote Shakespeare all night long if you listen," explained John.

Gordon's smile was boyish. It made him look not only younger but slightly dashing, like the poets of old. "Guilty, as charged."

Matt was beginning to wonder if he was going to have competition for Sierra's attention. Gordon and Sierra did seem to have an awful lot in common. "Sierra, are you about ready to eat?"

"Sure." Sierra looked at John and Kay. "Are you joining us?"

"I think we can do that," chuckled Kay, who seemed

to be getting a kick out of joining their date. "As long as you don't mind a fairy princess who isn't known for her table manners."

"What about you, Gordon? Are you heading for dinner too?" Sierra seemed to be enjoying herself making new friends, or maybe she was just being polite. Either way, their dinner together was getting awfully crowded.

"I would love to join you all. Dinner eaten with lively companions is always so much more interesting than dining alone." Gordon walked over to the trash receptacle and proceeded to knock the lit tobacco out of his pipe and into the sand container on top.

Matt stood helplessly by as their quiet dinner for four grew to an entire tableful. Austin and Tyler had hit it off so well this afternoon that he knew they would have entertained each other throughout the meal, leaving him plenty of time to get to know Sierra better. Now he was going to be lucky to get a word in edgewise or even be seated next to her.

"Tyler, what do you have there?" Kay frowned at her son's hand.

Matt glanced over and saw a long fuzzy caterpillar wiggling on his nephew's palm. Austin's nose was practically touching the insect.

"It's a caterpillar, Mom. I found him under the bushes and wanted to show Austin."

"Is that what you put in your pants pocket?" Kay didn't look too pleased with her son. At Tyler's hesitant nod, Kay said, "How many times must I tell you, no live animals in your pockets?"

Matt had heard the story about Kay, wash day, and one angry frog at least four times now. By the look on Sierra's face, he knew he would be hearing it again tonight. The tale had all the earmarks of becoming a family legend.

"No dead ones either," added John just in case there was a question in Tyler's mind. "Go put the little fellow over there by the trees." John pointed to a clump of trees, right off the sidewalk.

The boys scurried off to do what Tyler's father told them to do, and Gordon rejoined the group. Morgan was twirling around in circles making everyone dizzy just from watching her. If her dinner stayed in her stomach tonight, it would be a miracle. This evening couldn't possibly get any worse.

"Hey, look, Matt, there's Paul, Jill, and the kids." John pointed down the street where another of his brothers and his family were heading right for them. He bit the inside of his cheek to keep from groaning. All they needed was the last of his brothers, Ned, and his fiancée, Norah, to join them.

Three-year-old Hunter, Paul's son, went running over to see what Tyler and Austin were doing. Introductions were flying fast and furious. Sierra, who stood five feet ten inches, actually was getting lost in the crowd. Matt noticed that she grabbed Austin's hand as the group walked across the street to the church.

Morgan's sparkling wand whacked Matt in the side. His brother had been right. The darn thing hurt. He stopped to rub it, and Jill ran over his foot with the baby stroller his three-month-old niece, Amanda, was sleeping in.

"Sorry, Matt," said Jill, and she hurried along with Kay.

Gordon was talking to Sierra about something. Whatever it was must have been interesting, because Sierra was smiling. Short of stepping in a pile of dog-doo this evening couldn't possibly get much worse.

"Hey, Matt, look who's waiting for us by the door!" John's voice was shaking with laughter.

He glanced over and groaned. His mother and father, along with Ned and Norah, were standing by the Methodist church's main double wooden doors waiting for them. Morgan's wand bashed him on the knee as he stumbled.

Great! This wasn't a date. It was a migration.

Chapter Three

Sierra nearly fell off the seat when the boat hit a rough patch. That's what she got for sitting halfway on the seat facing the rear of the boat to keep an eye on the boys. Matt's hand reached out to steady her. "Thanks." His hand felt warm and strong as he cupped her elbow.

"Just be careful," Matt said as he released her. His large, work-roughened hand reached for the throttle and he once again slowed down the boat.

The small boat hadn't been going fast, Matt had obviously sensed her concern for Austin, who was sitting in the back with his new best friend, Tyler. Matt was handling the boat like a little old lady driving to church on a Sunday morning with a dozen eggs on her lap. Both boys were wearing bright orange life preservers and were behaving themselves. Neither had left his seat, but they had been twisting and turning in every direction to see as much as possible. They hadn't stopped talking since they'd met at the docks right after breakfast.

The boys didn't miss a thing. Every splash or curious wave was thought to be a mermaid. Matt had been indulging them by steering the boat in whatever direction the boys commanded him to go. Sunday mornings were a perfect time to go mermaid watching. The sun was shining brightly and the warm sea-scented breeze felt wonderful.

While Mermaid Bay hadn't produced a legendary creature yet, they did spot a curious harbor seal and more than a dozen puffins to amuse the boys. She loved to watch the puffins fly by and then quickly dive straight down into the water, only to shoot back out of the water with their shimmery catch hanging out of their beaks. Puffins were extremely fast fliers, and they beat their wings so fast that they became a blur. The funny little birds resembled black and white flying footballs.

No one could watch them without smiling.

All along she had thought puffins were just tiny penguins with orange and yellow beaks that happened to live off the coast of Maine instead of Antarctica. Matt had told her that although they both were birds and expert swimmers, they weren't the same. Penguins couldn't fly, and puffins could.

Matt made an excellent tour guide. He had filled the boys' heads with tales of where mermaids had been spotted in the past, pirate treasure, and phantom ghost ships that had been sighted off the coast of Maine. The boys were hanging on his every word.

"Then what happened, Uncle Matt?" Tyler was eager for his uncle to continue the story of the mermaid and the sailor she had saved from drowning during a storm and a horrible shipwreck back in the 1700s.

"The sailor was found the next morning, lying on the rocky beach by Hancock Point. He was barely alive, but clutched in his fist was a gold necklace and the fattest ruby anyone had ever laid eyes on."

"What's a ruby?" asked Austin, who was sitting on the edge of his seat absorbing every word.

"It's a very expensive gemstone, like a diamond, but it's red," Sierra answered her son.

Matt turned his head and looked at the boys. "This one was red all right. Blood red."

She tried not to laugh as both boys' eyes grew wide with excitement. Matt seemed to be enjoying himself as much as the boys. The old saying about not being able to take the boy out of the man came to mind.

"What happened to the sailor and his riches?" asked Tyler.

"The story goes that he traded the gold chain for an old boat and cashed in the ruby and sent the money home to his poor mother and a bunch of younger brothers and sisters." Matt winked at her. "As soon as he had recovered from his near-drowning, he got into his boat and headed out to sea. No one ever saw him again."

"Really?" asked Austin.

"Yep." Matt turned the boat toward the open ocean. "They found his boat three days later just bobbing out in the ocean. No one was on board."

While both boys thought about that, Matt gave Sierra another wink. "Legend has it that he joined the mermaid under the sea, and they are still living happily ever after."

Tyler wrinkled his nose. "No way. He'll drown again."

"True, but how do mermaids breathe underwater?" Matt headed the boat toward a tiny island in the distance. "I just think it's strange that ever since then, not one sailor ever lost his life to the sea along this part of the coast. There have been a couple wicked storms causing shipwrecks, but no one has died. All the sailors have found their way to the shore. Some even claimed a mysterious young sailor dressed in old sea-faring clothes had helped them."

"Wow," Austin said as he looked around, hoping to spot the young sailor or the mermaid.

"I hope you guys are hungry," Matt said. "I packed enough to feed an army."

She had noticed the large cooler shoved in between the front and back seats. Tyler's feet, with their little blue sneakers, were resting on its lid. "I could have brought something." She was more than capable of packing a picnic lunch for four, but she couldn't ignore the special little thrill knowing that Matt had wanted to impress her. She hadn't been on a real picnic since . . . heck, she couldn't remember when. The afternoon fishing with Austin on Lake Tahoe didn't count. They had given up their packed lunch in the hopes of catching a trout or whatever kind of fish would have been hungry enough to bite a chunk of a bologna sandwich.

"Today's my treat." Matt gave her a wicked grin. "If you really want to feed me, I'll take one of those southwestern omelets you fed Lenny Holmes the other morning. The man swore it would burn the roof off my mouth and I'd be begging for more."

Sierra wasn't sure if there was a double meaning behind that request. Was Matt asking for just the omelet, or was he hinting at being there for breakfast one morning? It was a very intriguing thought, one that gave her abdomen a warm tug of desire. She looked away from Matt's strong profile and glanced at her son in the back seat. A deliciously wicked thought that would never happen. She was a mother with a very impressionable young son. There would be no sleepovers in her near future, and without Austin's nanny there to help out, there would definitely be no hanky-panky, as Rosemary liked to call it, during her Maine vacation.

"Sure, I can make you an omelet." It wasn't like she was going to be doing anything more interesting with her time. "Name the day and time." It was one way of finding out if Matt was thinking six a.m. or six p.m.

"Wednesday night, if you're still talking to me." Matt maneuvered the boat closer to the island.

So much for him wanting to be there for breakfast. "Why won't I be talking to you?" She waved the boys back into their seats as the boat drew closer. She could see a small patch of sand, but the rest of the island looked windswept and uninhabitable. The island looked to be about a mile long and maybe half as wide.

"My family wants me to invite you and Austin to a cookout at my parents' house on Tuesday night. The whole gang will be there."

"And you don't want me to come?" She had met his entire family last night at the spaghetti dinner. They had been loud, opinionated, and wonderful. Everyone had made her and her son feel very welcome. She and Austin had both had a great time. Maybe she had misjudged Matt's interest.

Matt looked at her as if she had lost her mind. "Where would you get that idea?"

"You're the one who said I wouldn't be talking to you, remember?"

Matt cut the engine and shook his head. "I figured after spending another night with my family you would have had enough."

"Enough what?" She thought she understood what Matt was trying to say, and she thought it was cute. Her family consisted of Austin, a dear friend who happened to be her ex-husband, Rosemary, and her father. Dad couldn't have cared less about the guys she had dated. He had it in his mind that she would marry Jake Morley, his heir apparent, and that was the end of that. The year after she'd graduated from college, she had married Jake. Although it hadn't been her worst mistake in life, it hadn't been one of her brightest moves either.

"Enough, you know, matchmaking." Matt's cheeks turned red and he quickly turned away and threw the anchor over the side of the boat.

"They do this often?" She tried to contain her chuckle, but she had a feeling she'd failed when Matt's back stiffened.

"Every chance they get. I'm the last one who's single. They all feel it's their duty to throw every available woman at my feet so I can trip my way up to the altar." Matt took off his sneakers and in one smooth move slid over the side of the boat.

The water came up to his thighs but his gaze never left hers. "I would understand if you prefer to skip the cookout."

"Not a chance." She gave him a big grin. "I like your family."

"If you say so." Matt gave her a funny look that she couldn't decipher, before turning his attention to his nephew. "Come on, Tyler, you first."

Tyler must have known the drill, because he flew into Matt's arms. The small boy who looked so much like his uncle said, "See you on shore, Austin."

Matt carried Tyler the twenty feet to shore and set him down. "Stay right here, where I can see you."

"Can we go exploring later?" Tyler was hopping up and down, ready to take off into the shrubs.

"You have to eat your lunch first, and then only if

Austin's mom says it's okay." Matt turned to the boat and waded back out.

Sierra watched the way the ocean lapped at Matt's thighs, and refused to acknowledge what her treacherous mind was thinking. Rosemary would not only be trying to wash out her mind with soap, but she would be saying a whole lot of Hail Marys while doing it.

"You have a choice, Sierra. I could carry you ashore, or you have to wade."

"I'll wade." Matt's arms looked way too tempting. She took off her sneakers. "I can carry Austin." She sat on the side of the boat and dipped her toes into the cold water. All of a sudden, wading ashore lost its appeal.

"I'll get him." Matt held her gaze as he put both of his hands onto her waist and slowly lowered her into the water.

Her eyes went wide as the heat from Matt's body caressed the front of hers and freezing water lapped at the hem of her shorts. "Oh!"

Matt's gaze started to smolder. "You can say that again." He reluctantly released her and then reached into the boat. Matt handed her her sneakers and the big tote she had brought along. "You're going to need these."

"To eat?" She winked at Austin, who was watching them closely. Her son looked confused by her and Matt's closeness. She took a step away from Matt and her toes sank into the sand.

"No, to explore the island." Matt smiled at her son. "You okay with me carrying you to shore like Tyler?"

Austin nodded his head and reached out his arms.

Matt plucked him from the boat and made his way to shore. She trailed behind them, watching her son. Austin looked over Matt's shoulder and grinned at her. She smiled back. Her son seemed very comfortable in Matt's capable arms. Lucky boy.

She hurried up onto the small area of sand. It might be August, but the water felt like November. "Doesn't the water heat up?" She had swum in the Atlantic Ocean before, down in Miami, Hilton Head, Atlantic City—where the water was warm and the beaches plentiful. Maine's coast felt like another country, not just another state.

"This is warm." Matt grinned as he lowered Austin to the ground. "You should go wading in March."

"Hey, Austin, come look at this," shouted Tyler, who was perched on one of the rocks at the edge of the small sandy beach.

Her son hurried off without a backward glance. Nothing was more fascinating to a four-year-old than a tide pool. She watched as Austin scrambled up onto the low boulder next to Tyler. Both boys bent their heads over what was so fascinating and started whispering to each other.

She glanced off into the surrounding trees and brush. "Any animals or other inhabitants I should be aware of?" It looked like a deserted island, but there was the whole other side she hadn't seen. As far as she knew the place could be home to a herd of moose, and she and the boys would have to swim for their lives.

"None worth mentioning." Matt called out to Tyler, "Try not to get too wet. We didn't bring along a change of clothes."

Tyler's mischievous grin flashed across the distance.

Matt shook his head. "I'm going to get the cooler and blanket. I'll be right back." He nodded in the direction of the boys. "Keep an eye on Lewis and Clark over there."

She watched him wade back out into the water. It was a better view than the scrub pines that had been battered by the weather for centuries. Khaki shorts with big cargo pockets and a light blue T-shirt that clung to very impressive muscles did a girl a world of good. In fact, Matt Porter was the most interesting thing in Misty Harbor.

Although the town was charming and quaint, she wouldn't classify it as interesting. Las Vegas was exciting. Los Angeles was the cultural hub of the hip and upcoming. New York never slept, and Miami pulsed to the Latin beat. Misty Harbor wasn't even a beep on the rich-and-famous radar. So why was her father looking to build the next Randall Hotel in the middle of it?

It didn't make sense to her, but her job wasn't to make sense out of it all. Her job, and the reason she was vacationing in a tiny fishing village on the coast of Maine, instead of Bar Harbor or Kennebunkport, was to see if the property that was going up for sale was worth the asking price, and to see if the town could support an exclusive hotel.

Her first reaction was that her father and her ex, Jake, had sorely misjudged the town's size and accommodations. First impressions had been known to be wrong before, so she was biding her time, sitting back and enjoying this time with her son. Mermaid watching was giving her a whole new perspective on life.

Matt joined her back on the shore and handed her a blanket. "Hope you and Austin like chicken salad sandwiches, iced tea, and cookies."

She spread the blanket on the only spot and hoped the tide wasn't coming in. If it was, the blanket was going to get wet. Sand was at a premium on the small island, and she just covered it all. "What kind of cookies?" she asked teasingly. It really wouldn't matter. She'd never met a cookie she didn't like.

"Chocolate chip and oatmeal raisin." Matt sat the

cooler down at the edge of the blanket. "I couldn't make up my mind, so I packed both." Matt gave her a charming smile that must have gotten him out of a whole bunch of trouble when he was a young boy.

"Smart move." She looked over to where the boys were playing and called, "Lunchtime."

Austin and Tyler put whatever they were playing with back into the shallow tide pool and came scampering onto the blanket. "We're hungry," Tyler said to his uncle.

Matt dug into the cooler and Tyler wiped his hands on the seat of his pants.

"You boys have to wash up first." She reached for her tote bag.

All three males looked at her as if she was talking Greek. "Sierra," said Matt, "in case you hadn't noticed there isn't anywhere to wash up."

She raised a brow but kept on digging through the tote. "I noticed." She was a mother to a four-year-old and came prepared for anything—short of nuclear holocaust or an organ transplant. She took out a small bottle of antibacterial gel and a plastic carrier of moist wipes.

Austin obediently held out his hands. She squirted some of the gel on his hands and he started to rub them together.

Tyler shrugged and held out his hands for the same stuff.

She handed Austin and Tyler each a moist towelette. Tyler wiped his hands and then gave them a sniff. "They smell funny," Tyler said.

"It's strawberry." She took the trash from the boys and deposited it into an empty Ziploc bag she had dug out from the bottom of the tote. "Your hands are now sterile. Eat up."

Matt looked at the tote with much speculation. He

handed the boys and her a sandwich. "I packed extras, so if you're still hungry after eating one, there's more."

"Uncle Matt," said Tyler. He took a big bite of his sandwich. "After we eat, can I show Austin where the dead guy was?"

"Don't talk with your mouth full."

Her hand froze in midair. Her sandwich was halfway to her mouth and her gaze flew to Matt. "There's a dead man on the island?"

"We're on Dead Man's Island," Tyler replied around a chunk of his sandwich.

Matt glared at his nephew. "There are no dead men on the island, Sierra."

She looked at Matt and it suddenly hit her. How well did she know Matt? Just because Lenny Holmes gave him a "thumbs up" and said Matt was "one of the good ones," what did that mean? Come to think of it, how well did she know Lenny or anyone else in town?

Logic told her there probably weren't any corpses lying under the battered shrubs and she was overreacting. Austin and she were fine. "So how did the island get its name?" She took a calming breath and took a bite out of her sandwich.

"It's haunted too!" added Tyler.

She nearly choked on her lunch. Tears filled her eyes as she wondered if they were going to have to rename the island after her. Her gaze collided with Matt's as she gained her breath.

Matt reached into the cooler and pulled out a bottle of water. "Tyler, that's enough." Matt smiled reassuringly at Austin, uncapped the bottle, and handed her the water. "Drink something, Sierra. This place isn't haunted."

Tyler pouted.

She took a tentative sip of water and was thankful her throat was still working. "Want to explain how the island got its name?"

"In the mid-1700s someone came out here to explore the island. They found the bones of a man. He was staked out in the middle of the island, and there was still a cutlass through his rib cage. He obviously had been there for a while."

"Pirates," whispered Tyler to Austin.

Her son's eyes grew big and he wasn't eating. "It's okay, Austin. This happened hundreds of years ago," she said in a reassuring tone. "There are no pirates now, and there most definitely isn't a body on the island. It's just a story."

"The bones were taken back to the mainland and given a proper burial, Austin." Matt reached over and ruffled the top of her son's head. "I've been on this island hundreds of times, and I've never seen a dead person or a pirate."

"Tell them about the treasure, Uncle Matt." Tyler took another bite of his sandwich.

"What treasure?" Now she was the one intrigued.

"Legend has it that pirates buried their treasure somewhere on this island. The captain and the poor soul who was killed here probably came to shore and buried their loot. To keep the location a secret, the captain probably killed the guy to keep him from talking."

"How do you know he killed him?" She loved a good legend. Especially if it had a treasure.

"What? You think he tripped over his own cutlass and ended up with it through his rib cage?" Matt tried not to laugh.

She rolled her eyes. "Point taken." She glanced around with interest. "So, you think there really is a treasure?"

"No." Matt grinned. "My brothers and I spent most of our summer vacations out on this island searching and digging. Every boulder, rock, and pebble has probably been moved a dozen times in the past twenty years."

"Hmmmm . . ." She glanced at the trees and scrub pines. If she were a pirate, where would she hide the treasure? "No luck?"

"Not even a gold coin. Everyone eat up, and then we can go check it out." Matt shook his head and started in on his sandwich.

Half an hour later Matt stood next to Sierra and tried not to laugh. She looked so disappointed.

"Are you sure this is the spot?" Sierra walked around a pile of boulders and over tree roots. Most of the soil had been stripped away by the harsh weather. She shook her head.

"Positive. I warned you there wasn't anything here." As far as being the pinnacle of the legend, it didn't look like much. Rocks, straggly looking trees, and some dirt marked the spot. One lone wildflower was resiliently pushing its way up between two rocks and blooming a bright yellow. The coast of Maine wasn't for the weak.

"Has anyone looked under these rocks?" Sierra frowned at the rock in front of her. It was the size of a desk. Not a student's desks, but one of those big old teacher's desks that looked so impressive to a second-grader.

"If it was only the captain and the dead pirate who buried the treasure, How would just the two of them move a rock that size?" he asked. Sierra's question had been reasonable. It was one his brothers and he had asked, and answered. "It took all three of my brothers, two of their friends, and me to move those boulders and dig."

"What did you find?" Sierra looked impressed by the heroic feat.

"More boulders. Bigger boulders." He didn't want to ruin her notion by telling her it had been harder than it looked. Teenage boys didn't give up easily once they had their mind set on finding a treasure and becoming millionaires. He could still remember what they had all wanted to buy first. His brother Ned wanted an entire mountain. Paul had wanted a big fishing boat. He was going to buy the old lighthouse. Hours of backbreaking work had been a small price to pay for those dreams.

That's all they had been: dreams. Young boys' dreams.

"Hey, Uncle Matt," called Tyler, who was crawling around with Austin under some nearby trees. "Did you check under here?"

"Yes." He didn't have the heart to tell his nephew those trees weren't old enough to have been on the island back in the early 1900s, let alone the 1700s. The landscape of Dead Man's Island had been reshaped many times over in the past couple hundred years. Tyler deserved a chance to dream.

Sierra chuckled softly as she sat on a rock and watched the boys. "They look like they are searching for Easter eggs, not a chest full of coins and jewels."

He sat down beside her. "Give them a couple years and they'll be planning ways to get a backhoe out onto the island to find their fortune."

"Is that what you did?"

"We tried." He chuckled at the memories. "A couple of the locals had metal detectors out here searching."

"Did they find anything?" Sierra kept an eye on the boys as they scrambled from one spot to another.

"Mostly change that other searchers had dropped." He watched the way the breeze lightly played with Sierra's long blond hair. Today she had pulled it back into a ponytail and wore a baseball cap with a puffin and the word MAINE sewn onto it. Tiny denim shorts highlighted her long, lean legs and a pink tank top bared her arms to the sun.

Sierra would have looked like any other tourist who flocked to the Maine coast during the summer months, except for one thing. Sierra was gorgeous. There was no other way to describe her. She was five feet ten inches of willowy perfection. She also was a heartbreak waiting to happen.

He knew to avoid summer affairs of the heart. When the cool breezes started to blow into Misty Harbor, the sightseers and vacationers packed their bags and headed out of town. The locals had officially christened August "Heartbreak Month." The name said it all.

"Mom, come here," called Austin. "Look at this!"

Sierra hurried to her son's side. Austin was holding a large shell in his hand, one that obviously had been tossed onto the island by a major storm, or left there by a person. Seashells didn't sprout from rocks or trees. Matt smiled as Sierra held the shell to her son's ear.

There was something special about Sierra. He couldn't quite put his finger onto it yet, but he was getting closer. She was gorgeous but wasn't vain about it. A vain woman wouldn't leave the house without her makeup on. Today he couldn't detect any makeup except maybe lip gloss or whatever they called it. Something made her full lips look shiny. Sierra's lips had a just-kissed look. Since he hadn't done any kissing, they were driving him nuts.

Sierra had a laugh that was sexy as hell. But what really turned him on was the true love and affection she showed her son. It was plain to see that nothing was more important to Sierra than her son.

"Can we take it home with us, Mom?" Austin was cradling the shell.

"I can't see why not." Sierra looked around them. "I think we should try to find something for Tyler to remember this day by."

He knew Tyler wasn't interested in shells. His nephew would probably want some sea creature washed up into one of the tide pools. His sister-in-law Kay would kill him if he allowed Tyler to bring home another animal. He needed Kay's cooperation to keep stealing her son, and he needed Tyler to keep Austin happy, which allowed him to keep seeing Sierra. Animals were definitely out. He stood up and joined the trio. "How about a cool piece of driftwood, Tyler?"

Tyler frowned. "A piece of wood?"

"Driftwood—there's a difference." He started heading down the barely distinguishable path toward the water's edge. The boys immediately started to follow him. Sierra brought up the rear. "Sometimes if you're real lucky, a piece of an old pirate ship can wash ashore."

"Really?" Tyler didn't look convinced.

"Sure thing." He winked at Sierra to let her in on the game. "I once heard of a guy finding an entire helm washed up on Deer Isle."

Austin tugged at his mom's hand. "What's a helm?"

"It's the wheel that pirates used to steer their ship," he answered for Sierra.

"Come on, Austin, I'll beat you to the shore." Tyler took off in a flash.

Austin carefully handed his mother the shell and then ran after his new friend, calling, "Wait for me."

Sierra's laugh sent a bolt of heat straight into Matt's gut as she hurried past him on the path. "Come on, slow-poke, before we lose sight of them."

He watched as Sierra nearly sprinted after the boys. Her long tanned legs ate up the distance. Visions of what else those long legs would be good for teased his mind. He particularly liked the one where she wrapped them around his waist. If he wasn't careful, he would need a dip into the cold ocean to cool off.

The boys and Sierra disappeared from sight, but he could still hear them. He wasn't worried about Sierra getting into trouble, but his nephew was a different story. Tyler was like Velcro. Wherever trouble was, it stuck to him. He hurried after them.

He caught up to Sierra on the rocky shore. She was slowly following the boys as they scampered over rocks and the occasional fallen tree. "Did they find anything yet?"

"Just a couple branches." Sierra gave him a beautiful smile that made her eyes dance. "You and your brothers must have been a handful. Your poor parents."

"They survived." He loved the way her eyes turned greener when she laughed.

"Did that guy really find a helm?"

"He sure did." He helped her up onto a big boulder. The boys were a couple yards away. "Only it wasn't from a pirate ship. It was made of plastic and about ten years old." He chuckled as Austin picked up a piece of wood covered in dried seaweed. "Bet you that smells."

Sierra shook her head. "Great. I'm never going to get him clean."

Austin dropped the stinking wood and went on to the

next discovery. His second choice didn't appear any better than the first.

"He's a boy."

"Are you saying girls can't get dirty?" Sierra looked insulted.

He shook his head and laughed. There was no way he was going to get into that argument with her. "I'm not used to girls. My niece, Morgan, is only three and I refuse to take her anywhere until she learns she doesn't have to totally undress to use the potty."

Sierra grinned as she jumped to the next boulder. "Will you bring her treasure hunting?"

"Of course." He cupped her elbow as she maneuvered her way over the next set of rocks. "As soon as she can handle all that potty stuff on her own."

"Chicken," Sierra teased.

"Uncle Matt, Uncle Matt!" shouted Tyler. He was holding something big in his hands and jumping up and down. "I found it, I found it!"

"Found what?" It looked like a piece of lumber to him, not a tree branch. The wood looked to be six inches by about twelve inches.

Tyler was showing Austin his treasure by the time Sierra and Matt joined them. "What did you find, Tyler?" Sierra asked.

"Part of a pirate ship." Tyler proudly held out the board to him. "See, that's the ship's name."

Matt carefully took the board and held it so Sierra could see too. It was a piece of weathered board that at one time must have been part of a wine crate. Now it was dried and bleached by the sun. In fancy faded green print were the words *Château Ausone*. "Looks French to me."

He knew only two things about wine. It came in white

and red. He was a beer man. Something told him that whatever *Château Ausone* was, it had to be expensive.

Sierra leaned in close and whispered in Matt's ear, "It's a Saint-Emilion wine."

"French?" Tyler frowned at the board. "Can pirates be French?"

"Sure can." Matt handed the board back to his nephew. He wondered how Sierra knew the wine. "From some of the stories I heard about French pirates, they were the worst kind."

Sierra rolled her eyes.

Chapter Four

Gordon Hanley heard the bell above the door to his shop announce a customer. He turned to the doorway opening into the shop and yelled, "I'll be right there."

A unfamiliar woman's voice politely called back, "Thank you."

He chuckled as he pulled a stack of books out of one of the cartons that had arrived this morning. Most of the book shipments arrived on Tuesdays. Today was no exception. Today was also the day a customer was thanking him for keeping them waiting. Amazing. What would be next? He could win the odds on Olivia Wycliffe delivering a healthy baby boy by midnight. So far, the odds were fifteen-to-one against him. If Olivia had the baby today, he would win enough to purchase himself another early birthday present. This time he was thinking about a Larsen pipe.

Sheriff Larson frowned on the bookie operation he ran from the back room, but someone needed to keep the odds, collect the losses, and handle the payouts. His book and tobacco store was centrally located in town, and people trusted him. What could he say—he was good at numbers.

The birth of Ethan and Olivia's baby was the only bet he had going at the time. Last week Daniel Creighton won the pot by guessing not only the day but also the sex of Erik and Doc Sydney Olsen's first child. The Olsens had welcomed a tiny baby girl, named Inga. Gordon's money had been on a big husky boy, like his father, making an early arrival.

Live and learn. Predicting babies was a lot harder than figuring out who was falling in love or who would be catching the biggest tuna of the year. Babies were an unpredictable lot. Erik had known his wife's due date, and even he had been off by two weeks. The big Norwegian was so in love with his little daughter, he had happily handed over his losses while passing out cigars.

Erik had purchased Gordon's most expensive box of cigars for the special occasion.

With a towering stack of the newest hardbacks balanced in his hands, Gordon left the tiny stockroom and headed for the front of the shop. A customer awaited.

Gordon put the books on the counter and eyed the woman standing in front of a bookshelf. From the back it was hard to tell her age, but he would guess between twenty and forty. Long, nearly black hair was past her waist. He had to wonder if she could sit on it. A long, flowing brown skirt with light blue swirls came to her ankles, and chunky sandals were on her feet. The light blue sleeveless top and the swirls on the skirt saved the woman from blending into the walls. He preferred his shop, the Pen and Ink, dark and dreary. His eyes were extremely sensitive to the light, adding to the mystery.

After all, he had a reputation to maintain and protect.

What kind of vampire would he be if he allowed sunlight to flood his shop?

He watched as the tall, thin woman reached for a book. Her hands were much younger than forty, but she didn't wear all the jewelry young people wore. A plain brown leather–banded watch was on her right wrist. What he found most interesting was the book she had selected, a relatively old hardcover that had been sitting on the shelf for years: *Shakespeare's Sonnets.*

If he had been thirty years younger, he would be halfway in love. Any woman who appreciated William Shakespeare had his undying devotion and attention. The day was indeed looking up. With the way his luck was running today, this customer might be able to hold up her end of a conversation on dear old Will.

"'A hundred thousand welcomes. I could weep and I could laugh, I am light and heavy. Welcome.'" He quoted the Bard, as a way of a greeting. It was his way of testing her knowledge on the subject he held dear to his heart.

"Coriolanus. I'm impressed." The young woman turned around.

Gordon felt his heart slam against his chest and his breath leave his lungs. He wondered if this was going to be the last face he'd see on this earth. If it was, he'd go gladly. Before him stood his daughter. "Juliet," he whispered in astonishment.

The young woman froze.

This was the daughter he had never met. Hell, he hadn't even known she existed until eleven years ago, when out of the blue a letter arrived from Victoria Knox, a woman he had met when teaching English literature at a small college in Rhode Island. A woman he had fallen in love with. Victoria had explained how his daughter thought someone else was her father. Victoria had begged his forgiveness, and his silence. For months he had stared at the photo of his fifteen-year-old daughter, Juliet, that Victoria had enclosed with her letter. He could never bring himself to destroy her safe and secure world, so he held his silence.

He paid his penance.

The five-by-seven color photo had been placed in an antique sterling silver frame and was still sitting on his nightstand upstairs.

"You recognize me?" Juliet seemed uncertain, awkward, and shy.

Juliet really hadn't changed much in the past eleven years, but she had grown more beautiful. His daughter had grown from an awkward fifteen-year-old into a beautiful young woman. Gone were the braces. Gone were the glasses and the high-buttoned blouse that had seemed so out of date on the young, serious-looking girl. He would have recognized her on any street in the world. This was his daughter. There was no mistaking the Hanley in her. She didn't resemble Victoria at all. The poor kid looked like her dad.

"I would have known you anywhere." He was uncertain what to do. He wanted to pull her into his arms and never let go. In the twenty-six years since she had been born, he had missed everything.

"Mom said that she had sent you a picture." Juliet clutched the book in front of her like a shield.

There was no mistaking the sheen of tears in her eyes. "Is Victoria all right?" He knew there was an edge of panic in his voice, but he couldn't help it. Something must have happened to Victoria. Why else would Juliet be standing in his shop after all these years?

Juliet must have sensed his panic and quickly said,

"Mom's fine." His daughter glanced around the shop. "She knows I'm here." Nervous fingers toyed with the book held in their grasp.

"Is she all right with that?" Juliet looked like she was ready to bolt out of the shop at any second. "How is your mom doing?" Ordinary questions that seem so inane, but he didn't know where else to begin. The hard questions would scare her off. He wanted to put his daughter at ease. He definitely did not want to ruin this moment.

"Mom's fine."

"And your . . . father? How is he?" What else was he supposed to call the man who had raised Juliet as his own? In the letter eleven years ago, Victoria had told him that Juliet thought Ken Carlyle was her real father. Obviously the truth had finally gotten out. One had to wonder why, after all these years.

Juliet hesitated for a moment. "Dad passed away two years ago."

"I'm sorry to hear that." And he was. Victoria had written that Ken Carlyle was a caring, devoted, and loving father.

"Thanks." Juliet looked around the shop. "So this is the Pen and Ink?"

His daughter looked about as uncomfortable as he felt. "Would you like a tour?" He gave a sigh of relief when she slowly nodded. "As you can see, you're standing in the book section." His hand waved to the counter behind him. "That's the cash register." A turnstile filled with postcards was beside the counter. The wall between the double front entry doors and the counter was crammed with magazines, newspapers, and the typical tourist information brochures.

He took a couple of steps to his left. "This is the rest

of the books, a small stationery section, and of course pens. Can't have the Pen and Ink without the pens."

Juliet walked over to the display of pens and seemed impressed. He didn't stock normal, everyday pens that one could purchase across the street at Krup's General Store. He carried only a few top-of-the-line luxury pens. Most were fountain pens, some ballpoint, and a few rollerball. All of them were neatly displayed in two locked glass cases and had price tags that gave the local residents sticker shock. The pens weren't for the locals. They were for the tourists.

Rich tourists.

People who were willing to shell out more than a hundred dollars for an onyx and sterling Aurora, or a Cartier, or a Cross. Some had platinum, some gold. They were expensive finger jewelry for the businessman or woman.

"Do you sell many of these?" Juliet gazed at the pens like most women looked at diamonds.

"A dozen or so during the tourist season." He moved to the room at the back of his store. "This is what the shop was before I purchased it."

Juliet looked into the room and wrinkled her nose. "A tobacco shop."

"How did you ever guess?" he chuckled. A wall humidor case that was stocked with tobacco and cigars took up the entire far wall. Other display cases held humidors that were made out of everything from crystal to silver plate to Spanish cedar. A few of the humidors were new, but most were prized antiques. Pipes lined another case. In the center of the room was a small mahogany table with a chess board, set up and ready to play. Two comfortable leather chairs that were way past their prime flanked the table. Ashtrays and pipe holders were everywhere. Most were for sale, but a few were used by customers, chess players, and himself. An old, and at one time very expensive, rug was faded, worn, and had quite a few burn marks.

He frowned at the rug and counted his lucky stars that the rug and entire shop hadn't gone up in flames. He would have lost not only his shop but also a place to rest his weary head. The entire second floor of the shop was his apartment, his home.

"Don't you think that books and tobacco make a strange combination?" Juliet walked around the room, but she didn't linger like she had over the books and pens.

"I know, the smoke." He nodded toward the counter, where his pipe of the day was lying unlit. "I smoke a pipe, so I don't notice it as much as other people."

"What do the customers think of the books smelling like a pipe?"

"Most don't mind it, and the few that do, we work out other arrangements." He had never had to justify his pipe smoking to anyone before. "I was going to turn the whole shop into a bookstore, but a lot of the locals asked me to continue to stock their tobacco and smoking items. At the time I figured 'why not,' since the display cabinets and inventory came with the price of the shop." He chuckled at the memory. "Next thing I knew, I was smoking a pipe, selling books, and playing chess with the locals during the slow days."

"Is that how you spend your days?"

"Most of them." He looked at the clock above the register. It was a little after one. "Have you had lunch yet? Are you hungry?"

"I had a sandwich and a soda at the general store right before I came in here." Juliet gave him a small smile. "I was trying to work up the nerve to walk in here and meet you."

"I'm glad you did."

"I wasn't sure what to expect, so I kept walking up and down the sidewalk all morning. I must have passed the shop a dozen times, but I couldn't see in the windows, so I wasn't even sure you were here." A flush stained her cheeks. "I think people were starting to notice me."

"They would have to be blind not to notice you, Juliet." He marveled once again at the woman standing before him. "You're a beautiful woman."

Juliet's flush turned darker. "Thank you. My unannounced appearance isn't going to cause any problems, is it? I'll leave if there are."

"Problems? What problems?" As far as he knew, the only thing wrong with this meeting was it was happening twenty-six years late.

"Mom wasn't sure if you had married, or if you had children. My being here could cause all types of problems."

"I have one child, Juliet, and that's you." He understood her concern, but it was groundless. "I never married, but if I had, you always would have been welcome." He had no idea what Victoria had told her, but he wanted Juliet to know he would have wanted her, if he had known.

Juliet slowly smiled. "Thank you."

"You have nothing to thank me for." This had to be the most awkward conversation he'd ever held in his life. "How about I go upstairs to get us something to drink, and we can relax a bit? Maybe sit in there." He waved toward the smoking room. It was the only place in the shop to sit, besides a stool he kept behind the cash register.

"That sounds good." Juliet's shoulders seemed to relax a bit.

He was halfway to the stairs that led up to his apartment when a thought occurred to him. "I have no idea what you like to drink. I only have diet soda, orange juice, and milk. I could make a pot of coffee or tea, if you would prefer."

"Diet soda is fine."

He hurried up the stairs and rushed around his kitchen gathering anything he thought she might like. His fingers were shaking so badly that he dropped two ice cubes onto the floor. After a couple of deep breaths he convinced himself Juliet would still be there when he went back down. She had driven all the way up from Boston to see him. She wasn't going to disappear.

Searching the cabinet, he found a box of cookies with a couple left and a new box of fancy crackers. He added those to the tray and hoped she wasn't allergic to anything. His father had had a reaction to strawberries, and he had to wonder if it could have been passed to his daughter.

He frowned down at the tray, wishing he had something more impressive than sick-looking blue glasses that he had bought more than twenty years ago, and mismatched plates. At least the tray was an elegant silver-plated antique he had picked up in London two years ago. Or it would have been if he had bothered to polish it once in a while. There wasn't anything he could do about the tray, or the dishes. He carefully carried the tray down the stairs that ended in the tobacco room.

Juliet was struggling to open the windows. One was open, and she was mumbling under her breath as she tried to raise the other one. The windows were very seldom opened. The reason for that was obvious. They were a bitch to get up or down.

"Here, I'll get that." He placed the tray on the table next to the chess set and put his weight behind trying to open the wooden-framed window. Either the frame was swollen by too many winters and summer storms, or it had been painted one too many times. It took him a few minutes, but he finally managed to get the window up. A cool summer breeze blew sea-scented air into the room.

Juliet pulled her hair to one side, then sat down in the chair closest to the window. "Thank you. I hope you don't mind me opening them."

"Not at all." He moved the chess set to the top of a display case. "Sorry, I guess the aroma can be a little overbearing."

Juliet wondered if her eyes were watering. The stench of burnt tobacco and cigars permeated everything in the entire shop. How did Gordon Hanley, the man who was her biological father, stay in business? "You don't have to apologize. I'm just not used to smokers, that's all."

"It's a nasty habit."

She smiled. "Yet you do it." Her mother told her Gordon Hanley had been a dramatically romantic figure, that every college girl had dreamt about. She tried to picture what Gordon had looked like twenty-six years ago. Sitting across from him, she could see what her mother had meant. Gordon was still a good-looking man, in a Gothic sort of way. He must have been stunning back in his youth. He was tall and thin with an angular face and flowing long black hair that was now streaked with gray. The man who had fathered her looked like a poet.

"I've never touched a cigarette or a cigar. Now a pipe is a different story." Gordon picked up a glass of soda and relaxed into the chair. "A man needs a vice or two to stay sane in this world."

"I could think of worse vices." She now understood where she got her height, her dark hair, and her metabolism. Her mother and sister, Miranda, constantly groused about how she could eat anything and not gain an ounce, while they just looked at food and their jeans got tighter.

"Like having a child and never giving one dime of support?"

She worried her lower lip at the serious change of topic. A touchy subject, by the tone of Gordon's voice. "From what I've been told, you didn't know my mother was pregnant or about me till I was fifteen. My mother asked you not to interfere or contact us."

Gordon didn't deny that statement. "When did Victoria tell you about me?"

"Two months ago. We were having a family dinner when the topic of who had what blood type came up. Mom changed the subject and then asked me to stay after my brothers and sister left."

"Brothers and a sister?"

"You don't know?" She stared at Gordon Hanley, her father, and realized he knew about as much about her life as she knew of his. Absolutely nothing. "I have two brothers and a sister."

"Victoria had four kids?" He chuckled at the thought. "I remember her once telling me she wanted a large family. I'm glad she got what she wanted." There was a touch of sadness in his voice.

"Ken's twenty-four and a police officer with the Boston P.D. Brad's twenty-two and just graduated with a degree in criminal justice. He followed in Ken's footsteps last month."

"And your sister?"

"Miranda's twenty-one and the spoiled baby of the family. She has one more year of college and then she's determined to go to law school."

"They're all in law enforcement?" Gordon seemed intrigued by the idea.

"Dad, I mean my stepfather, was a detective for the Boston Police Department." For twenty-four years she had called Ken Carlyle Dad. Was she really supposed to be calling him stepfather now? And what was she supposed to call Gordon Hanley? She couldn't bring herself to call him Dad, and "Mr. Hanley" sounded asinine considering the situation. "Gordon" had the best ring to it, but so far she had avoided calling him anything.

"What do you do?"

"I've always been the oddball of the family. I'm an elementary school teacher. I teach third grade at a school right outside the Boston city limits." No wonder she'd never felt the slightest desire to follow in her father's footsteps like the rest of the kids. Ken Carlyle hadn't been her father.

"You're not odd." Gordon seemed insulted by the very idea.

"No, I guess I'm not." She had to smile at it now. "I did follow in my father's footsteps after all. Mom told me you were teaching English lit when you two met." Her mother really told her that she had been one of Professor Hanley's students.

Gordon cringed. "It wasn't as bad as that sounds. I was only twenty-nine, and your mother wasn't some nineteen-year-old freshman. She was twenty-six, intelligent, and a beautiful woman."

"I also understand that she did most of the chasing." Her mother hadn't portrayed Gordon as a seducer of young, naive coeds. "The story I heard was that you gave her quite a chase."

"It only appeared that way." Gordon shrugged. "I didn't run that hard or that fast. Victoria Knox stole my breath the first day in class. I knew I was in trouble. I knew it was wrong."

"What happened?" She knew what her mother had told her, but she wanted to hear Gordon's side.

"By Christmas we were having a secret affair. I would have lost my teaching job and messed up my career if the school had found out. Victoria said she didn't mind, but I knew she did. I hated the sneaking around. By May the school year was drawing to a close, and I broke off the relationship. Victoria was going home for the summer and I was heading to England. I thought it would be for the best. Time and distance would take care of the rest."

"Did it?" She knew her mother had loved Ken Carlyle and their marriage had been a happy one. But there had been something special in the way her mother had talked about Gordon Hanley.

"In August, when I returned to teach I discovered Victoria hadn't returned for her senior year. I made some inquiries and discovered she had gotten married during the summer."

Juliet was the one to cringe now. "Ouch." She knew why her mother had married Ken in July of that summer. She had been born on December 11. "That must have hurt."

"I figured our relationship hadn't really meant that much to Victoria."

"Why did you leave teaching?" Juliet loved teaching, and from what her mother told her, so had her father.

Gordon shrugged. "I was born and raised in a town near here, East Sullivan. The coast was in my blood, and I was ready to return." Gordon took a long drink of his soda. "During spring break I discovered this shop was going up for sale. By June my name was on the deed."

There was a lot left unspoken. She knew it, and he knew it. What right did she have to poke into her father's private business? "Why give up teaching? I'm sure there must have been a school somewhere in the area that could have used your experience, your love of Shakespeare."

"You know about my obsession with the Bard?"

"My mother named me Juliet." She raised a brow and bit her lip to keep from smiling. When she had been younger, she had taken quite a bit of ribbing on the name. "Romeo, Romeo" had been shouted frequently within her hearing. By today's standards, Juliet was a very normal name. In the three years she had been teaching she had seen and heard kids named after just about every state, mythical god, and constellation that dotted the universe.

"Juliet is a beautiful name."

"My sister is named Miranda, from the *Tempest*. Thankfully, Dad got to name the boys, or they would have ended up with names like Hamlet or Othello."

Gordon chuckled. "Victoria always did love Shakespeare."

"She still does. Mom volunteers a lot of her time directing at a theater for underprivileged and troubled teens. Most of her time is usually spent fund-raising, though. And she's not above getting the rest of the family involved when she's shorthanded. I spent many of my weekends painting scenery. Miranda's a great seamstress when push comes to shove, and Brad can usually get the lights working for an entire performance. Ken and a couple of fellow cops keep the stage from collapsing around their heads. It's an old theater in a not very desirable part of town. Though the city enforces the building codes, it doesn't see fit to help pay for any of the costs."

"Sounds wonderful and challenging." There was a glow in Gordon's pale hazel eyes.

"You sound like my mother." Her mother got that same glow in her eyes when she talked about the theater.

Before Gordon could reply, two women walked into

the shop. Gordon glanced at the customers and muttered something under his breath that she didn't quite catch.

"Gordon," called the heavyset woman, "I'm here to pick up Roy's order."

Gordon gave Juliet an apologetic look. "Excuse me for a moment. I'll be right back."

"Take your time. I'm fine." Juliet smiled pleasantly at the woman. The other customer was lost from sight.

He went out to the front part of the shop, where Priscilla Patterson stood waiting. "Good afternoon, Priscilla." He spotted the bird-like figure hiding behind Priscilla's bulk. "Norma." The two women, though totally opposite in appearances, went everywhere together. He once referred to them as mismatched bookends.

"Did we interrupt something?" Priscilla was staring at Juliet and the tray of snacks.

Gordon rolled his eyes and winked at his daughter. This was going to get sticky. "Priscilla and Norma, I would like you to meet Juliet Carlyle." How was he supposed to introduce his daughter. "Juliet's the daughter of an old acquaintance of mine." It was the truth.

Juliet stood up and smiled. "Hello."

He hurried over to the wall humidor and found Roy Patterson's standard weekly order: a small tin of McClelland Arcadia and pouch of Sir Walter Raleigh Aromatic. Roy was one of the locals who had convinced him to keep the tobacco part of the shop open. Roy couldn't play chess worth a damn, but he appreciated fine tobacco.

"What brings you to Misty Harbor, Juliet?" Priscilla couldn't care less about her husband's tobacco. She wasn't known to be the town's biggest gossip for nothing.

"I've never been to Maine, and I heard this area was lovely."

"Are you just visiting, or do you plan on staying?"

"Just a short visit."

"Here's the order, Priscilla. Is there anything else I can get you?" He wanted Priscilla and Norma gone. He wanted to spend the day getting to know his daughter. Too late he realized he should have put the CLOSED sign up on the door of the shop. He headed for the cash register, hopefully to ring up Roy's order. Priscilla never lingered in his store because he never had anything new or interesting to tell her.

"Roy's birthday is coming up," Priscilla said as she glanced around the shop. "I've been thinking about buying him a new pipe, but I don't know which one he would like."

He froze and slowly turned to Priscilla. More than twenty-five years he had been running this shop, and never once had Priscilla taken any interest in Roy's tobacco choices or pipes. "Roy usually picks out his own pipes."

"I know, but I wanted to surprise him this year." Priscilla's gaze wasn't on the pipe display case. It was darting back and forth between him and Juliet, measuring and studying.

Norma's hungry gaze was locked on the cookies.

It took him an hour, all the cookies, and a trip upstairs for more soda and crackers, but he finally got Priscilla and Norma out of the shop. He also ended up selling Priscilla the top-of-the-line Peterson pipe that was going to make Roy one happy fellow.

He turned to Juliet, who was browsing the bookshelves. "Sorry about that."

"No need to apologize. They were customers."

"They were on a fact-finding mission." He couldn't believe the questions Priscilla and Norma had asked

Juliet. Priscilla was smart enough to suspect something, but Norma had been more interested in the crackers. Juliet had been taking it all in stride, but he had put his foot down when Priscilla tried arranging a date between her nephew Gregory and Gordon's daughter.

"Can I ask you a question?" Juliet frowned at the shelf before her.

"Sure."

"Why do you stock your books by color, instead of by title or author's name?" Juliet's fingers ran over a row of red spines. "Doesn't it make it difficult for the customers to find what they are looking for?"

"There are two types of book buyers. There are ones who know exactly what they are looking for. I know where every book is stocked, so I can find it for them." Gordon looked around the shop and grinned. "Then there are the buyers who have no idea what they want. So they browse the shelves, and usually something interesting catches their eye that they never thought of reading before."

"People don't mind?" She shook her head at large overflowing shelves of black books.

"Tourists come in for two kinds of books: the latest bestseller, or books on Maine. The locals are used to my system and have adjusted fine. I have quite a few regulars who are working their way through the colors."

Juliet laughed and shook her head. "I must admit, it's different."

"Thank you." He took that as a compliment. "How long are you planning on staying in town?"

"A couple days, maybe a week." His daughter looked uncertain. "If you don't mind."

"Mind? Of course I don't mind." His heart would have been crushed if she had turned around and driven out of his life so soon after entering it. "Do you have a place to stay?"

"Not yet. I wasn't sure what I would find, so I didn't make any hotel reservations." Juliet relaxed a bit. "I did pass a Motor Inn on the way into town."

He made a rude sound. "You can't stay there. I can call a local bed-and-breakfast to see if they have a room, or you can stay here with me. I actually have a very small guest room upstairs in my apartment. My brother and his wife make use of it whenever they come to visit. The choice is up to you." How desperate did that sound, offering his daughter the guest room?

"The bed-and-breakfast sounds nice."

He tried not to let his feelings show. After all, he was a complete stranger to her. He headed for the phone. "I'll give Olivia a call and see if she has room." Olivia Wycliffe was due any day now, but he knew she had someone helping her with the bed and breakfast she owned.

Two minutes later, Juliet had a room, and the bill was coming to him.

"Now it's only a couple streets away from here." He drew a quick map on a piece of scrap paper. "You can't miss it."

"I'm sure I can find it." Juliet took the map and turned to the front door. "You really don't have to take me out to dinner. I'm sure you have something better to do with your time."

"There is nothing on this earth that would give me greater joy than taking you to dinner tonight." Hell, he didn't even want her to leave the shop. He was scared to death she would disappear from his life for another twenty-six years. At fifty-six years old, he wasn't sure if he had another twenty-six years left in him. "I'll pick you up a little before seven. The Catch of the Day is the best restaurant in town."

"I'll be waiting." Juliet gave him a sweet smile and walked out the door.

Chapter Five

Matt had a feeling that the family cookout would head in this direction, and he would be powerless to stop it. At least his father and brothers looked as helpless as he felt. The women were sitting at one picnic table discussing Ned and Norah's upcoming wedding, while the men were supposed to be watching the kids and getting dinner on the table.

It was easier said than done.

Three-month-old Amanda was screaming her head off, and if the aroma coming from that direction was any indication, he didn't envy his brother Paul's job. His father was manning the grill while Ned and Norah's new stepfather, Karl James, were in the kitchen getting things together. He and John were supposed to be watching the older kids as they ran around the backyard.

Herding kittens would have been easier.

Tyler and Austin had joined forces with three-year-old Morgan and Hunter. Between chasing chipmunks under the shrubs, trying to ride Ned's big black Newfoundland, Flipper, or teasing Zsa Zsa, the Pomeranian with an attitude, it was impossible to keep track of them all. Three-year-old

Morgan had been trying to get the pink bow out of the tiny dog's hair. Zsa Zsa wanted no part of Morgan and her sticky fingers. The four-pound Pomeranian had big brown eyes only for the 150-pound Newfoundland.

"Morgan, get away from Zsa Zsa before she snaps at you," called John, who was dragging Tyler out from under a bush. "Your mother said not to get dirty." John shook his head at his son. The entire front of Tyler was coated in dirt and dust. A twig was sticking out of his hair and half a back pocket on his shorts was hanging by a thread.

It was a typical Porter barbecue, only this time, he had two invited guests, and with Ned's future in-laws there, his father had to set up a folding table to handle the overflow. Sierra and Austin blended right in with the rowdy crowd. In fact, since they'd arrived, he hadn't been able to talk to his own date. He couldn't kid himself any longer—this was a date.

He was dating a tourist and her son. No wonder his brothers were looking at him with sympathy in their eyes. Everyone knew August was "heartbreak month" in Misty Harbor. The way things were going, his heart was going to at least get stepped on, if not crushed. Sierra was becoming very important to him, and he hadn't even kissed her yet. He watched as Sierra and Norah bent their heads over a pad of paper. Night and day. Norah had short, red, spiky hair and about twenty earrings glittering in her ears. Sierra's long blond hair was let down tonight in a classic style.

He knew the women were talking about Ned and Norah's upcoming wedding, but he didn't understand what all the jabbering was about. How difficult could it be to plan a wedding? The way the women were going on, someone would think the queen of England and the president were going to be invited.

"Hey, Matt, grab Austin before he hurts himself," called his father.

He glanced over to where he'd last seen Austin and felt his heart plummet to his knees. Austin was hanging upside down from a tree limb. He sprinted across the yard and grabbed the little monkey. "Hey, how did you get up there?" Austin hadn't been too far off the ground, but someone had to help him reach the low limb.

Austin grinned but remained mute. Tyler and Hunter looked guilty.

He glanced over at Sierra to see if she'd noticed Austin's Tarzan imitation. She had one finely arched golden brow raised and she gave him a look that made him extremely thankful that nothing had harmed her son. He grimaced but smiled back.

Austin waved to his mother. "Mom, did you see me?" he shouted.

"Sure did, sweetie," she said before turning her attention to Matt. Sierra gave him another long look and then winked.

"We're hungry, Uncle Matt," complained Tyler.

"What else is new?" Matt wondered if the wink meant he was forgiven. "Let's go see what's holding up the food." Surely once the food was brought out the women would cease their planning and he would be able to talk to his date. He headed for the house with Austin on his shoulders and Hunter and Tyler bringing up the rear. His brother John was busy chasing his daughter, Morgan, who was running after Zsa Zsa with an evil look upon her face and a butterfly net clutched in her fist.

The first thing he noticed as he entered the house was the smell. By his brother Paul's "goo-gooing" and "gaa-gaaing" he could tell that baby Amanda was being changed in the other room. His niece wasn't the cause of the stench. "What reeks?"

His brother Ned was standing in front of the open oven door and wearing huge red lobster pot holders. He was holding a casserole dish. "Mom's beans."

All he could see was a thick layer of ash that was slowly bubbling. "What did you do to them?" His mother's baked beans were horrible, but they usually didn't resemble the city of Pompeii.

"I didn't do anything to them," Ned said as he placed the dish onto the counter. "Mom set the timer, and I was supposed to take them out when it went off."

Karl James tugged at his beard, trying to hide his grin from the boys, who were staring at the dish in complete fascination. "Joanna gave your mom her recipe for them."

"Do your wife's baked beans look like this?" Ned picked up a fork and poked one of the bubbles. A small cloud of ash billowed into the air.

Karl took the fork from Ned's hand and poked at another globule of air. Another small explosion of ash rose above the casserole dish. "Can't say that I've ever seen anything like this."

Tyler's eyes grew wide and he shuddered. "Do we have to eat that?"

"Yuck," added Austin. From the boy's perch on Matt's shoulders, he had a clear view of destruction.

"Don't you guys worry about it. We'll figure out something." He had no idea what, but there was no way anyone could eat that and be healthy enough to attend Ned's wedding in two weeks. They also couldn't hurt his mother's feelings. Peggy Porter had feelings beneath her tough facade. Of course she might knock a couple of her sons' heads together while expressing those tender feelings.

"How about we all help get this stuff outside?" The countertop and table were overflowing with food. He plucked Austin off his shoulders and set him on his feet. "You can carry the mustard and ketchup." He handed Austin the plastic containers and then started handing out the other stuff for the youngsters to carry. Light and nonbreakable was the rule.

Karl and Ned each picked up a large bowl of salad and headed out back. Paul was still in their parents' room changing Amanda, and John was out back. Why was he always stuck with the dirty job?

With the kitchen empty, there was no time like the present. "Leave no witnesses" had always been the Porter boys' motto when they were young. He moved out of the splash zone and, using a long spatula, pushed the casserole dish off the counter and onto the floor. The loud crash was heard out back. He could hear "What was that?" coming from a couple people.

By the time his mother and brother Ned rushed into the kitchen he had the dustpan out and was gathering up the broken pieces of the dish and the congealed glob of beans.

"What happened?" asked his mother, looking at the mess on the floor.

"I'm sorry, Mom, it slipped." He pretended not to hear Ned cough. "I'll buy you a new dish. I know how much you liked this one." He kept his eyes on the mess. If he looked at his brother he was sure to laugh. At one time or another, all through their youth, various dishes had slipped. Even his father had been known to drop a few.

"Well, clean up the mess." His mother stepped around him and grabbed the basket filled with rolls. "Krup's

General Store carries the blue set of cookware that matches everything else your brothers or father buy to replace what they break." Peggy Porter pushed opened the screen door and disappeared onto the back patio.

Matt cringed when he heard his mom say, "It's nothing. Matt, the klutz, dropped the baked beans, so we are going to have to do without them tonight. I swear, the men in this family have blubber on their fingers with the way things slip out of their hands all the time. How any of them manage to keep all their fingers and toes when they work around power tools is beyond me."

Paul, who was standing in the bedroom doorway with a now-smiling Amanda in his arms, laughed. "I bought her a new Crock-Pot last month and I had to drive all the way into Sullivan to pick up a bucket of chicken to replace the tuna stew she had made." Paul shuddered at the memory.

Ned got some paper towels and wet them. "I remember the tuna stew. Norah told me the wedding was off if I made her eat any of it."

"So why didn't you drop the Crock-Pot?" groused Paul. "The new one she liked set me back fifty bucks and now Jill is complaining that my mother has a bigger Crock-Pot. She wants a new one too."

"You got to it first." Ned smiled and handed Matt the wet towels.

He took the towels. "Hey, a little help here." The beans had splattered everywhere but thankfully none had landed on him. There were even beans dripping down the cabinet doors. He'd saved the family from having to choke down the beans, or finding ways to dispose of them off their plates without his mother seeing them. The least his brothers could do was help clean up the mess.

Paul and Ned both laughed, picked up the remaining food, and headed out the door. "Why should we help? We weren't the ones to drop it, klutz."

He uttered a curse as the screen door slammed. Great, now Sierra was going to think he was a klutz. He cleaned up the major part of the spill and tossed everything into the garbage can.

Armed with the roll of towels and some orange spray cleaner, he started to wipe down the cabinet doors.

"Need any help?" Sierra had quietly sneaked up on him.

"Thanks, but I got it." Now he felt like a real idiot. Thankfully most of the mess was history. "I'm usually not this clumsy." It was a little hard to explain how broken baking dishes could prevent food poisoning. It would be stupid to even try.

"Norah just let me in on the secret." Sierra leaned her hip against the counter and frowned at the few remaining cabinet doors he had yet to wipe down. "I've never seen baked beans that color before. Why are they gray?"

"No one knew, and no one was brave enough to taste them to see what secret ingredient my mother might have added to this batch." His mother once had added sardines to spaghetti sauce.

"Why is it smearing like that?" Sierra bent down to study the gray smear left behind after the first wipe. She reached out a finger and touched the streak. A gray residue coated the tip of her finger. "It's powdery."

"It's ash." He sprayed the cabinet and wiped it clean. "Now you know why I accidentally dropped the dish."

"Smart move." Sierra stood up, walked over to the sink, and washed her hands. "So you're not only a nice guy and a great brother, but a hero too."

"How do you figure that?" He cleaned the last cabinet

door and tossed the used paper towel. He joined Sierra at the sink.

"You're nice because you didn't want to hurt your mom's feelings"—Sierra playfully bumped his hip with hers and reached for a towel to dry her hands—"and you're a hero for not making any of us eat whatever that was in the dish you broke."

"'Hero' is stretching it a bit." He wasn't a hero. Just a simple coward who had eaten one too many meals his mother had fixed. The first allowance he had ever received had been spent on a bottle of Pepto-Bismol.

"I think it's cute." Sierra handed him the towel.

For the first time he noticed he had Sierra alone and all to himself. No Austin, no brothers, and no other family members to distract her. "So you think I'm cute?" he teased as he dried his hands.

Sierra's laugh was low and seductive. "There is that, but that's not what I said."

He loved her smile. It was reflected in her eyes. "So you do think I'm cute." Hell, no man wanted to be known as "cute," but he wasn't about to get choosy at this stage of the game. He'd take "cute." They both were crowded into the corner of the kitchen. He could smell the light scent of her perfume. Sierra wore the fragrance of a fresh, cool summer breeze with just a hint of flowers. The perfume alone raised his blood pressure. He watched her eyes as he reached out a finger and slowly traced her lower lip.

Sierra's eyes flared opened with heat, and she seemed to have stopped breathing.

Whatever he was feeling, Sierra was feeling it too. He hadn't been imagining this connection between them.

"Hey," called Ned as he opened the screen door,

"everyone is looking for you two." Ned grinned as he strolled into the kitchen.

Sierra blushed and quickly stepped away. Matt turned to his brother and wondered what he could chuck across the room to wipe that smile off his face. "Was there anything else you wanted, Ned?"

"Mom sent me in for the deviled eggs Jill brought." Ned walked over to the refrigerator and pulled out a tray. Two dozen deviled eggs slipped and slid across the plastic tray but thankfully none landed on the floor. "She also said for you two to knock off whatever you're doing and get your butts on out there."

He wanted to bury his face into his hands and howl. Sierra was going to think his whole family was crude and insensitive. "Tell her we'll be right there," he muttered between clenched teeth.

"I have to go check on Austin." Sierra hurried out the door without a backward glance.

"Oops." Ned shrugged. "I guess I interrupted something."

"You could say that." He had no idea what Ned had interrupted, but whatever it was, the heat of the moment had been about to consume them both.

"Matt, I don't want to rain on your parade, but she'll be leaving come Labor Day." Ned gave him a sympathetic smile.

"You don't think I know that?" he snapped as he left the kitchen and joined the party.

Sierra walked the yard in silence; studying every angle. She could hear Norah and her mother behind her arguing about something, but she tuned out the volume of their voices until it sounded like a bee droning. She learned that little secret years ago. Without getting her own bearings first, she wouldn't be able to come up with solutions to the growing list of problems.

And the list was long and various.

Norah and Ned's wedding was a little over two weeks away, and as far as she could tell, the entire event was a disaster waiting to happen. The good news was that the wedding party consisted of four people, and that included the bride and groom. Matt was going to be the best man, and Norah's college roommate was to be the maid of honor. Matt and Ned both had purchased new suits for the occasion. Norah's dress was ordered, fitted, and guaranteed to be ready on time. The maid of honor was bringing her own gown of pale pink. Beyond that, nothing was settled.

Sierra looked around the yard of Joanna and Norah's cottage. The small house was right next door to Matt's parents. On the plus side, the yard was large enough to hold an outside wedding, which was what Ned and Norah wanted. On the minus side, the yard wasn't what she would call landscaped. Someone had started some nice gardens, but that was as far as he or she had gotten—the starting point. The yard had a long way to go to match any of those pictures Norah and her mother had marked or ripped out of the countless magazines they had shown Sierra earlier.

"Who's the gardener?" She had seen enough. Now it was time to offer up some solutions.

"I am," answered Joanna, Norah's mom. "When we first moved here in June, I started to play a little bit with the yard, but I didn't manage to get very far."

"Karl swept her off her feet, and the next thing I knew my mom's married and has left home." Norah grinned at her mom and teased, "Of course Karl's gardens look wonderful."

"How was I supposed to know that you had your heart set on a garden wedding?" Joanna looked upset and frazzled.

"Mom, it's okay." Norah hugged her mom. "We'll think of something."

"How many guests are invited?" Sierra didn't waste time worrying about things that couldn't be changed. The past was one of them.

"Between two hundred fifty and three hundred." Norah looked shocked as she quoted that figure. "Ned said the entire town is going to show up."

Matt's mom and sisters-in-law joined them. "That's right, Norah. There will be no stopping it. Ned was born and raised here. He knows everyone."

"But that will mean the bride's side will have only a handful of people." Joanna looked distressed. "We have only about a dozen relatives coming in, and a few friends Norah has made at work."

"Then why have a bride's side and a groom's side?" She looked at Norah. "A garden wedding isn't as formal as a church one. You don't have to have sides."

Norah looked intrigued.

"Besides, who's going to seat them? You don't have any ushers, just Matt as the best man. It would take Matt a long time to properly seat three hundred people."

"I always thought the bride's side versus the groom's side was stupid," Jill said. "At our wedding we had people who were friends with both of us, and they had no idea which side to take."

"Taking sides does sound ridiculous," added Kay. "You go to a wedding for the whole couple, not just half."

Norah grinned. "Okay, no sides. So how do we set up the chairs?"

"I was thinking over there." Ned's mom pointed to the left.

"I thought over here would be better." Norah's mom pointed to the right.

"What about there?" Kay waved her hand toward the very back of the yard.

Norah's gaze bounced from person to person. The bride-to-be looked confused, rattled, and ready to elope.

"I have a question," Sierra said calmly. "Norah, do you still want the arbor with all the climbing roses as the center stage where you and Ned will exchange your vows?"

"Ned and I both love that idea, but I don't see how we can do it." Norah glanced around the yard. Only two rose bushes were in bloom, and neither was over three feet high.

"Let's pretend we can get an arbor and the roses. Where would you like to see it set up?"

"Over in the far corner of the property." Norah pointed to the corner where their property met Ned's parents'. It was filled with trees and bushes. "If it was set up in front of the trees, they would act as a lovely green backdrop, and the guests wouldn't have a view of the other neighbors' fences and backyards."

She smiled. "Perfect." It was where she would have put it. "You place the arbor, arch, altar—or whatever you want to call it—and then set the chairs up so they are all facing it."

"Ummm . . . Sierra, you're forgetting one thing," Norah said with a smile. "We don't have an arbor, arch, fence, or even a tepee that roses or any other plant could climb up."

"Arbors and roses are easy." She grinned at Norah. If there was ever a woman in love, she was standing right in front of her. "It's that true love part that's a little more difficult to come by. Enjoy it."

"If only Ned would wait until next summer. I can have this garden blooming like crazy." Joanna looked at the yard in dismay. "Norah and Ned both want a garden wedding, and I have no idea where to even begin."

"They should get married in the church," said Jill. "Then we can have some flowers brought in to give it that garden feel. They can even have the reception in the social hall or down at the fire hall."

"Ned said I have till the middle of August to pull this together," Norah added, "or he's kidnapping me and taking me to Las Vegas to get married by an Elvis impersonator." Norah shuddered at the thought.

Sierra laughed. "Then I suggest we get moving."

"We?" Norah raised a brow.

"We, if you want my help." No one in Misty Harbor knew her, so she couldn't blame them for being cautious. "I'm an excellent expediter, and I can delegate like nobody's business."

"But you're on vacation," Joanna said.

"This is a vacation to me." She wasn't about to tell them the real reason she was spending a month in Misty Harbor. Once people found out she was scouting the area for a major hotel, the truth was harder for her to see. Everyone started having agendas. People had strong opinions on whether they wanted to see a hundred fifty–room elegant hotel go up in their town. Either they would be profiting from the extra tourist trade and employment or they would be losing business, losing their employees, and losing their small town. Once a Randall Hotel went up, Misty Harbor would cease to be a small town.

Things would change. She was aware of the fact that most people didn't like change.

"You wouldn't mind helping?" Norah seemed thrilled with the thought.

"Of course not. I volunteered, didn't I?" She was practically knocked to the ground when Norah threw herself at her. Norah was an itty-bitty thing, but if you added all the weight of her jewelry, she weighed as much as Flipper, Ned's Newfoundland.

"Have you ever planned a wedding before?" Joanna asked.

"No, but I've attended many, and my best friend is a wedding planner. Lianna's in L.A. right now, but she'll help us." The Randall Hotel Corporation had Lianna on a retainer for when important guests needed that particular service. Either Lianna came personally, or she worked closely with the event coordinator at the hotel.

"Do you really think we can pull this together?" Norah looked hopeful. "I really don't want to get married by a guy in a white sequined jumpsuit."

"We can't find a caterer," Peggy Porter said.

"None of them will take on a big affair on such short notice." Joanna picked up Zsa Zsa, who had come running across the yard.

"I suggested the women's guild at the church, but every one of them has been invited to the wedding," Jill said.

Kay added, "No one wants to miss the reception."

"What if it rains?"

"We can't find a band."

"We found a place that rents tables and chairs, but they don't have tents."

"What about a DJ?"

"We need a bridal bouquet and centerpieces."

"What about a bar? Who's going to be serving drinks?" Peggy asked.

The questions and complaints were coming fast and furious. Sierra looked at Norah. The poor gal looked shell-shocked and ready to cry.

"Stop!" Sierra raised her hand and her voice. "We're upsetting Norah."

Everyone looked at the bride-to-be and started to apologize. Sierra shook her head and tried not to laugh. Not one constructive thing with the upcoming wedding had been accomplished, and they had been talking about it for hours. Before dinner, during dinner, and now after dinner, the entire conversation had been about Ned and Norah's wedding. The men of the family figured all they had to do was show up for the ceremony and enjoy themselves. The females were all running around like Chicken Little with the sky about to fall.

She reached for Norah's hand and pulled her from the mob. "Norah, do you trust me to help? I know pulling a wedding together in two weeks is a challenge, but I'm up for it. Plus I have a whole bunch of free time." She was more than up for the challenge. She needed a challenge.

"You really don't mind?" Norah wiped at a lone tear. "I think we could use your help."

"I would love to." Sierra felt the thrill of being needed for what she could do, not for who she was. "This is Norah's wedding. What she says goes. Our job, ladies, is to give Norah the wedding of her dreams." Sierra glared across the yard to the Porters' backyard.

All the men were sitting around the picnic tables drinking beer and relaxing like they didn't have a care in the world. Karl James appeared to be telling an amusing story. Amanda was asleep in her stroller, and the kids were all blowing bubbles. Someone had been smart enough to pack plastic bubble bottles. Her money would be on one of the mothers.

"Do you know what the first thing we are going to do is, ladies?"

All the women had followed her gaze across the yard. "What?"

"We are going to get the men involved. It's Ned's wedding too, and he's the one who put a time limit on this affair."

Peggy chuckled. "You want Ned to plan his own wedding? Lord, we'll all be hiking up mountains at sunrise or some such nonsense."

Norah groaned. "He'll want to spend the honeymoon in a tent."

"We won't let him plan a thing, Norah." She gave the bride-to-be a hug. "Remember, we're delegating."

"What will we have them doing?" Joanna didn't look like she was going to trust her daughter's big day to a bunch of Porters.

"Come, I'll teach you all a lesson in delegating." She gave them a big wink and then led the women back to the picnic tables. They all sat down.

Sierra reached into the pile of magazines Norah had brought with her and started to flip through them. Norah had all the pages marked. She found the one she was looking for. "Norah, is this what you want?" The glossy picture was of a bride standing before a white arbor covered in pink roses. The advertisement was for some expensive fragrance.

"Yes, that's the look I want." Norah wasn't talking about the gown.

Sierra smiled and looked across to the table where all the men were sitting. "Ned, I understand you're a very good carpenter."

Ned grinned and his chest puffed out with pride. "Most think so."

"Hey," Matt said, "he puts together overgrown Lincoln Logs. If you need a perfectionist, I'm your man."

Paul made a rude sound. "I taught them both everything they know about wood."

"And who, pray tell, taught you?" John Sr. crossed his arms over his chest and glared at his four boys.

She fingered the page of the magazine and tried not to smile. Men were so predictable sometimes. "So you all are handy with tools?"

"Darn straight we are." Ned looked insulted that anyone would think differently. "There's not a thing we can't build with our own two hands."

"What do you need?" asked Matt. He tried to glance at the magazine she was holding.

"Doesn't matter what she needs," stated John Jr. "We can do it better than anyone else in town."

"Just keep Paul away from a chain saw and everything will be okay," joked Ned.

"Hey, that wasn't my fault. The darn thing kicked."

"What about the time you fell off the roof, Ned?" Matt was laughing at his younger brother.

"I was pushed!"

"You fell off a roof?" Norah looked horrified by the idea. "Why didn't you tell me?"

"I was only four at the time and Paul pushed me."

Sierra felt her stomach lurch. What was a four-year-old doing up on a roof?

"I did not." Paul glared at Ned. "You lost your footing and almost pulled me down with you."

"Did you get hurt?" Norah's gaze was traveling over Ned, looking for signs of an old injury.

"Only my pride." Ned grinned.

"And my holly bush," Peggy Porter added. "Fell right on top of it and broke it to pieces."

"He could have been hurt," cried Norah.

"Ah, he had a good two feet of snow to break his fall." Ned's father didn't look upset.

"What were you doing up on the roof, anyway?" Norah asked her husband-to-be.

"We were waiting for Santa Claus." Matt answered like it was nothing.

"Yeah, all four of them sneaked up there about midnight one Christmas Eve. I believe the plan was to sneak some more toys for themselves once Santa went down the chimney."

Sierra looked at the Porters' house behind her. It was a two-story home, and the roof looked a long way up. "How did they get up there?" Austin was four and she never would have thought about him climbing up on some roof—Santa or no Santa.

"Climbed out the bedroom window and shimmied right up onto the roof. The older boys had to help the younger ones." Peggy glared at the boys. "Nearly gave me heart failure when little Ned came falling past our bedroom window screaming like some banshee."

The Porter men all laughed, while the women whacked them on the arms.

Sierra's stomach dropped to her knees as her gaze sought out Austin. Her son was having a wonderful time with the Porter kids. Austin was safe.

"What do you need, Sierra?" Matt was watching her.

She glanced down at the magazine in her lap. Now she didn't feel so bad at springing this on them. Ned and his brothers owed their mother big time for that fright. There were probably a hundred more frights just like that over the years.

Sierra looked at Ned and smiled sweetly. "It's just a little project we need for the wedding." She held the picture against her chest. "I'm sure between you and your brothers and father it will be a snap to build, considering all your skills and talent combined."

"I think we've been had, boys," John Sr. chuckled.

Ned groaned.

She handed Ned the magazine and lightly tapped the picture of the arbor. "Norah likes this one, and we need it done and in place two days before the wedding."

Ned looked at the picture and then up at Norah. "This one?"

Norah slowly nodded her head. She looked uncertain, but her eyes were smiling with love and hope.

"All you had to do was ask, honey." Ned leaned forward and kissed her.

Matt and the rest of the Porter men were staring at the ten-foot-by-twelve-foot elaborate Victorian arbor in pure horror.

Karl James whistled softly.

Somewhere behind her she heard Peggy and Joanna chuckle with appreciation. Peggy's deep voice muttered something about delegating.

Tyler looked at his Uncle Ned and his soon-to-be Aunt Norah and made fake choking sounds. "Yuck!"

Ned and Norah still hadn't come up for air.

Chapter Six

Matt liked the silence of the night and the darkness as he walked Sierra and Austin back home. After a couple hours in the company of his family, he needed the peace and quiet. He and Sierra each held one of Austin's hands, and they were swinging him between them with every step.

They looked like a family.

"You don't think I was too pushy, do you?" Sierra asked as they neared her front door. For the first time this evening, Sierra looked uncertain.

"I think you did a masterful job of managing my brothers." She also managed him like a pro. He had a piece of paper stuck in his back pocket with a list of things he had to do for the wedding. Everyone had a list, and Sierra controlled the master list.

He didn't mind. Much.

He had been racking his brains trying to figure out how to help Ned and Norah with their wedding. Ned kept saying they needed the help, but no one got around to telling anyone what to do. Sierra's lists told them in minute detail what to do and how to do it, and heads would be rolling off those who lagged.

He had to give Sierra credit. There was only one other woman who could control and manage all the Porter boys at once, and that was their mother. Peggy Porter wasn't what anyone would classify as a feminine mother. He loved his mother dearly, but he knew more about putting a wedding together than she ever would. And he knew squat.

Ned insisted on an outdoor wedding and a very short time frame to pull it off. Norah had always dreamed that when she got married it would be in a garden—her mother's garden. For once the bride and groom were in perfect harmony.

Now all they had to do was pull together a garden, order some food, hire a band, and call the minister and Norah would have her perfect dream wedding. Ned wanted whatever made Norah happy. The Porter boys had always stuck together through thick and thin. Norah and Ned were going to get that dream garden wedding. If Sierra was the person to pull it all together, that was fine by him.

To his way of thinking, a strong-minded woman was a turn-on.

Matt released Austin's hand as they reached the front porch of the house. "Someone looks sleepy." The last couple of feet, Austin barely swung. The little boy appeared to be half asleep on his feet.

"Would you like to come in for coffee?" Sierra dug out the key to the door.

"Sure." He followed them into the house. He couldn't remember ever being in the Alberts' L-shaped rancher before. "Nice place."

Sierra flashed him a grin. "Thanks, but it's not mine." Sierra guided her son toward the back of the house while calling over her shoulder, "If you put the coffee on, I'll get sleepyhead here ready for bed."

"I can do that." He had seen his brothers and sisters-in-law trying to get kids ready for bed before. Horrible screaming, crying, and laughing battles went on behind closed bathroom doors. The end result was always the same. His niece and nephews came out all squeaky clean, wearing cute pajamas, and looking like angels. His brothers and sisters-in-law came out soaking wet, exasperated, and battle weary. He'd take coffee duty any day of the week.

The Alberts' kitchen opened into an eating area and was done in what designers called "country." He called it normal. The coffeemaker was sitting on the counter, along with some dirty dishes, tourist brochures, two unopened bottles of wine, and four C batteries.

He looked in the cabinets and found the filters but no coffee. "Hey, Sierra, where do you keep the coffee?" he yelled in the direction of the bathroom.

Sierra's voice was muffled by the closed door, but he heard, "In the refrigerator."

Confused, he opened the refrigerator door, and sure enough a can of ground decaf was sitting on one of the shelves. Sierra obviously had a thing for fresh fruit and vegetables; the fridge was packed with them, along with milk, wine, and six fruit juices. Not a beer in sight. With the can of coffee in his hand, he yelled, "Why do you keep it in the refrigerator?"

"It stays fresh longer that way," came Sierra's reply over the sound of running water.

He chuckled at the thought of coffee going stale in any of the Porters' households. Never would happen. He made the coffee and eyed the mess sitting on the kitchen table. The only sound he could hear coming from the bathroom was running water and laughter, both Austin's and his mom's.

While the coffee brewed, he studied the mess. A remote-control car took center stage. The red car had its guts ripped open and its antenna was bent in half. A few loose wires hung from the undercarriage and three of its wheels were off. One of the axles looked bent and the hood was crinkled. There appeared to be a set of puncture marks in one of the doors. Someone had had a major wipeout. The controller was also opened, and the batteries were everywhere, along with four screwdrivers, a pair of needle-nose pliers, and a butter knife.

He closed his eyes and tried not to imagine what Sierra had used the butter knife on.

Short of seeing if there was a ball game on television or twiddling his thumbs, he didn't have anything better to do at the moment. In his experience, dates really got ticked off if you turned on a ball game. He pulled out a chair, sat, and picked up the car.

Fifteen minutes later, Sierra and a squeaky-clean Austin walked into the kitchen. Matt was so engrossed in what he was doing, he didn't even hear them.

"Wow!" Austin exclaimed as he hurried over to Matt and his racing car. Her son climbed up on the chair next to Matt. "Can you fix it?"

Matt chuckled. "No guarantees with this one, Austin." He reinserted the now-straight axle. "What did you do to it? Drive it off a cliff?"

Austin pouted. "Mom did it, not me."

Matt slowly turned in his chair and stared at her. "You did this?"

She felt like an idiot and could almost hear the women-driver jokes that Matt was smart enough not to voice. "Yes, and no." She hated feeling stupid. "I was holding the controller at the time of the incident." She could tell Matt was trying not to laugh at her.

"Want to explain the incident?"

"Elvis did it!" Austin was stacking the car's tires on top of each other.

"Elvis?" Matt's grin was contagious. "The King wrecked your car?"

"To be more accurate, the King bit Austin's car during its maiden voyage and then ran with it through half of Misty Harbor before we could catch him."

"Ah . . . that explains the puncture marks in the door." Matt held out his hand, and Austin placed a small plastic tire in it. "Did you get his autograph?"

"Whose?" Sierra poured Austin a small glass of juice.

"Elvis's, who else?"

"Elvis is a dog. A big, overweight hound dog that lives next door and has nothing better to do with his days than to chase remote-control cars and terrorize the neighborhood."

She placed the juice in front of Austin. "Are you still hungry, hon?"

"Cookies?" Austin gave her that hopeful pleading look, that usually worked. Tonight, it wasn't going to.

"No. You had enough snack food over at the Porters'. You can have an apple, a banana, or some grapes." With the amount of junk food Austin had consumed, she didn't know how he could possibly be hungry. There had been enough food at the Porters' barbecue to feed the entire town. Instead of trying to find a caterer for the wedding, they should just hold a barbecue.

"Nah, not hungry now." Austin sipped his juice and played the pit crew for Matt, who was putting the car back together.

She'd figured as much. She got down two mugs and poured the coffee. She added sugar and cream to hers and left Matt's black. With a mug in each hand, she joined them at the table.

Matt attached the last tire just as she set the coffee in front of him. "You remembered how I take it?" Matt seemed impressed.

"Black, no sugar, right?" It had been ingrained in her mind since the morning out at the lighthouse when he had shared his coffee with her. She had never tasted a stronger cup of coffee in her life. It was like drinking espresso, and she disliked espresso.

"Thanks." Matt smiled at her, before turning his attention to Austin. "You ready to test this out, Crash?" He held up the car.

Austin excitedly slid off the chair and reached for the car. "Make it go fast."

Matt chuckled and reached for the controller. "Fast it is."

Her son placed the car on the floor and took a step back. Matt put the batteries in the controller and snapped the case closed. "Ready?"

Austin nodded. "Ready."

Matt fiddled with the knob, and the car made a right-hand turn and crashed into the baseboard. "Hmmm . . ." Matt fiddled some more, reversed the car, and started to drive it in and out of the chair and table legs. "There she goes, just like new." He made an exceptionally great turn and stopped the car right in front of Austin. "Want to give it a try, Crash?"

Her son nodded and moved closer to Matt.

Sierra sat back in her chair and watched Matt patiently explain the controls to her son. She sipped her coffee and smiled as Matt's large hand covered her son's and showed him exactly how to maneuver the small joystick. Within minutes Austin had the car weaving in and out of chairs and she had to resort to putting her feet up on a chair to save her toes. Of course it looked like a deranged game of bumper cars, but Austin was having a blast. By all the sound effects, Matt seemed to be enjoying himself just as much.

She hated to be the spoilsport, but it was way past Austin's bedtime. "Hey, Crash, just a few more turns around the table, and then it's hit-the-hay time."

"Aw, Mom . . ."

"Aw, Austin . . . ," she mimicked right back. It was a nighttime tradition between them.

Her son grinned. "Can I play with it tomorrow?"

"Sure can." Jake, Austin's father, had sent the car to him as an enjoy-your-vacation gift. They had been in Misty Harbor for only a week, and so far Jake had called four times to make sure they were okay. The first two times he'd called, it had been sweet that Jake had been so thoughtful. By the fourth call she was beginning to suspect that Jake might not fully think she was capable of handling her own life and taking care of their son.

"Hey, Crash, I'm coming for dinner tomorrow night." Matt ruffled the top of Austin's head. "You can show me what you can do then, okay?"

"Is Tyler coming with you?" Austin seemed more concerned with his new best friend than his mother inviting a man to dinner.

"Afraid not." Matt looked at her. "But if you and your mom aren't doing anything Saturday morning, we could go fishing out at Sunset Cove."

"Will Tyler be there?" Austin had a one-track mind and wasn't afraid to speak it.

"Sure, but it's up to your mom, Crash. She might have other plans already made." Matt gave her a pleading look that matched her son's.

"Please, Mom, please!"

Two against one was unfair odds, but how could she resist? "We don't have any fishing gear," she teased. Krup's General Store had everything they would need, but she didn't want to appear to be a total pushover. Both with her son, and Matt.

"No problem. I'll fix you both up with everything you'll need." Matt winked at Austin.

She laughed at her son's attempt to wink back. "I know when I've been outnumbered. Fishing on Saturday sounds fine."

Austin threw his arms around her neck. "Thanks, Mom."

She kissed his cheek. "You should be thanking Matt, not me. I'm not the one who will be baiting your hook." She looked at Matt to make sure he got that message loud and clear.

Matt grinned. "What about taking the catch off the hook?"

"Nope, not me." There was no way she was touching any slimy worms or flopping fish. There was a reason she had been born a girly-girl. "And I'm not cleaning or cooking them either."

"Got anything against eating them?" Matt chuckled.

"No, I love fish and any other kind of seafood."

"So how do you usually get the fish you claim to love?" Matt asked.

"I order it off a menu." Usually phoned in to room service, but she didn't want to sound too much like a wimp. Matt seemed to be having a hard time realizing she didn't do the fishing thing. The women in Maine seemed more in tune with the outdoors. Kay, one of Matt's sisters-in-law, even went hunting.

Matt's laughter filled the kitchen. Austin joined in,

even though she was pretty sure he didn't know what he was laughing about.

"Come on, Crash, say goodnight to Matt." She stood up and took the controller away from her son. "You'll see him tomorrow night."

Austin's "Goodnight, Matt" was barely out of his mouth before he sprinted from the room.

"I'll be right back, Matt. Help yourself to another cup of coffee and make yourself at home." She followed her son to his room.

Austin was already in bed with the light blanket tucked to his chin. "You cold?" His window was open, but it didn't seem too chilly.

"Nope." Austin wiggled some more.

"What has you so excited?" She knew her son's moods. If she wasn't mistaken, it was going to be a long time before he allowed sleep to claim him. "Santa doesn't come for another four months."

"Tyler told me a secret today."

"He did?" Best friends were always telling each other secrets. She was happy that Austin had found a friend, one he seemed very comfortable to be around. This vacation was doing them both a world of good.

"Want to hear it?" Austin's smile was infectious.

"Only if you want to tell me."

Her son wiggled his finger and whispered, "Come closer."

She bent closer.

"Tyler told me that Matt likes you." Austin giggled.

"Does he now?" She had already figured that one out for herself. Why else was the man sitting at her table drinking coffee and playing hot rods with her son?

Austin nodded. "Tyler heard his mommy say it to Hunter's mommy."

"Well, they must know." She brushed a lock of her son's brown hair off his forehead. "What do you think about Matt liking me?" In the two years since the divorce had become final, she had never mixed her dates with her personal life. Matt was different. There was no separating him from Austin. Without Rosemary there, she had Austin with her twenty-four/seven.

"Matt fixed my car and he's taking us fishing." Austin smiled as he snuggled into his pillow. "I like Matt."

"So do I, hon. He's a very nice man." She kissed her son's cheek. "Now get some sleep. You had a busy day."

"Night, Mom." Austin's voice sounded sleepy, but she knew he was thinking about all the adventures with Tyler to come.

She headed for the door, and turned out the light, "Night, hon." A night-light near the bed gave Austin enough light to see by, if he needed it. She closed the door until there was only an inch or two of space and grinned.

So Matt liked her.

The first thing she noticed was Matt wasn't in the kitchen, the glass part of the sliding door to the back patio was open, and someone had turned on the patio light. She looked out back and spotted Matt sitting on the swing enjoying the moonlight and the cool breeze. He should have looked ridiculous sitting on the flowered seat cushion, under the matching canvas awning.

Kathy Albert had a thing for pink flowers. The master bedroom was done in pink, and the living room couch was a solid burgundy, and the two matching chairs had a pink flower print. Even the outdoor furniture was different shades of pink. One had to wonder what her husband thought about Kathy's decorating choice.

The thing was, Matt didn't look silly sitting there

surrounded by all those bold Hawaiian flowers and banana leaves. He looked seductive as all get out. The bright print highlighted his masculinity. The one quality Matt oozed was virility. Matt was what one called a man's man.

This made her attraction toward him seem strange. She usually wasn't tempted by the rugged, outdoors type of man. Business suits, luxury cars, fine restaurants, and tickets to the latest sellout show were her usual dates. Not barbecues where kids fed the dog under the table, conversations that went from hunting to diaper rash, and pickup trucks. Every male Porter owned a pickup truck. Their wives drove big hulking SUVs filled with car seats, baby paraphernalia, and sporting equipment.

The Porters weren't in her usual social circle, but she liked their laid-back, unpretentious style. Tonight she had barely spoken half a dozen sentences with her date. She was too busy keeping up with his family and laughing at their antics.

It could be all the fresh ocean air that was making her act out of character. Or maybe it was the relaxing pace of the town, or the fact she was on vacation.

Or maybe it was Matt Porter.

With that thought in mind, she stepped out back and softly closed the screen behind her. If Austin got up, they would hear him. The night seemed too perfect to miss. Taking the clue from Matt, she sat next to him on the swing.

"All tucked in?"

"For now." She liked how Matt always seemed interested in her son. Most of her dates didn't even know she had a child, unless it came up somewhere in the conversation during the evening. "I won't be surprised if he gets up, though. He's awfully excited."

"About?" Matt started the swing gently swaying.

"Everything—Tyler, the way you fixed his car, our upcoming fishing trip. You name it, and Austin wants to talk about it."

"Is that good?"

"Yes, it's good and different." She leaned back, closed her eyes, and enjoyed the quiet of the night. Matt was easy to talk to, easy to be around. "I work a lot of hours, so we don't usually get a lot of one-on-one time together." She was beginning to wonder if that was a mistake. Rosemary was great with Austin, but she wasn't his mother. She was, and she was never around much for her son. Did that make her a bad mother? "This is our first really long vacation together, just the two of us."

Matt's arm slid across the back of the swing. "How long has Austin's father been out of the picture?"

"Our divorce has been final for over two years. Jake and I are still great friends. I know it seems odd, but there it is." She and Jake had been friends long before they became lovers and had gotten married. "Jake and I make better friends than husband and wife."

"Is Jake remarried?" There was a quiet curiosity in Matt's voice.

"Jake's married to his job." So was she, in a way. Or at least she had been until Austin came along. Her father wouldn't, or couldn't, believe a woman could take over the company, so Jake was his handpicked and trained heir apparent. She was an only child. It made perfect sense to everyone that Jake and she get married and keep it all in the family. So they had, and learned it took more than friendship and a child to keep a marriage together. It took love.

"I heard you tell my mother and Norah that you're an expert expediter. What do you do?"

"Well"—she chuckled—"that is a pretty good description

of what I do. You need something, I get it. There's a
problem, I solve it. I'm a jack-of-all-trades, and I move
around and slide into any spot that needs a helping hand. I
have a degree in business management." She had a fancy
title in the Randall Corporation. Being the boss's daughter
gave her a vice presidency, a nice salary, and huge perks, but
there was one major drawback. She took her orders from
and reported to her father. Dad gave her busywork, most of
it unchallenging and boring. She should have left the corporation years ago, but she wanted to prove to her father that
she could handle his job.

She needed to prove it, both to herself and to her father.
She was strong and capable, and she had guts when it
came to being a business kind of woman. She wasn't like
her mother, who had been sweet, dependent on her husband, physically frail, and emotionally fragile.

So far Sierra had taken every assignment and done it
to the best of her ability. She hadn't failed once and usually had succeeded beyond her and everyone else's ex-
pectations. Her father was constantly praising her and
sometimes she received a nice bonus in her paycheck.
But she never could figure out if he was doing it because
of a job well done or because she was his daughter.

"I'm sure Norah and the rest of the family really appreciate what you're doing with the wedding and all, but
you don't have to do it, Sierra. You're supposed to be
on vacation. Austin and you should be relaxing and enjoying yourselves. Somehow I feel responsible for putting all of this on you."

She opened her eyes and looked at Matt. He was serious. "You didn't make me do anything." She shook her
head at the absurdity of it. "I want to help, Matt."

"Really?"

"Really." She turned in the seat and brought her legs

up under her. "This to me is fun, Matt. Austin and I are really enjoying ourselves. Where else can we go mermaid watching, cook marshmallows over a grill, and get to go fishing at Sunset Cove? Which by the way, I never heard of."

For the first time, she felt appreciated for what she could do, and not because her father was Lucas Randall, the owner of the Randall Corporation, which owned and operated a string of luxury hotels across America. "Norah and her mom, with all your family's help, could pull this wedding off without a hitch, Matt. I'm not kidding myself, thinking they need me. But right now, for them, it's like not being able to see the forest because of the trees."

"Trees? What do trees have to do with a wedding?"

"It's a metaphor. The forest is the wedding, the trees are everything that has to get done to pull off that wedding. Men don't understand it, but it's a complicated business, getting married."

Matt chuckled. "If you say so."

"I say so." Her wedding to Jake had taken nine months of intense planning and had been Lianna's first high-society wedding. It had been the make-or-break wedding of Lianna's career, and her best friend had pulled it off beautifully. The reception had been a little harried, with Lianna being the wedding planner and the maid of honor. Her college roommate had managed to give her father, the man footing the bill, the wedding of his dreams while keeping Sierra's taste in mind.

"Oh, and tourists don't know about Sunset Cove. It's the town's secret, so let's keep it that way." Matt gave her that teasing little-boy smile that tugged at her heart.

"Why is it a secret?" *Whom could I possibly tell about the secret cove? The only ones in town I know and are friendly with are the Porters, and they obviously know about it already.*

"We need a place that isn't overrun by tourists and commercialism. If visitors find out about the cove, they'll want rowboat and kayak rentals, a snack stand, and guided hikes along its trails. There's a couple of local residents who live right on the cove. They don't need or want strangers walking through their yards scaring away the wildlife and trampling their gardens."

She cringed. "Point taken. Is it hard living in a tourist town?"

"I wouldn't classify Misty Harbor as a sightseeing mecca. We get nice flow-through traffic, usually in the summer months. If you take into account all the inlets, coves, and bays, Maine has over three thousand miles of coastal land. Plenty of space to keep all the tourists happy."

"I take it you're not impressed with rich visitors who like to open their wallets and boost the economy?" She could hear it in his tone. The kind of visitors Randall Hotels catered to.

"You couldn't pay me to live in Bar Harbor. Most of the stores close up in October and don't reopen till May, plus the traffic is horrendous." Matt gave the swing another push. "None of the shops in Misty Harbor close and lock their doors come fall, and we have only a few snowbirds."

"Snowbirds?"

"Residents who live here during the nice months, and then head south for the winter. Living in a town full of empty houses all winter would be depressing."

"That it would." She hadn't thought about that aspect. "I also noticed that there aren't too many places to stay in town. I stumbled upon the Alberts' house rental by sheer luck on the Internet. Walking around for the past week, I saw only three bed-and-breakfasts and the Motor Inn."

"That's more than enough rooms to accommodate a few tourists."

The way Matt was talking, one would get the idea that sightseers were the enemy. "So there are no plans in the works for a major renovation of the downtown area? No splashy hotels? No dance clubs and bars?"

Matt snorted. "Misty Harbor's chief income comes from fishing. If you block up the harbor with fancy yachts, and crowd our shoreline with hotels, nightclubs, and millionaires' mansions, how will the residents survive? Sure, a few of the more enterprising souls would get rich, but the majority of the town would suffer. Taxes, to pay for all the improvements and expansion, will go through the roof. Property values will skyrocket. Over half our citizens are having a hard time meeting their tax obligations now. They would have no choice but to sell their homes, and possibly their businesses."

"I see you've been giving this some thought." And she obviously needed to give it a lot more. Her father was expecting a report by the end of August on Misty Harbor and its potential to support a Randall Hotel.

"Thinking is free." Matt moved an inch closer. "There is one good thing about all those tourists and sightseers flowing in and out of town."

"What's that?" She could tell by the warmth of Matt's smile she was going to like his answer.

"It brought you and me together." Matt leaned in and lightly kissed her.

She felt the warmth of his lips and wanted more. Matt's gaze was screaming heat. She wanted that heat. For days she had been thinking about their first kiss. It was inevitable that they were going to kiss. She had known that since sitting across from him at the Methodist church eating spaghetti. They had been surrounded by his family and half a dozen kids, and all she could think about was kissing Matt. She had almost gotten that kiss in his mother's kitchen early this evening. Matt had been a breath away from taking her into his arms when Ned had ruined the moment.

"Is that how they kiss in Maine?" Austin put more *oomph* into one of his kisses.

Matt slowly shook his head and smiled. "No, I didn't want to frighten you off."

"I'm not running, Matt." Just to prove her point, she slid the tip of her tongue over her lower lip.

Matt's gaze follow its path. "Where exactly did you say you were from?"

"I didn't." She had never gotten around to explaining her hectic lifestyle to Matt. "But we flew in from San Diego, California, if that helps."

"Ah . . . ," whispered Matt as he reached over, picked her up, and placed her right on his lap. "That explains the tan."

Sierra wrapped her arms around his neck, either for balance or to bring herself closer. She didn't know which. She didn't care. "You got something against tans?"

"Yeah." Matt tilted up her chin until their mouths were perfectly aligned.

"What?" Her gaze was locked on his lips, so she saw his answer more than she heard it.

"The lines." Matt captured her mouth with heat, passion, and a demanding tenderness.

She felt the swing sway wildly beneath them, or maybe it was just her world. Whatever it was, she didn't care. She opened her mouth and deepened the kiss. Matt tasted like coffee. She loved the taste of coffee.

Matt pulled her closer and groaned before playfully tugging at her lower lip with his teeth.

Her hand cradled the back of his head and forced him to kiss her again. Short silky hair ran through her fingers as she slipped her tongue into the heat of his mouth. She could feel Matt's response growing beneath her. Lord, how long had it been since she had been loved? Satisfied?

Over two years. Jake and her marriage had been sweet, gentle, and satisfying. Where was this heat? Was this what she had been missing all those years? She had kissed other men and never experienced the burning desire to rip the clothes off of them and have her way.

Her way. Matt's way. It didn't much matter. She wiggled to get closer.

Matt's hands held her hips still as he broke the kiss. "Ummm . . . Sierra?"

"Hmmm . . . ?" Her lips trailed down his jaw and across his square, stubborn chin.

"We have to stop now." Matt moved her off his lap and stood her up on her own feet as if she weighed nothing. "Not that I want to; it would just be the smart thing to do." He stood up next to her.

It took her a moment for his words to sink into her passion-fogged mind. She could feel a fiery blush sweep up her cheeks. What had she been thinking? Obviously she hadn't been thinking, or she would have remembered her son was thirty feet away, hopefully sleeping in his bed. She glanced toward the screen door and prayed she wouldn't see Austin standing there looking at her.

The doorway was empty.

Matt's fingers touched her chin and brought her head up. "He's not up, Sierra. I would have heard him."

She knew she wouldn't have heard her own son if he had been yelling for her. The only thing she had heard was the sound of her heart pounding in her chest and her rapid breathing. Or was it Matt's heart she heard beating and his deep breathing? Did it matter? No. She hadn't been acting like a very responsible mother.

"I'm going to go now, okay?" Matt's lips brushed hers in a tender caress. "Am I still invited for dinner tomorrow night?"

"Of course." She had been the one to lose control, not Matt. "Austin is expecting you."

"I'm more concerned about what you want, Sierra." Matt's gaze locked with hers.

She could handle any awkward situation. Even this. She gave Matt a small smile. "I would very much like for you to come to dinner tomorrow night." *And I promise not to jump your bones.*

Matt kissed her again. "I'll be here by six." He walked to the side of the house, then disappeared into the darkness around the corner.

She sat back down onto the swing and wondered what had just happened. How could a simple kiss get so far out of control so fast? The answer was easy.

There had been nothing simple about Matt's kiss.

Chapter Seven

Juliet left Olivia's bed-and-breakfast at exactly two minutes past nine. The Pen and Ink didn't open its doors until nine, and she didn't want to appear too eager even though she was so excited that she had barely slept last night. Her mother had hoped that Gordon Hanley hadn't changed that much over the years. From her mother's memories, Gordon was not only a perfect gentleman, good looking, and intelligent, but he was a very nice man as well.

Her mother's memories hadn't been wrong. Juliet had been especially thrilled to discover she had so much in common with her biological father, from their mutual love of Shakespeare to poetry. They shared not only an amazing amount of physical characteristics but mental ones too.

The first order of business they had discussed had been what she was going to call him. "Mr. Hanley" seemed ridiculous, and there was no way she could call him Dad. She already had a father, and his name had been Ken Carlyle. They had settled on plain and simple "Gordon."

Gordon had taken her out to dinner last night to what had to be the best restaurant in town, the Catch of the Day. He had entertained her with stories about the town and some of its residents. She returned the favor by highlighting some of her childhood memories. Gordon hung on her every word and had a million questions. It should have been odd or awkward having dinner and conversing with the man who had fathered her, but it hadn't been. Although they couldn't finish each other's sentences, they could finish each other's quotes.

Only her mother could keep up with her and recite back some Shakespeare. Both of her brothers were more apt at reciting Monty Python or Mel Brooks movies. *Blazing Saddles* and *The Holy Grail* were two of their favorites. Her sister, Miranda, leaned toward Disney movies and the color pink. Juliet had teased Miranda about always wanting to be a princess and that her brother Brad looked like Igor from *Young Frankenstein*.

Life in the Carlyle house had never been dull. Well, it was never dull for the other three Carlyle children. They were always coming and going and getting into everything. They had joined, and exceeded in, every sport available to them, headed up committees, and volunteered for anything under the sun. She preferred to read in the quiet of her room and get lost between the pages of a great book. Her brother Ken had christened her with the nickname Bookworm, and it had stuck.

She had hated that nickname as a young teenager. It was just another reminder of how out of sync she had been with the rest of the family. She now understood why. Her brothers and sister did not share the same father with her. They had all inherited Ken Carlyle's physical abilities, while she had been born with the proverbial two left feet and her nose in a book. It just went to prove that heredity, not environment, played a more important role in shaping a child.

Juliet pushed the memories of her childhood away as she walked down White Pine Street. She enjoyed the morning sunshine and cool ocean breeze on her face. She could see part of the busy harbor as she neared Main Street. The whale-watching boat was boarding its passengers for the morning tour.

A tall, good-looking guy was collecting tickets and waving a family of four on board the boat. The kids seemed to be enjoying themselves, but it was the ticket collector who caught her eye. From a distance, he appeared to be around her age, in his mid-twenties, nicely built, and tall. Being five feet nine inches tall herself, she tended to pick out the tall guys in a crowd. Not that the wharf was crowded this morning. He had tawny hair that was blowing all over the place and she could tell he was smiling. Now there was some nice sightseeing. The town ought to advertise him in one of their brochures.

The residents of Misty Harbor, or maybe they were other tourists, were a friendly bunch. Everyone greeted her or waved. An old man with a gray beard, wearing an old oily baseball cap and driving a beat-up old truck, honked and waved as she hit Main Street. She waved back, and by his grin, she might have made his day. Well, at least his morning.

She looked toward the dock for a last look and froze. The tawny-haired stranger was staring at her. She knew a blush was sweeping up her cheeks, but there was no way he would see it. The honking must have caused him to glance in her direction, but it didn't explain why he was still looking.

She didn't consider herself beautiful. Passable, in a quiet and shy way. In Regency times, she would have been a wallflower. Miranda, on the other hand, was vibrant and outgoing, and left a string of broken hearts in her wake. Miranda also had a lush figure and blond hair that men fawned over, while Juliet was stick thin and flat chested, had nearly black hair, and wore glasses. Miranda brightened any party, while she served the appetizers with cute plastic toothpicks sticking out of them and tried not to spill the tray.

A boarding passenger distracted the man's attention and broke the spell. Giving her head a shake, she hurried on her way. She turned right onto Main and headed for the row of shops. Gordon's bookshop was nestled in between Bailey's Ice Cream Parlor & Emporium and a store called Harbor Gifts.

Juliet glanced in the gift-shop window. A touristy T-shirt and ball cap were on a cardboard cutout. A porcelain lighthouse, a pillow, a rubber crab, and a stuffed red lobster completed the display. The shop was dark inside and the door appeared locked. The list of hours, posted on the plateglass door, told her that whoever was in charge of opening the store was late.

She walked to Gordon's store and was surprised to see the front double doors wide open. A cast-iron doorstop shaped like a lobster was keeping one open. The other managed to stay open all by itself. She walked inside and saw Gordon struggling with the back windows in the tobacco section. The windows were giving him a devil of a time. "Morning."

Gordon turned around and smiled. "Morning, yourself. You're up early." He gave the window frame a hard whack with the palm of his hand and tried it again. This time he managed to work up the swollen wood frame.

The cool morning breeze was now blowing in both windows. Although the shop still smelled, it wasn't quite as overwhelming as it had been yesterday. She doubted that the odor of cigars, pipes, and cigarettes that had been smoked over the past hundred years would ever leave the shop. There was history in the shop, and it penetrated every square inch of the place.

"I said I'd be by first thing." She knew Gordon had purposely opened the door and windows for her. "Thanks." She nodded toward the windows.

This morning Gordon was dressed in a pair of black pants and a retro gray and black fifties-style shirt. His black and silver hair was pulled back neatly in a ponytail, giving his face a more angular look.

"Realized last night that you were right. It does smell like an ashtray in here."

She didn't know what to say to that comment. The shop did smell. "Opening the door and windows also lets in the natural light so customers can see what they're looking at," she said. The display window for the shop was covered with a burgundy curtain that obstructed every ray of light from entering the shop.

She had studied the display case yesterday before entering the shop, trying to figure out what kind of man Gordon Hanley was. The display window hadn't given her much hope. Except for one current best seller propped up in the corner, the entire display could have been set up in the eighties, or even the sixties. Dark, thick tomes of literature were piled haphazardly and an assortment of pipes was scattered about. Prince Albert tobacco still came in a can and the pipe cleaners had faded from the sun. There was nothing about the display to invite a person in to browse around and shop. There also hadn't been a clue about the owner besides a certain lack of creativity, or his lack of interest in the shop.

"Maybe you can tie back the display window curtain.

It would let in plenty of light to brighten up that section of the store." Last night Gordon had asked her for some ideas on the shop and how to improve it. Her mind had raced with one idea after another all through the night. This morning she would offer up some simple suggestions and let Gordon do what he wanted. It was his shop, after all.

Gordon walked over to the thick curtain and frowned. "How about we take the whole thing down? It's not like we don't want people to see what's in the shop."

"True." The curtains on the back windows that were pushed aside were another problem. Who wanted to see the current view of a back alley? "I can take them down for you." She was itching to brighten up the place. Maybe even wash a window or two.

"I'll get them. I don't want you to fall." Gordon headed for the back storage room. "I put on a fresh pot of coffee and even picked up a box of donuts from the food store this morning before I opened." He pointed to the small area next to the cash register. "Go help yourself to some."

"Thank you." She loved coffee, but she wasn't a big sweets person. Gordon had gone to a lot of trouble for her, so she helped herself to one of the store-bought powdered donuts. Last night at dinner, Gordon had taken his coffee black. This morning a mismatched creamer and sugar bowl sat next to the coffee machine. The creamer was filled with cold milk. He had thought of everything.

Gordon carried the small stepladder over to the drapes and unhooked the rod from the brackets. The heavy drapes and rod fell to the floor in a cloud of dust. Gordon waved the air and coughed.

She pretended not to notice the dust and bit into the donut. White powder scattered down the front of her dark green tank top and onto her skirt. She brushed at the powder, while Gordon hauled the drapes out back and, from the sound of it, into a garbage can.

Gordon walked back in and blinked. "Geez, I might have to wear my sunglasses in here from now on."

"It's not that bright." She chuckled as she stirred milk into her coffee. There was a marked difference in the shop, but she couldn't say it was better. With all the added light she could see the dust and disorganization more clearly. So would the customers.

"I have light-sensitive eyes." Gordon poured himself a cup of coffee.

"Oh, I'm sorry. Let's put the drapes back up." Why hadn't he said something before taking them down?

"Not after what they just landed in." Gordon chuckled. "It's not that bad in here, Juliet. I was kidding."

"You don't have light-sensitive eyes?" When they had walked to the restaurant last night, he had been wearing sunglasses. He hadn't worn them when he walked her back to the bed-and-breakfast, but by then evening had fallen.

"Those I have." Gordon glanced around the shop and squinted. "I take it you don't?"

"No, but I do wear glasses." She smiled over the edge of the cup. "Or, like today, contacts."

"When I knew your mother, she wore glasses for reading." Gordon's squint wasn't quite as pronounced.

"She wears them all the time now. She hates contacts and is too chicken to get laser surgery. None of my brothers or my sister wears them."

"You're the only one?"

"Yep. Dad said it was because I wore my eyes out by reading too much." It felt funny talking about her dad to her biological father.

"There's no such thing as too much reading." Gordon seemed appalled by the blasphemy.

She laughed. "That's what Mom told him."

"Good for Victoria." Gordon glanced around the shop and seemed happy about the work he accomplished. "So what are you planning to do today?"

"Hang around here."

"You can't be serious."

"Why can't I be serious?" She didn't see what the big deal was. How else was she to get to know her father?

"You're on vacation. You need to get out and meet people your own age. Why would you want to hang around a dusty old shop?"

"Because you're here." She started to wonder if she had misread Gordon. Maybe he didn't want her in town and in his shop. "You're the reason I came to Misty Harbor. Of course, if you would rather I leave . . ."

"No." Gordon's voice was sharp and held a note of panic. "I mean, please don't go. I want you here, it's just that I'm afraid you'd be bored within an hour."

"Of you, or the shop?"

"Both," Gordon said.

"Lord, what fools these mortals be!"

"You're quoting Shakespeare to me?" Gordon chuckled. "Careful, I might take that as a challenge."

"Feel free." Her smile matched his. "So are you going to allow me to help you in the shop?"

"Do I have a choice?" Gordon didn't look too concerned about her decision.

"I could always go back home."

"I could always close the shop," Gordon countered.

She shook her head. "No deal. The shop stays open." She didn't know much about Gordon, but from the little she had seen, he didn't strike her as being rich. As far as she knew, the store was his only income. Considering the amount of customers, or the lack of them, he could use every dollar he made. "Since the bed-and-breakfast won't take my credit card, I'll be helping out here during my stay. It's the perfect solution." She winked. "Besides, bookstores are my favorite places."

"Okay, but there's one condition."

"That would be?"

"You'll take time away from here and do some sight-seeing, relax, and pretend you're on vacation. I'll take some time off and show you some of the sights."

"Such as?" She didn't need anyone to point out the rocky coastline, and the town wasn't big enough for her to get lost in.

"We can take a ride out to Bar Harbor, go into Bangor for a day, maybe even do a whale-watching cruise."

"I would like that." *Especially the whale-watching tour.* "It's a deal." She glanced around the shop. "So what do you want me to do first?" She had spent count-less hours volunteering at the local library back home, and more time than she cared to think about wandering, browsing, and getting lost in bookstores. There wasn't a doubt in her mind that she would be able to handle whatever Gordon threw her way.

Gordon shrugged. "Wait for a customer."

"What do you usually do?" She couldn't sit on her backside and wait.

"Read a good book, drink coffee, or smoke my pipe." Gordon's smile was contagious. "Being a shop owner is hard work. You can do whatever you like."

She couldn't very well tell him the shop needed a good cleaning. "Well, since I want to browse your shelves, I think I'll dust them as I go."

"I gave up dusting them years ago. It's a thankless job that never seems to end."

"Since I'm going through the books anyway, I might as well dust them." She glanced under the cash register where there seemed to be a collection of junk. "Where do you keep the cleaning supplies?"

"Back room." Gordon seemed uncertain. "Are you sure you want to do this?"

"Go through your stock? Darn straight I do. I noticed yesterday that you have some great books hidden away." She headed for the stock room in search of a rag before Gordon came up with another excuse.

Matt sat in his pickup truck in front of Sierra's place and wondered if he was making a colossal mistake. Sierra was all wrong for him. She had a child and they would be leaving in a couple weeks. Although those things were important, they weren't his real worries. Sierra never came out and said it, and there wasn't anything to give it overtly away, but his gut was telling him that Sierra came from money. Big money. Her style and sophistication wasn't married into or learned; it was inherited.

It was six o'clock at night and big, bad Matt Porter was scared of a beautiful woman and a little money. That wasn't quite true. He wasn't scared of money, he was intimidated by it. Money was power. Money bought dreams. Half the time he disliked the rich on the size of their wallet alone.

His dream since he had been eight years old was to buy and live in the Misty Harbor lighthouse. The abandoned lighthouse was run-down and was in dire need of repairs. Now that he was an adult, he knew he couldn't live in the actual lighthouse, but he could rebuild the lighthouse keeper's house, which at one time had been connected to the lighthouse. Over the years he had collected three old black and white photos of the house, and for his twenty-fifth birthday his family had given him what had passed for blueprints of the original house. All he needed to do was to convince Millicent Wyndham to sell him the property for a reasonable amount, an amount he could afford.

His dream was about to crumple. The Randall Corporation, a major U.S. hotel chain, had made Millicent a substantial offer for the lighthouse and the coastal acreage it sat upon. He would need two lifetimes and a winning lottery ticket to match the financial offer.

He considered himself a practical man, one who didn't mind working hard for a living and saving for what he wanted. One who didn't believe in rich, unknown relatives passing away and leaving their stock portfolio to him or relying on a fairy godmother to appear in a pumpkin patch. He had been saving for his dream since he was eight. With the current price of coastal property, he could now afford a couple dump trucks worth of rocks, a swimming pool of seawater, and enough grass to hold a Wiffle ball game on. The lighthouse wasn't the expensive part of the deal, it was the land.

He snorted as he got out of the truck. What did he have to complain about? Millicent, knowing how much he wanted that piece of property, had given him the heads-up two weeks ago, before the town had found out. His savings account looked impressive. There was more than enough to buy a nice-size piece of property outside the town's limits and to start building a home.

Besides, he had more important things to think about tonight—mainly a beautiful woman who might or might not be rich but who sizzled when she kissed. He had returned to his small apartment last night achy, hard, and lonely. The window air conditioner had been cranked on high all night, but he had gotten no relief.

He had kissed his fair share of women in his life. None had the effect Sierra had had on him last night. By three o'clock in the morning he had convinced himself he had imagined the whole thing. Not the kiss—that had been real enough—just his reaction to it. No kiss could have been that wondrous, that perfect, that hot.

He walked up onto the porch, rang the doorbell, and grinned. Just to prove his memories wrong, he would have to kiss her again.

Austin threw open the door. It banged against the closet door behind it. "Matt!"

He could see Sierra hurrying out of the kitchen. "Austin, I told you to wait for me." She came to a halt next to her son and scolded him. "How many times must I tell you, you cannot open a door unless I'm with you."

Austin looked at the tip of his sneakers, "Sorry."

Sierra looked up at him standing there. "Hi. Sorry about that. Austin loves to answer doors and phones."

"Hey, Austin, listen to your mom on that one." He knelt down so he was on a more even level with the small boy and ruffled the top of his hair. "Your mom is right. You shouldn't be opening doors on your own." He wasn't worried that something would happen to the boy in Misty Harbor. Austin didn't live here, but the world out there wasn't as safe and friendly as the small coastal town.

"Mom said it was you." Austin pouted.

"I said, 'That should be Matt.'" Sierra swept her son up into her arms. "'Should be' and 'is' are two different matters. I was in the kitchen, so I couldn't see who was ringing the doorbell. I was guessing."

"Can I answer the door when I get bigger?"

"Yes." She gave him a hug. "Now go get your car so you can show Matt that trick you've been doing all day." Sierra put her son back down and he sprinted into the back part of the house.

"Trick?" He tried to think of a trick a four-year-old could do with a remote-control car. He drew a blank.

"He thinks it is." Sierra closed the door. "He makes it go in circles, and circles, and circles." Her eyes and finger were doing circles in the air.

He chuckled at the thought of how many times Sierra had been privy to that trick today. "Can't wait to see it."

"You'll regret those words." Sierra headed for the kitchen. "Come on back. There's been a change of plans."

"Oh?"

"Don't worry, I'm still feeding you, but you'll be doing some of the cooking."

He wasn't sure he liked the sound of that. He didn't mind cooking, he just wasn't very good at it. "What happened to omelets?"

"I witnessed the amount of food the Porter men put away last night and at the spaghetti dinner. An omelet would never do for dinner, unless I threw a pig on a spit to go along with it."

Sierra reached the kitchen counter and handed him two sealed packages. One contained an average-size steak, the other a huge piece of meat that made him question the size of the cow it had come from. "Are you planning on feeding my entire family?" He chuckled at the size.

"Not for dinner." She pointed to the smaller steak. "That's mine. I like it medium." Her fingertip tapped the side of beef. "That's yours. Your job is to start the grill out back and cook them."

"What's Austin eating?" He loved a good steak, but he didn't think he could finish this one on his own.

"Chicken nuggets. He doesn't like steak." Sierra went back to chopping a tomato for their salad. "I have potatoes already baking in the oven."

He saw that the table on the patio had been set for three. A vase filled with flowers was in the center of the table, surrounded by three burning mosquito-repellent candles. There was also a vase of fresh flowers on the kitchen table, and another had been on the coffee table in the living room. Either Sierra loved flowers, or the eligible bachelors of Misty Harbor were at it again. He swore he wasn't jealous. "What's with all the flowers?"

"Austin and I went nursery hopping this morning. I felt that I should at least purchase something at each stop."

He glanced at the tower of bakery boxes sitting on the counter. "Are you planning a party?" Everyone knew that the pink and white striped boxes came from Jolene's out on Route 1 in East Sullivan. Jolene's had been voted the best bakery in Maine three years running.

"No, that's for our guests."

"What guests?" As far as he knew it was going to be only Sierra, Austin, and him this evening.

"Your family."

"My family?" There went his fantasy about kissing Sierra, just to make sure she was as delicious as he remembered. Why couldn't his family leave Sierra and him alone?

"Only the female members. We needed to hold another planning session for the wedding. The guys are all heading over to your parents' house to start on the arbor." Sierra started to slice a cucumber.

"So I'm supposed to head over there?" Some date this was turning out to be. They weren't even going to be in the same house.

"Well . . . no. Your mother kind of volunteered you." Sierra stopped slicing and gave him a sympathetic look. "Since you were going to be here anyway, your mother said to leave you in charge of the kids while we work on the wedding details. With five kids running around she was afraid we would be distracted."

"Four."

"Four what?"

"It's four kids running around. Amanda doesn't even crawl yet." He'd rather go cut wood and nail something, but he'd be a good sport about it. For tonight. Next planning session, Paul or John could watch their own kids.

"Do you mind?"

"Not really, as long as you're okay with this. You're the one who is supposed to be on vacation."

"I am on vacation." Sierra grinned. "I had fun today haggling and exchanging ideas with the nursery owners."

"Is that what all this stuff is?" He motioned toward the kitchen table, which had paperwork, pictures, and magazines spread out all over it. He could barely see an inch of wood beneath all the paper.

"Norah's mom, Joanna, dropped some stuff off to me on her way to work this morning."

A length of pink silk was tossed over one of the chairs, and some see-through netting in a rainbow of colors was strangling another. The bouquet of flowers on the table matched the material, and he wondered if that meant anything. He stepped closer and spotted a couple pictures of towering wedding cakes, some complete with bridges, pillars, and stairways climbing from layer to layer. Icing flowers in every color imaginable tumbled down the sides and across the white layers. Plastic brides and grooms, bells, or birds were perched on the top layer. One creative cake had two feathered swans, a waterfall, trails of ivy, and what appeared to be a pond of whiskey sours set up next to the cake.

Ned was going to think the whole thing was ridiculous. Norah was going to go along with it only because of her mother. He now understood why his own mother had been absolutely no help when it came to planning her sons' weddings. Peggy Porter would rather wrestle an octopus than decorate a wedding cake with a fake swan.

"Are you sure this isn't too much for you?" He was getting a headache just thinking about it. Last night he had overheard Ned whispering in Norah's ear something about eloping. He personally agreed with his brother.

"Oh, please," gushed Sierra, "this is a walk in the park for me."

"If you say so."

Austin ran into the kitchen, carrying his car and the remote. "Want to see, Matt? Want to see?"

He chuckled at the excitement in Austin's voice. Ah, to be four again and express yourself so everyone knew what you were feeling. "Of course." He held up the steaks. "Let's go put these on the grill first, and then you can show me out on the back patio. We'll leave your mother to the fixing of the vegetables"—he lowered his voice and growled—"while we men handle the meat."

He headed out back to the propane grill.

Austin looked at his mother and in a low voice said, "We're handling the meat." He followed Matt out back.

Chapter Eight

Sierra knew she should be concentrating more on what was being said around her than on the enticing view on her back patio. Matt Porter had a very dangerous way of distracting her. Austin was having a ball playing with the Porter kids, and Matt seemed to be holding up rather well under the circumstances. Four to one were lousy odds, even for a six-foot-three-inch hunk.

"Are you sure that's going to look okay?" asked Paul's wife, Jill. "I mean, mixing silk roses and leaves in with the real ones? Won't you be able to tell?"

Sierra pulled her mind back into the discussion but was saved from answering by Joanna.

Norah's mom looked intrigued by the possibility. "I think we can pull it off, providing we get good-quality artificial rose vines in the right colors."

"That's not a problem. I talked to Lianna last night and she has an excellent supplier. You can get anything your heart desires." Sierra's old college roommate had been more than willing to help in any way she could. They had spent two hours on the phone catching up on each other's lives and discussing the wedding. After they had hung up, Lianna had been a busy girl out on the West Coast. When Sierra had turned on her laptop this morning, there were pages of attachments and e-mails and a promise of an overnight package that would arrive the next morning.

"Can we get them in time?" Norah, who had put in a full day at work, looked a little tired and frazzled. She obviously wasn't getting enough sleep, either due to the chaos of the upcoming wedding or Ned.

Sierra's money was on Ned. She had never seen two people more in love. "We need to place the order by Friday morning, and there should be no problem."

Joanna glanced through a stack of photos Sierra had printed from her digital camera this afternoon. "All three nurseries are willing to sell us the mature climbing rose bushes?" Joanna seemed surprised that nurseries would indeed sell the plants and bushes they were using in their own displays.

"There's a couple of conditions. There won't be a guarantee on them, and there is no way to get all ten climbing rose bushes in the same color. Plus they are going to cost more than regular potted bushes with only a couple blooms on them. All the nursery managers were in agreement, though: we'll need at least ten mature climbers and six regular bushes to fill in both sides of the arbor nicely. After the rose vines are wrapped and in place, we go through and add the artificial ones to fill in the bare areas."

"Can we still do the lights?" asked Joanna.

"As long as the guys get us an electric line out there, I don't see a problem with that. We'll wrap the lights when we weave in the fake roses." The reception part of the wedding would be going into the evening hours. They were going to need lights everywhere.

Joanna seemed pleased. "I contacted the wedding

supplier out in Bangor. We can rent white or brass candelabras, but not the black or the ironwork ones. They were already taken." Joanna handed Norah three sheets of paper. "They faxed the pictures of them to Ethan's gallery for me, and I have to call them first thing in the morning to let them know how many and which ones."

"What about the candles for them?" asked Peggy.

"Candles are easy, we just need the size and color." Lianna had sent her lists from three suppliers that could do a rush order. "Norah, you have to decide on colors tonight."

"Where do I begin?" Norah looked at her mother for some help.

"Chelsea is wearing pink, right?" Joanna started gathering up all the digital photos of the roses.

"Right, the maid of honor will be in pink." Norah reached for the pink silk draped across the back of her chair. "This is the color: light pearly pink."

"The only thing we are really limited in, colorwise, is the roses. You need to make your choices from them." Joanna started to spread out the photos and everyone got out of their seats to get a better look. The mother of the bride had taken control.

Everyone started talking and offering advice at once.

Sierra got up and walked over to the counter. As far as she could tell, they were on the right track and really didn't need her help making this decision. It was time to get out the goodies. She busied herself putting on a pot of coffee and keeping an eye on the kids in the backyard. Matt had them all on their hands and knees, trying to teach them how to play leapfrog.

It wasn't working. She chuckled as Morgan threw herself on her cousin's back. Hunter collapsed under the weight. Tyler was trying to do a somersault, and Austin was

following wherever his new best friend led. Matt was shaking his head while hauling Morgan off Hunter.

Jill, who had picked a fussing Amanda up out of the stroller, walked over to her and looked out the window. "He's quite good with children."

"Yes, he is." She could have played stupid and pretended not to know whom Jill was talking about, but she didn't like games.

"Austin seems to like him." Jill snatched a cookie from one of the bakery boxes Sierra had just opened.

"That he does. Matt and Tyler are all he's been talking about since the Blueberry Festival." She picked up the pink glass platter that had been sitting next to the boxes, and started to place the fancy cookies onto it. The Alberts had two sets of dishes: one was everyday white with pink flowers. The set in the china cabinet was vintage pink Depression glass. Kurt Albert was either very tolerant of the color pink, or he was color-blind.

"You're not going to serve the kids on Kathy's good dishes, are you?" Jill bounced Amanda in her arms. The little girl gave a big drooly smile.

"Nope." She reached behind Jill and picked up a stack of paper plates. "I even have juice boxes in the refrigerator."

"Spoken like a true mother." Jill cuddled her daughter and glanced back outside. "So you and Matt are getting along?"

"Subtle, Jill, real subtle," Kay said as she joined them. "What she wants to know, Sierra, is do you have the hots for our brother-in-law?"

She tried not to choke or blush as Matt's mother hooted with laughter. "That's Kay, speaking her mind once again." Peggy Porter gave Sierra a wink. "So what do you think of my last unattached son? Matthew's a

good boy, knows how to pick up after himself, and is a hard worker."

Sierra wished the floor would open up and swallow her whole. "He's very nice." What was she supposed to say? That Matt's kisses made her forget she had a child in the other room?

Peggy snorted. "Well, if that ain't the kiss of death, I don't know what is." Peggy snatched a cookie right out of Kay's hand. "Here I had high hopes of getting my last little chick settled down. Oh, my dainty heart can't stand the strain of seeing Matthew without a family of his own."

For the first time in her life, Sierra snorted. "I didn't picture you as a drama queen, Peg." There was nothing dainty on Peggy Porter. Her heart was probably as big as a Volkswagen.

Peggy stood six feet one inch tall and had broader shoulders than most NFL players. Her brown hair was cut ruthlessly short and was sprinkled with gray. Wind-burned cheeks and chapped lips gave evidence that if a jar of moisturizer was sitting on her bureau back at home, it wasn't being used. Tonight, for the occasion of hammering out some finer points for her son's wedding, she wore a faded Grateful Dead T-shirt, a pair of jeans cut off at the knees, and what appeared to be size twelve construction boots. Peggy could wrestle a grizzly and win.

Jill and Kay both sputtered, "A drama queen? Peggy?"

"She started it." She sounded childish, but by the gleam of mischief in Peggy's eyes, the older woman was having fun teasing her. Sierra noticed for the first time that Matt and Peggy had the same color eyes, light sky blue.

"You're the one who called my son nice."

"What did you want me to call him?"

Peggy crossed her arms over her massive chest, tapped

her steel-toed boot, and stared her down. "Since he's the spitting image of his father, I think you should call him handsome, hot, and sexy." A small smile was tugging at the corner of the older woman's mouth. "Stud-muffin, even."

Every woman in the room burst out laughing. "Stud-muffin" was a word no one would ever have expected to come out of Peggy's mouth. If Peggy had started sprouting the names of top Paris designers, they wouldn't have been more surprised.

"I don't see what's so funny," huffed Peggy. It was easy to see she was faking her disapproval. "I call his father that all the time."

The room went nuts with laughter. Baby Amanda started to fuss. When she got herself back under control, Jill cuddled the baby as the noise quickly died down.

"Well, how do you think I got those four strapping boys? I didn't pick them in a cabbage patch, that's for sure."

Matt and all four kids were standing at the patio screen door staring in. They had probably heard all the laughter and had come to investigate.

Matt stared at his mother. "I really don't want to know what's going on, do I?"

Sierra wasn't sure, but Matt might have been blushing. She busied herself with placing some cookies on a paper plate and tried not to laugh.

"Just giving Norah some tips for the honeymoon, son." Peggy swiped another cookie and popped it into her mouth.

"Matt, why don't you take the kids to the picnic table and get them situated? I'll bring out some juice and snacks in a moment." Sierra felt sorry for Matt. The poor man had no idea what he had stepped into. His own mother was trying to pawn him off as a stud-muffin to a tourist.

Matt hesitated for a moment before saying, "Okay." All the kids ran to the picnic table shouting for cookies. Matt slowly followed.

Sierra looked at Peggy. "You should be ashamed of yourself."

"Why? For trying to fix my son up with you?"

"No, for teasing him like that." Sierra grinned. Her father never teased her, and from the few memories she had of her mother, neither had she. Rosemary had on the rare occasion, and it had usually involved boyfriends. She liked how the Porters, and their extended family, teased one another. It was their way of showing how much they did care, how much they loved one another.

"Wait till I tell Pop Pop John that's he's a stud-muffin." Jill couldn't resist teasing her mother-in-law.

"Peggy, in case you didn't notice, Matt and Sierra were already together before we showed up," Norah added, but her gaze never left the pictures in front of her.

"Besides, Sierra's a tourist, she's heading back for . . ." Jill frowned. "Where are you from, anyway?"

"Austin and I flew in from San Diego." It was the truth. They had been out in California for the past four months. Two months before that it had been Seattle. Before that had been Dallas, Miami, and Boston.

When Jake and she first got married, they had bought a house in Seattle. They had barely used it. By the time Austin made his appearance, she realized that what she and Jake had wasn't really a marriage. What they had, and still have, was a deep, loving friendship.

"See, Peggy, she'll be going back soon enough."

"That's why it's so important that we highlight all of Matt's good points. She doesn't have the time to find them out for herself."

Norah gave a very unladylike snort. "Trust us, Peggy,

Sierra's seeing Matt's good qualities." Norah gave Sierra a wink. "Leave her alone, and come here and give me your opinion on this color combination."

Everyone gathered around the table as Sierra went back to fixing the snacks for the kids.

She gathered a bunch of juice boxes from the refrigerator and watched as the women in her kitchen jokingly teased each other. They were what a family should be: loving and tolerant of each other's differences.

Peggy Porter and her two daughters-in-law looked like they could handle any problem or situation that came their way. Jill and Kay, while not as imposing as Peggy, were formidable females in their own right. Norah, with her red spiky hair and bright clothes, and wearing more jewelry than most department stores carried, looked like a tiny gypsy moth. Joanna, Norah's mother, was dressed almost identically to Sierra. Both she and Joanna had chosen linen slacks and a silk sleeveless top for this last-minute get-together.

She frowned as she loaded up the tray with plates full of goodies and drinks for the kids. What did that say about her sense of style if the one she most resembled was the mother of the bride?

"What's wrong, Sierra?" Jill was standing by the table watching her frown down at the tray. "Something wrong with the cookies?"

"No, just mind wandering." She picked up the tray and smiled. "As soon as I deliver this to Matt, I'll finish getting the rest ready. Jolene's Bakery is hoping to get the cake order for the wedding, and hopefully a few other orders to go along with it."

She nodded toward the remaining pink and white striped boxes. "I was talking to Jolene about how we were meeting tonight to work out some finer points on the wedding, so most of what's in there are free samples to entice us."

"You got free samples out of Jolene?"

She gave a small secretive smile. Jolene was not only a world-class baker, she was also a businesswoman who recognized a good thing when it landed in her lap. "She heard just about the entire town was invited to the wedding. Not only does that mean a big order, but think of the advertising opportunity this presents for her business."

"I'm sure everyone in town has been in Jolene's at least once," Kay said.

"I'm sure they have." Considering what Jolene's cookies tasted like, she couldn't imagine that they hadn't been in there a lot more times than that. "It never hurts to remind your customer base of what they are missing."

She carried the tray out back and sat it in the center of the table. "I want you three to listen to your Uncle Matt." She ruffled the top of Austin's hair. "You may have three cookies and one brownie. Not a bite more." Her son had eaten all of his dinner, but she didn't need him bouncing off the wall on a sugar high before bedtime.

"Those rules apply to you three too." Matt looked at his nephews and niece.

"I just made a pot of coffee. Would you like me to bring you out a cup?" Matt and she had finished off the partial bottle of wine she had in the refrigerator with dinner. The juice boxes sitting on the tray just didn't seem Matt's style. "Or I could open another bottle of wine."

"Coffee's fine." Matt shook his head as the kids practically climbed onto the tabletop to reach the cookies. "What about me?" Matt teased. "How many cookies and brownies can I have?"

"You can have whatever you want. You're a big boy." Matt raised a eyebrow. "Whatever I want?"

The kids all giggled and then fought over a particularly large chocolate iced cookie.

The hunger in Matt's gaze had nothing to do with Jolene's brownies or cookies. She felt the hot slide of desire pool low in her gut. Heated, sheet-rumpling possibilities were in his eyes. Possibilities she was oh-so-tempted to explore. "Within reason."

Matt's gaze turned hotter. "How will I know if it's within reason or not?"

Right now there wasn't anything he could do that wouldn't be within reason. Matt was making a simple vacation a lot more complicated and exciting than it should have been. She realized how much she was enjoying herself and grinned. "If you have to ask, it's not within reason."

Matt groaned as she walked away.

Two hours later Matt practically pushed his family out Sierra's front door. Considering they were Porters, there was a lot of pushing to do. He'd clean the mess in the kitchen himself if it gave him some alone time with Sierra. The woman was playing havoc with both his mind and his body. He loved his family dearly, but there was a limit to his patience.

He had hit that limit an hour ago when his father, Karl James, and all of Matt's brothers showed up at Sierra's door. They had made short work of that towering pile of Jolene's Bakery boxes, coffee, and whatever else Sierra had set before them. A horde of Porters had invaded the kitchen, and Sierra now would have to do more food shopping.

It was not the impression he wanted to make with her. A beautiful single woman invites him to dinner, and somehow he was roped into babysitting four kids for almost two hours. If he believed in reincarnation, he would have to say he must have done something very bad in a previous life to deserve such a fate.

"My," exclaimed Sierra, standing in her living room looking a little dazed at the mass exodus that had just trampled through her living room. "Your family leaves as fast as they come."

"They're quick on their feet." His brothers had been dragging their feet, the stroller, diaper bag, and anything else they could use to slow down their departure. They also had been silently laughing and egging each other on, because they knew how badly he wanted them all to disappear. Surprisingly, his main ally had been his mother. *Strange*. If he hadn't been seeing things, she had even given the short hairs on the back of Paul's neck a tug to get him to move faster.

When his mother tugged, you moved.

Matt looked over at Austin, who was standing there looking like he had lost his best friend. "Hey, buddy, don't worry. The way your mother is heading up this whole wedding, you'll be seeing Tyler again real soon."

"Of course you will, honey." Sierra bent down on one knee and hugged her son. "I think someone is extra sleepy tonight. Let's go get you ready for bed."

"I'll clean up the kitchen." He wasn't about to leave that mess for Sierra.

"I'll get that later." Sierra looked torn on what to clean first: the pile of dishes on the counter, the table littered with paperwork, or her son.

"You take care of Austin. He's about asleep on his feet." The boy was starting to get that blank stare his nephews got right before they crashed. He headed for the kitchen. "I do know how to load a dishwasher." His mother had made sure of it. Peggy Porter had taught her boys to clean and cook so she could spend her days out on the fishing boat. It was an unconventional upbringing, but once people tasted his mother's cooking, they understood why none of the Porter boys ever complained.

Sierra softly smiled and said, "Thanks." Then she tugged Austin into the hall.

Matt stared at the kitchen and wondered where to begin. If Kathy Albert ever saw her kitchen looking like this, she would double, if not triple, Sierra's rent. He opened the dishwasher and started loading the dishes in.

Half an hour later, Austin was tucked into bed and Sierra was drying the pieces of antique pink Depression glass he had hand-washed. "You didn't have to wash these, Matt. I'll get to them later."

"They're almost done, and there wasn't that much to wash." Most of the dishes were in the dishwasher, but he didn't think the pink glass platters or the crystal wine glasses they had used at dinner should go in there.

"Most men would rather dry than wash." Sierra placed the plate into the china cabinet.

"I'm not most men." Besides, she had been tucking Austin into bed when he had started to wash them. What kind of man would be afraid of a little water and bubbles? His small apartment in town didn't have a dishwasher, so who did she think cleaned up after him? Last time he looked, the cleaning fairy hadn't once deemed fit to pay him a visit. He put the wet wineglass into the white plastic drainer and pulled the plug in the sink.

"I noticed." Sierra picked up the glass and started to dry. "Your family is nice."

He chuckled. "They take some getting used to." The

Porters en masse had been known to make little kids hide and grown men to think twice.

"Well, I think they're sweet."

He looked at Sierra to see if she was joking. She wasn't. "Are you sure we're talking about the same family that was just here?" No one had ever called his family sweet before.

"One and the same." Sierra put the glass away and hung up the damp towel.

"Didn't you see my mother arm wrestle Jill to see who had to make centerpieces for the tables or haul and set up the chairs and tables the morning of the wedding?" Neither of them wanted to deal with centerpieces and flowers.

"I saw that." Sierra grinned. "Jill had her there in the beginning, but your mom is built for endurance."

"Mom's slowing down some. I guess being a grandmother will do that to you."

Sierra laughed. "I would say so. I'm mother to a four-year-old, and I'm slowing down."

"Jill wasn't too happy to lose."

"Don't worry, I found her a new job instead of making the centerpieces."

"What, and who's making them now?" Matt walked over to the kitchen table and shook his head at the mess of papers. He was afraid to move anything in case there was a system to the chaos. He prayed there was some secret female order to things, or his brother's wedding was going to be a mess. Ned wanted a picture-perfect garden wedding for Norah.

"Jill's going to help set up the two tents that are being rented, and Ned found a DJ who knows where to rent a wooden dance floor." Sierra started to gather up the papers, magazines, notepads, and pictures. "I'm doing

the centerpieces. Norah wants them simple, with colorful flowers, and absolutely no balloons."

Matt shook his head and took the pile of papers out of
Sierra's hands and placed it back on the table. "Come,
we have to talk."

Talking wasn't what he really wanted to do with her,
but it would be a start. Since arriving here for dinner
they hadn't had a moment to themselves. Between
Austin's thousand questions during dinner, the invasion
of every female and kid in his family, and then the arrival of everyone else, he had barely gotten time to thank
her for dinner.

He held her hand and walked into the living room.
The night breeze had gotten chilly enough to close the
patio door, so sitting outside wasn't an option. He
tugged her down onto the couch next to him. "Take a
moment to relax, Sierra. From the sounds of it, you've
been running around since first light." If she didn't
knock it off, she was going to need a vacation from her
vacation.

Sierra kicked off her sandals and tucked her legs up
under her. "I was still in bed at first light. Where were
you when the sun came up from the sea?"

He chuckled at her reference to Austin's belief that the
sun did in fact rise from the sea every morning. "Watching it." He didn't want to think about Sierra still snuggled all warm and sleepy-eyed under the covers. He had
pictured it quite vividly this morning while sitting on a
cold boulder having his first cup of coffee.

"You do that a lot?" Sierra reached up and slipped the
dangling earrings out of her pierced ears. She placed them
on the coffee table and then absently rubbed at her ears.

"Every chance I get." He watched as her thumb and

forefinger rubbed at the delicate lobes. "Why do you wear earrings if they bother your ears?"

Sierra immediately dropped her hand. "Habit."

"Habit? Rubbing your ears might be a habit, but wearing earrings?" He thought she looked adorable curled up on the couch. There was a slight disheveled look to her appearance, like she had just entertained a houseful of guests and given a four-year-old his bath. He liked her better now, all mussed up, than how prim and proper she had looked when he first arrived.

"Okay, you got me." Sierra gave a small smile. "I'm vain, and I love costume jewelry."

Matt laughed. "Norah *loves* costume jewelry. You, on the other hand, like it well enough to wear it even if it bothers your ears." His soon-to-be sister-in-law actually jingled and jangled when she walked. A rolling tambourine would make less noise than Norah.

"You wouldn't think so if you ever saw my jewelry boxes."

"Boxes, as in plural?" Women were wondrous, beautiful creatures who deserved to be pampered and bejeweled. Why any one of them would need more than one jewelry box was still beyond him, though. Then again, if he tried to imagine the size of a jewelry box Norah would need, all his mind could conjure up was the thirty-six-gallon plastic tote where his father stored drop cloths and tarps on the top shelf in his garage.

"As in multiple." Sierra laughed at the look that must have been on his face. "Relax, eighty percent of it is costume."

"What's the other twenty percent?" Her answer to that question would answer his concerns about her being wealthy or not.

"Mostly family heirlooms."

That answered that question. If you had heirlooms, you

were rich. "The only heirloom I ever received was two antique fishing poles that were my Great-Uncle Harvey's." He wouldn't dream of using either one of them for fear he would damage it. They currently were on display above the living room window in his apartment. Neither pole had ever impressed any date he had brought home. "Your family must have different heirlooms than mine."

"I inherited it all through default." Sierra shrugged, as if it didn't really mean anything to her. "I'm an only child of parents who were only children themselves."

"Default? Nothing of Great-Uncle Harvey's was given out by default except his straggly old cat, Jasper. The decrepit old beast went to Ada, Harvey's female companion on the occasional Saturday night, if you know what I mean." He wiggled his eyebrows and Sierra giggled.

"Ada had to have been ninety, hated to wear her dentures, guzzled martinis, and sang Dean Martin songs everywhere she went. She used to scare the tar out of my brothers and me. She also drove a hard bargain. We had to deliver Harvey's bar and his entire stock of booze to her place with the howling Jasper or it was no deal."

Sierra's giggles turned into full-blown laughter. "You didn't."

"Of course we did. My father threw in a couple bottles of gin to sweeten the deal. Jasper was a demon hellcat." It had taken him, his father, and all of his brothers three hours to corner and cage the beast. Every one of them came out of the fight scratched, nicked, and bit to hell and back.

"So Ada and Jasper lived happily ever after?"

"In a way. The week after the funeral Ada hooked up with the captain of a fishing boat. Jasper lived out his life on the high seas, eating his fill and popping Dramamine to combat seasickness."

"And Ada?"

"Sad to say but within six months she followed Uncle Harvey to the great beyond. Doctors claimed the cause of death was pneumonia."

Sierra's face fell. "It was really a broken heart, wasn't it?"

"Nope." He grinned. "The fool woman went skinny-dipping in Sunset Cove in October."

Sierra threw a pillow at his head. "You're horrible."

"Hey"—he caught the pillow in midair—"I wasn't one of those idiots out there with her frolicking naked in freezing-cold water. Hear tell it, there were quite a lot of colds going around that fall." He held up the pillow and leaned toward Sierra. If it was a pillow fight she wanted, he'd be more than willing to oblige. "Legend has it that it was near epidemic proportions in Misty Harbor."

Sierra playfully leaned back as he leaned forward. There was a teasing glint of laughter in her sea-green eyes. "How many were out in the cove with her?"

"I don't know, it's a pretty big cove." He tossed the pillow aside. The last thing he wanted to do with Sierra was fight. He leaned forward and kissed her laughing mouth.

The kiss picked up where last night's kiss had left off—explosive. Whatever fuse he had, Sierra lit it like no other woman ever had. Hell, he hadn't even known he had a fuse until last night.

Sierra wrapped her arms around his neck and tugged him closer as she fell backward onto the couch. The kiss deepened with a bold swipe of her tongue. He followed her lead as he stretched out on top of her.

The couch was too short for their height, and his jeans were uncomfortably tight. It was perfect.

Sierra tasted like coffee and sin. Hot, silky sin. Her light floral scent enticed his senses and heightened his desire.

How could she smell like cool breezes and flowers when he was burning up inside?

He broke the kiss and trailed his mouth over her jaw and down her slim throat. He could feel the rapid pounding of her heart under his lips. The beat matched his own—wild, untamed, and nearly out of control. His tongue traced the speeding pulse.

Sierra tilted back her head and gave him greater access to her neck. A deep-sounding purr vibrated in the back of her throat. One of her hands tugged at his shirt until it was released from the waistband of his jeans. Smooth, cool fingers skipped up his backbone as his hand found its way under her top.

The warm, silky skin of her stomach beneath his fingers caused him to groan against her throat. Her skin wasn't warm, it was hot. Hotter than their kiss.

His mouth continued its downward path until the barrier of her blouse stopped him. His hand slid up and cupped her lace-covered breast.

Sierra arched her back and softly called his name.

He could feel the hard bead of her nipple beneath his palm. She wanted him as much as he wanted her. They were both mature, unattached adults who wouldn't hurt anyone if they continued along this path.

It should be so simple. It wasn't.

The first of many complications was sleeping thirty feet away in the other room: Austin. They would be hard-pressed for an explanation if Sierra's son woke up from a bad dream and walked into the living room this very minute.

Matt gently released her and pulled his hand out from underneath her top.

Sierra's eyes opened. He could see the desire swirling in their depths, and the question, Why had he stopped?

He slowly sat up, pulling her with him. "It's getting late. I should be going."

"Why?" There was hurt and confusion in Sierra's voice.

"I just realized something." He ran his trembling fingers through his hair and stared at her beautiful face. The flush of desire colored her cheeks and her long hair was tangled around her shoulders. "Something important."

"What?"

"I think I may be falling in love with you."

Chapter Nine

Juliet looked at the man who was her father and tried to picture what he had looked like twenty-seven years ago. Gordon Hanley must have been devastatingly handsome, but not in the pretty-boy, Brad Pitt way. Gordon was too thin and angular to be classically handsome. He resembled a tragic poet of old, except for the retro fifties-style shirt and the tinted glasses.

Gordon had been only twenty-nine when her mother had had him for a professor in college. Juliet understood the attraction of a young, good-looking professor. She had had a crush on one or two herself over the years. Her mother had not been nineteen or twenty, but a full-grown woman of twenty-six when she had met Gordon in her junior year.

Victoria Knox didn't do crushes. Her mother had worked her way across America and then traveled through Europe before heading off to college. Juliet hadn't inherited her mother's sense of adventure. Stepping into Gordon's shop two days ago was probably the bravest thing she had ever done.

"Are you sure this is going to look right?" Gordon

finished shoving the last of the empty eight-foot-tall mahogany bookcases into place.

"It's looking great." They had spent all day yesterday and a good part of the previous evening rearranging the shop on paper. Today was moving day. "I don't know what creaked more, the bookshelves or your knees," she teased. "How old did you say you were?"

"I didn't," Gordon huffed, not because he was insulted by the question. He was just out of breath. "These things weigh a ton, and they probably haven't been moved since before I was born."

Considering the age of the shop, he was probably right. "You're the one who wouldn't let me help." She had shown up at the shop by seven, two hours before he usually opened. She had worn an old pair of jeans and an old T-shirt that advertised a Shakespeare festival that had happened three years ago. Her hair was tied back into a ponytail and she hadn't bothered putting in her contacts. Between the dust in the shop, the smoke that still clung to everything, and staying up late into the night reading a book Gordon had recommended, her eyes were a mess.

She was a mess.

The shop was a bigger mess, but at least it was smelling better. She had opened both front doors and all the windows before setting to work. The cool morning temperature was somewhere in the sixties, but after emptying all the shelves of about a ton of books, she was sweating. A red welt marked one cheek, where a book had tumbled off a high shelf and she hadn't been quick enough to catch it.

It was half an hour before opening time, and a customer wouldn't be able to walk through the place. She didn't think it mattered much. Gordon's shop hadn't been bustling with customers for the past two days. Most of the people who had stopped in were more curious as to who she was than they were interested in buying anything.

Gordon had introduced her to everyone as the daughter of a dear friend. It was the truth.

"I was not going to have you get hurt or pull a hernia by moving those cases." Gordon placed his hands on his hips and glanced around the shop. Towering piles of books were everywhere. A couple piles had lost the battle with gravity. "You can help restock the shelves."

"I planned on it. As soon as I wash fifty years of grime off of them and then give them a good polishing." She placed her hands on her hips, in an unconscious, perfect imitation of Gordon's gesture, and looked at the morning's work. All the bookcases were now in their new positions. "What do you think?"

"It opens up the place more. Gives the customers more room, plus it seems lighter in here." Gordon worked his way across the room and headed for the coffeepot next to the cash register. "Want another cup?"

"No thanks." She surveyed the two rooms and the bucket of cleaning supplies she had picked up at Krup's General Store yesterday afternoon. Gordon had sent her shopping for whatever she thought they might need to make the shop more pleasant. She hadn't been worried about it being quaint or welcoming. She was more concerned about the smell and the fact that customers couldn't possibly find what they were looking for. Whoever heard of shelving books by color?

"One thing we didn't discuss yesterday was how do you want me to reshelve the books?" She didn't want to hurt his feelings.

"Spines out." Gordon grinned.

"There's a name for people like you." She tried not to laugh. "And it's not very pleasant."

"I've been called worse." Gordon pulled the stool out from behind the counter and sat.

She imagined those names were whispered by the young kids in town. After spending two days in the shop, she couldn't help but notice the strange fascination the local kids had with Gordon. Tourists weren't bothered by him and neither was the occasional adult who stopped in. It was the eight-through-twelve crowd that acted funny. Groups of boys waited out on the sidewalk while one lonely kid walked in and usually purchased one of the comic books that Gordon stocked over with the magazines. The kid counted out his quarters with shaking hands and stuttered his thanks. So far only one young girl had braved the shop.

Strange, but they almost seemed afraid of Gordon. It was a mystery she was bound and determined to work out in the next couple of days.

"Do you want me to put them back up the way they were or in some other kind of order?"

"The original owners starting selling books years before I bought the place. They couldn't figure out if it would be better to shelve them by title, author, or subject matter."

"So they picked color?"

Gordon shrugged. "They weren't big on reading, I guess."

"So why didn't you change it?" Gordon was an avid reader. Yesterday he had given her the tour of his apartment above the shop. She was surprised that the weight of all his books hadn't caused the ceiling in the shop to cave in yet. Every available inch of wall space was covered with bookshelves. The overflow of books was piled on tables, on top of the television, and even in closets.

Gordon's apartment looked amazingly like hers.

"The locals were used to the system. Why change it?"

"So the tourists could find the kind of book they want. Isn't that the main idea of having a bookshop in a tourist town?"

"Misty Harbor isn't a tourist town. Bar Harbor, Camden, and Boothbay Harbor have the big tourist trade. We get them only a couple months out of the year." Gordon finished his coffee and stood up.

"So you want me to stock the books by color?"

"No, I'm thinking genres. Fiction, nonfiction, poetry. Sections like that."

"Why change now?" She didn't want Gordon to make all these changes for her. She was leaving in a couple more days, she had a job to get ready for outside of Boston. Classes would be starting right after Labor Day.

"It's time." Gordon gave her a small smile. "Besides, I'm getting expert female advice on decorating, and free labor right now. Be warned, for I might start on my apartment next."

She shuddered. "'Present fears are less than horrible imaginings.'"

"*Macbeth,* very good."

She stuck her tongue out at him.

Gordon roared with laughter.

"My help isn't free. You're paying my bill at the bed-and-breakfast." She hadn't been expecting that. Truth be told, she'd had no idea what to expect upon meeting the man who was her father. Resentment. Indifference. Anger that she had barged into his life.

She hadn't been prepared for a warm, intelligent man who seemed to hang on her every word. One who insisted on knowing everything about her. She wasn't comfortable talking about herself. She wasn't the interesting

Carlyle. Given a choice between the latest action-packed movie and a book, she'd take the book every time.

"Oh, I'm sorry." A woman stood in the doorway of the shop staring around in confusion. The little boy standing next to her had opened his eyes wide with wonder at the disaster before them. "I thought you were open."

"We are, Sierra." Gordon put the stool back behind the counter and out of the way. "Come on in—if you can manage it," Gordon added with a chuckle.

"Juliet, I would like you to meet Sierra Morley. She and her son, Austin, are visiting for a while. Sierra, this is the daughter of a dear friend of mine who has come to help get my shop into order, Juliet Carlyle."

Sierra looked around the shop. "Either she's just starting, or fire her, Gordon. The place is a disaster. I've seen tornadoes cause less damage."

Juliet looked at Gordon and sputtered, "You're blaming this on me?"

Gordon smiled while Austin crept farther into the shop. "Wow, you're in trouble," Austin muttered to her as he gazed around. Some of the piles of books were as tall as he was.

All three adults laughed. "I'm not in trouble, Austin. Mr. Hanley told me to take down all the books."

"Sure did, Austin." Gordon smiled at Sierra. "We're open, but customers enter at their own risk."

"I'll chance it." Sierra followed her son deeper into the shop. She glanced into the back room, which still held all the tobacco supplies, and now a bunch of books.

"Can I help you find something, or did you just want to browse?" Gordon chuckled at his own absurdity.

"My father's birthday is next week, and I hear that you have the best selection in town for pipes." Sierra made her way around another stack of books and the stepladder.

"I've got the *only* selection in town," corrected Gordon. "Do you have an idea of what he likes?"

"Dunhill."

Gordon whistled. "Expensive taste. They are considered the 'Rolls-Royce of pipes.'" Gordon followed her into the back room. "I have only one of their pipes in stock right now, but I can get you anything they make in plenty of time for his birthday."

Sierra stopped in front of a display case filled with vintage humidors. "These are beautiful."

"Some are made for cigars, some cigarettes, but most are just for tobacco." Gordon opened the case. "This one is an art deco piece that has never been used." He handed it to Sierra. "Hand-carved mahogany with Spanish cedar lining. But it's for cigars, as you can see."

Sierra opened the box and trailed her fingertip over the sweet-smelling wood. "What do you have for just tobacco? Something that would look good on a desk."

"I have quite a few vintage pieces in here." Gordon put the wooden humidor back and lifted out a crystal container with a silver lid. "The crystal is Fostoria, and the lid is sterling." He opened it up and showed the cork lining on the inside of the lid. This is about eighty years old, as close as I can tell, and it's in excellent shape."

Austin glanced at Juliet and looked totally unimpressed. She didn't blame him. "Hey, Austin, would you like to help me?"

"Do what?" Austin wrinkled his nose at the pipes in another display case.

"Gordon had me make piles with the books, but as you can see, some have fallen over." She was the oldest of four and knew what kept little kids quiet and happy. "If you help me rebuild some of the towers, I'll buy you any book in the store."

Austin looked at his mother. "Can I, Mom?"

"Sure. I'm right here with Mr. Hanley trying to find something special for your grandfather's birthday."

Juliet sat on the floor and grinned at her new helper. Austin was a cutie, and she was sure Gordon could use a sale. An actual paying customer was as rare as the Austrian porcelain humidor Gordon was now showing Sierra.

The strange-looking container was a monkey wearing a red jacket, and one of his little paws held a regular-size pipe. The monkey was old, hand painted, and creepy-looking in a way. The little fellow wasn't the cute, furry kind of monkey with a big smile and a twinkle in his eye. He looked sad, or maybe his expression was supposed to be wise. It was hard to tell.

Gordon was never going to sell the strange nine-inch monkey for the asking price of three hundred dollars.

The little boy sat down next to her, eager to help.

"Okay, Austin, how about I start with the blue books, and you do the yellow?"

A deep male voice asked, "What's wrong with the green ones?"

Juliet glanced up, way up. She tried not to groan. The man standing in the shop was the same one she had noticed the other day down by the whale-watching boat. He was even cuter up close. The tawny mane of hair wasn't as wild as it had looked the other morning, blowing in the breeze. Then again, it was now pulled back in a ponytail. He also wasn't quite as young as she had first guessed.

This morning she would put his age in the upper twenties. He was not right out of high school or college, as she had thought. He was freshly shaven and dressed in jeans and a clean khaki windbreaker with "Blake's Whale-Watching Tours" embroidered on it.

She felt like Cinderella, before the fairy godmother

made her appearance. Where was a magic wand when she needed one? "Hi." She couldn't remember what he had just asked. Something about books. Well, duh, they were in a bookstore.

Austin jumped to his feet. "Hi, I know you." The little boy ran to the stranger. "You showed me the whale the other day."

Sierra and Gordon came out of the back room. Sierra was still clutching the monkey.

"Steve, how are you doing?" Gordon asked. "Haven't seen you in about a week."

"Keeping busy." Steve nodded to Sierra in recognition. "Uncle Lawrence is trying to do an extra tour a day before the end of the season."

"That's Lawrence for you," said Gordon, chuckling. "Always trying to make a buck."

Steve looked at Juliet as she got to her feet. The only reason she stood up was she felt stupid sitting on the floor. Both men were six feet or above, and Sierra was close to that mark. It was hurting her neck to look up that far. When she had been sitting, she had been a condensed mess and praying to blend into the chaos around her. Standing, she was a five-feet, nine-inch mess. With the tip of her finger, she pushed her glasses back up.

Gordon looked at her, then Steve. "Steven Blake, I would like you to meet Juliet Carlyle. Juliet, Steven."

"Mr. Blake." She brushed at the dust covering one side of her T-shirt.

"Please, call me Steve."

"Juliet's the daughter of a dear, close friend of mine. She's visiting our town and helping me straighten up the shop, as you can see." There was a calculated gleam in Gordon's gaze. "I'm trying to get her to explore the area—you know, sightsee and enjoy herself—but so far she's done nothing but work."

"We can't have that." Steve reached into the pocket of his jacket and handed Juliet a ticket. "A complimentary ticket for the whale-watching tour."

She took the ticket. She wasn't sure if Steve went around handing out complimentary tickets all the time, or if there was something more behind the gesture. "Thank you."

"You're welcome. I hope to see you on one of the tours soon."

"I'll be there. It was one of the things I wanted to do while here." She had been planning on it since seeing him down at the docks.

Steve gave her a smile. "Great." He grinned down at Austin. "Gotta go, buddy. There's another tour leaving soon and the whales are waiting."

"Wow," Austin said.

"See you later, Gordon." He nodded at Sierra. "Ma'am." He gave Juliet a long look that seemed to study every angle of her face, before saying, "Juliet." Steve turned without saying another word and walked out of the shop.

She stared down at the red ticket in her hand. "My goodness." She wasn't in the habit of receiving complimentary anything from handsome strangers. "He didn't do any browsing?" Steven Blake hadn't even glanced at a book, pipe, or magazine.

Gordon grinned and teased. "I think he got exactly what he wanted."

For the first time she could remember, an appropriate quote failed her.

* * *

Sierra helped three-year-old Morgan reel in her line. It was easy to tell which line in the crisscrossing fishing strings was Morgan's. Hers had the Snoopy in the inner-tube bobber. As the plastic bobber left the water, Sierra saw what the problem was with the line. The hook was attached to a small stick with some gross-looking algae hanging from it. The worm was nowhere in sight.

"Not a fishie." Morgan poked her finger at the stick in disgust. The little girl had been hopping up and down hoping that she had caught a big fish.

She quickly caught the little girl's hand before the hook got her. "Don't touch, Morgan. Remember, the hook will stick you."

Morgan made a face and sat down on the pebble shore. Disgusted with the whole fishing experience, she began to play with the small stones.

Sierra tried not to laugh. Morgan was definitely Tyler's sister. The two were identical in their expressions.

Hunter, seeing that his cousin had already abandoned the game, handed Matt his little blue pole. "I'm done." Hunter joined Morgan on the ground, which was part dirt, part sand, and was covered with a lot of stones.

Ten minutes of fishing was obviously a three-year-old's limit. Now she understood why Kay had handed her a cardboard box filled with plastic shovels and pails to take along on their adventure. It was bad enough that they had to borrow Jill's SUV, which could hold four car seats and two adults, but it also held boxes of toys, half a dozen fishing poles and tackle boxes, a cooler filled with drinks, and a basket filled with lunch. There had also been Sunblock, a change of clothes for each child, and two blankets shoved into the mess.

She had traveled cross country with Austin and Rose-mary packing less.

"Matt, I'm going to run up to the car and get the box of toys." She gestured to the two three-year-olds fighting over a greenish rock. "Can you keep an eye on these two for a second?"

Matt looked up from where he was busy trying to untangle Austin's line from Tyler's. "I'll get it for you."

"You have your hands full." She would rather climb the slight slope up to the car than listen to the boys argue about whose line tangled up with whose first. "Austin, behave, please."

"Oh, Mom," Austin groused.

Tyler's chuckle earned him a stern look from his uncle. "I really don't need to say anything, do I?" questioned Matt.

"Naw." Tyler looked at Austin and grinned. "Sorry."

"Sorry," Austin said back with a smile.

Matt rolled his eyes as Sierra turned to climb the slope. She had never seen Austin happier than he had been these past two weeks. It wasn't all because he was spending time with her, and they were on vacation, and she wasn't constantly being pulled away with work. Tyler and the other Porter children were the main reasons. Her son had made friends.

It was going to devastate Austin when they had to leave. She should be registering her son in a preschool next month. Instead she had no idea where she'd be staying come the end of September. One thing she did know, she'd be wherever her father felt her expertise was needed.

She opened up the back hatch of the SUV and pulled out the cardboard box and a heavy blanket. She was thirty-one, and her father still ran her life. The hatch slammed shut with a little more force than necessary. By running her life, her father was now running Austin's too.

It had been okay in the beginning. Austin was such a

joy to take with her everywhere she went. He had been an expert traveler by the time he could walk, and besides, she had Rosemary to take care of him while she worked and handled business. Austin now needed a home—a real home, not a string of hotels where he was spoiled by every staff member in every Randall Hotel. Austin was, after all, Lucas Randall's only grandchild.

She carried the box down to the shoreline and saw the laughter and joy on Austin's face as Matt squatted next to him giving him tips and advice on how to catch the big one. Austin didn't get a lot of male attention. His father, Jake, was a workaholic. She had married and then had a child with a man just like her own father.

Although her own father loved her and would get her anything her heart desired, he never gave her what she had wanted the most: time, and acceptance for who she was and what she could do. Her father treated her like some fragile, emotional woman who would fall apart under the least bit of strain and pressure. She understood his reasons because her mother had been one of those physically delicate and emotional women.

She wasn't her mother, unless she looked into the mirror—then her mother's face stared back at her. Sierra had inherited her mother's looks, and her father's brains for business. For thirty-one years she had been determined to make her father see the difference between his daughter and his beloved deceased wife. No matter what she did, he still treated her with kid gloves.

Sierra placed the box on the ground. "Hunter and Morgan, there's all kinds of beach toys in here." She was happy to see that whoever packed the box had done a great job. There were enough toys to go around.

Morgan snatched up a pink bucket. "That's mine."

Hunter grabbed the biggest plastic shovel and the red sieve.

She found a dry spot to sit, spread the blanket, and enjoyed the family squabbling. This was what being a family was all about. This was what she never had being a child with no siblings or even cousins. She had never had anyone to fight with.

Matt joined her on the blanket. "This wasn't exactly what I had in mind when I invited you and Austin fishing."

She glanced over to where Austin and Tyler were standing about six feet apart so their lines wouldn't tangle again. Both were staring intently at their bobbers. Hunter and Morgan were busy emptying every toy out of the box and getting dirty.

Matt, on the other hand, looked clean, handsome, and totally irresistible dressed in cargo shorts, a T-shirt, and sandals. She had missed him yesterday while she and Austin had explored parts of Mount Desert Island. Long into the night she had laid in bed thinking about what Matt had said to her Wednesday night: that he thought he was falling in love with her. Logic told her to back away from him. She was leaving in a couple weeks.

Logic had nothing to do with the wonder she had felt at those words.

"I really don't mind having Hunter and Morgan along." When they had shown up at Matt's parents' house to pick up Tyler, the entire family had been there working on the yards. They would need both the Porters' backyard and Joanna's cottage backyard to hold the number of people coming to the wedding. "This gives their parents a chance to get some more work done on the yards and gardens. It's looking wonderful, by the way. You guys must have been at it pretty late last night."

"When it became dark, Kay and Jill took the kids home, but Paul and John stayed. We rigged up some lights to see by. I guess we worked till about eleven."

She had been impressed with the amount of work they had managed to do in one evening. "With the hedges ripped out and sod put down, the two yards combined will be plenty of room for the wedding."

"My mom's thrilled that her yard is getting a garden or two put in." Matt leaned back onto his elbows and stretched his legs out in front of him. "Joanna and Karl shopped for two full days to buy all those plants that now have to be planted, and the mulch is being delivered sometime today."

Sierra stretched out her legs. They weren't nearly as long as Matt's. The sun felt wonderful, while not being too hot and oppressive. "So, honestly, what would you rather be doing, digging gardens or fishing here?" The two bigger poles that Matt had brought for them to use were still in the SUV.

"Here"—Matt looked at her—"with you, of course."

She felt a tug of desire at his words. "So why were you fighting with Paul earlier?" She had seen the brothers exchanging words, but she couldn't tell if they had been teasing each other or not.

"We weren't fighting. He said that you and I were getting the easier part of the deal. I called his bluff"—Matt smirked—"and said fine, that he and Jill should take all the kids fishing and you and I would play in the dirt."

She chuckled. "I wouldn't have minded." As long as someone gave her detailed directions on how to do what needed to be done. The only time she had ever planted anything was during the summer she had been about eight. She had followed the gardener around everywhere, and once in a while, probably to shut her up, he had allowed her to help.

"You're supposed to be on vacation, Sierra." Matt

shook his head. "You've done enough with the wedding. Norah and Ned were singing your praises all last night."

"About?" She hoped Matt's sunglasses prevented him from seeing the blush sweeping up her cheeks. She didn't want kudos for enjoying herself. Besides, all the running around she was doing for the wedding was allowing her to see the surrounding area and towns, something she was supposed to be doing anyway.

"Everything. I hear you solved the catering problem."

"The idea fell into my lap. I can't take credit for it." She shook her head. "Your mom and sisters-in-law did a lot of the bargaining, and Joanna did the rest."

"How did that idea fall into your lap?" Matt leaned closer and stole a quick kiss while the kids weren't looking.

She grinned, even though it wasn't nearly the kind of kiss she had been hoping for. "On the way out of town Thursday, there was a car wash being run by the cheerleaders from the local high school. The rental needed to be cleaned, so while Austin and I were standing there, I overheard them complaining about how they were never going to reach their goal. Seems their squad is good enough to go to Dallas, Texas, for the championships, but they need some major fund-raising to do it. The mothers who were supervising were tossing around some more ideas to get money for the girls when it hit me: hire the squad to act as caterers for the wedding."

Matt laughed. "The Hancock High School cheerleaders are catering my brother's wedding? Please tell me they'll be in uniforms."

She lightly punched him in the arm. "You're horrible. They will not be wearing their uniforms. Nor will they be doing the actual cooking. Their parents and they will be serving, making sure everything is running smoothly, and handling the cleaning-up. They also will be making up cheese, vegetable, and fruit trays. Joanna got together with a bunch of the girls and parents Thursday night and worked out the details.

"Your mom, Kay, and Jill went to work on the Women's Guild at the Methodist church. They'll be doing the ham and roast beef, plus all the tables, chairs, and dishes are being rented from them. Ned used his pull and got the Catch of the Day to supply potatoes au gratin and hors d'oeuvres, and Norah threw herself on the mercy of a caterer in Ellsworth who has agreed to do up two kinds of salad. So, as you can see, I really didn't do much."

Matt looked at her in amazement. "All this came about because your rental car needed to be washed?"

She glanced at the kids, who were all too busy having fun to be paying her and Matt much attention. She leaned forward and brushed his mouth with a soft kiss that lasted longer than a peck but left her frustrated for more, just the same. "It was really dirty."

Matt groaned and tried to reach for her.

She moved out of arm's reach. "We have company."

"We *always* have company." Matt's smile softened his words. "Tell me the best part of your day yesterday. Did you enjoy Bar Harbor?"

"The town was packed with tourists. I did get to take Austin out on a lobster boat and he helped haul in a couple of big ones with Captain Bob."

"Captain Bob?" Matt smirked. "Sounds exciting."

"Only if you're four." She leaned back, kicked off her sandals, and playfully skimmed her toes up his calf. "My favorite part was the popovers at Jordan's Pond."

"In Acadia National Park?"

"Is there another Jordan's Pond restaurant?"

"Afraid not, there's only one." Matt kicked off his sandals. "So you like their popovers?"

"'Like' isn't a strong enough word for my admiration of them." She grinned. "Lunch wasn't bad either. I definitely have to go back before I leave."

"I'll take you to dinner there one night."

"It's a date." She didn't want to think about leaving yet.

"Good. Speaking of dinner, I have an idea."

"Which is?" She had lots of ideas to appease her growing appetite. None had to do with restaurants or food.

"My brother John and Kay have invited Austin to their place tonight for dinner and a kids' movie. They feel they owe us something for all the times we've taken Tyler with us. I said I'd leave that up to you, since I'm not sure how you'd feel about leaving Austin with them for a couple hours."

"What will we be doing while Austin's there?" Her mind conjured up all kinds of possibilities.

"I know a fantastic restaurant in Winter Harbor. It's an old mansion perched high on a cliff overlooking the ocean." Matt's toe trailed up her calf in retaliation for her teasing him. "Dinner is served by candlelight and there's usually dancing on the patio."

She didn't know what upset her more, that he hadn't suggested dinner in bed or that she hadn't packed anything slinky and sexy to wear during her vacation. She wanted to knock Matt's socks off, along with quite a few other articles of clothing. "Sounds wonderful."

Her mind was trying to calculate how much time she would need to run into town to that cute little boutique, Claire's, and still be ready in time. "If Austin agrees, I see no problem with him going over to Tyler's for dinner and a movie."

"Mom! Mom!" shouted Austin. "I got one! I got one!"

Her son was holding onto his pole for dear life and screaming at the top of his lungs.

"Hold on tighter, Austin," shouted Tyler, who then dropped his own pole to go help his friend.

Matt jumped to his feet and sprinted to her son. So much for their conversation. She couldn't compete with a bobbing bobber and a tight fishing line.

Men.

She stood up and laughed as Morgan shrieked with glee and started to run in circles, kicking up water everywhere. Hunter made a beeline for the mighty fisherman, shouting that he wanted to see.

Everyone was shouting and Matt was leaning over Austin, trying to instruct him on reeling in the line. Birds were chirping with their displeasure from being disturbed on a beautiful, quiet Saturday morning. Somewhere close by, a dog started to howl.

She loved her son dearly and was thrilled he had caught a fish. But tonight couldn't come soon enough.

Chapter Ten

Matt tried not to swallow his tongue as he held out the chair for Sierra. She wasn't just beautiful this evening, she was knockout gorgeous. Forks had literally frozen in midair when she had walked into the room. Every man in the room had followed her with his gaze as she walked across the room. The amazing part was Sierra didn't seem to notice. She was too busy checking out the architectural details of Cliffside Manor.

"This is wonderful, Matt." Sierra took her seat and smiled at the maître d' who had shown them to their table.

"I thought you would appreciate it." Matt took his seat and was thankful that their table was at least semiprivate. He didn't want strangers gawking at Sierra all through their meal. "Cliffside Manor dates back from the mid to late 1800s. The Parker's, who were heavy into steel, had it built for their summer home."

Sierra gave a soft whistle. "Someone had money. What happened to the Parkers?" She smiled politely at the waiter who stopped at their table and asked if they would care for a drink. "A glass of your house white wine would be fine."

"The same," Matt said as he handed back the wine list. "I don't know for certain, but the story goes that there was some type of tragedy that happened to the family around the time of the Depression."

"Lots of families lost all their wealth during that time."

"True, but the house never went on the market. It stood empty and abandoned till the mid-seventies. I think it has changed hands about ten times since then. Each owner poured a fortune into repairs and renovations, but it never seemed to work out. The first couple owners had it as an inn, then in the early nineties it was made into a restaurant."

Sierra glanced around the large, open room filled with fine antiques and lots of greenery that acted as a privacy screen.

He could see in her gaze the appreciation of the refined beauty. He knew what she was seeing: twelve-foot-high plastered ceilings, silk wallpaper, detailed molding, and eight-foot-tall windows with a commanding view of the ocean and the night sky beyond. The current owners had outdone themselves and had spared no expense. He should know—he had worked on the inn himself.

"Whoever did this," Sierra said, "is amazing."

"Thank you." He meant it. Sierra had no idea he had done most of the work in this particular room.

"You did this?" Sierra waved her arm and nearly upset the tray their waiter was carrying to their table. "Oh, I'm so sorry."

Matt chuckled. The young waiter actually blushed as he set their wine before them. "Thank you." Matt felt sorry for the tongue-tied waiter, but he knew that feeling. He had experienced it earlier himself when he went to pick up Sierra.

"There is no way you bought that outfit in Misty Harbor." He had lived in the town his whole life and never once had he seen a woman remotely dressed like Sierra. The silky light blue pants and sleeveless top shimmered and reflected the candlelight. It almost looked as if it changed color when she moved. Sierra had piled her hair on top of her head in a sexy twisting style and had paired the outfit with silver—glittery silver sandals, a silver bag, and waterfalls of silver dangling from each ear.

When they had dropped off Austin at his brother's, John and Kay had asked Sierra where she had gotten the outfit. Sierra had surprised both Kay and him by saying she had just picked it up at Claire's in town. His brother John had stood there with his mouth hanging open catching flies, until his wife rammed her elbow into his gut.

Sierra took a sip of wine and smiled at him across the rim of the glass. "Haven't you ever been in Claire's?"

"I walk past it a couple times a week." He'd seen the mannequins in the window wearing different outfits. None of them ever looked like Sierra did tonight. He would have noticed.

"In other words, you've never been inside." Sierra shook her head and opened her menu. "It's a wonderful shop, quite surprising in many ways."

He opened his menu and was happy to see they still carried a great selection of steaks. "Will you be wearing it to Norah's wedding?" He could foresee a truly miserable day if she was. Every male above the age of puberty would be drooling after her. Ned was going to be a bit upset when his best man started punching out some of the wedding guests.

Sierra looked up from the menu. "I'm not going to the wedding, Matt."

"Why not?" He snapped the menu closed. He already knew what he wanted.

"Ummm . . ." Sierra looked hesitant. "I wasn't invited."

"Of course you're invited." Why would she think she wasn't invited? Hell, if it weren't for Sierra, Norah and Ned would be saying their vows by a half-dead shrub, and the guests would be slicing off chunks of six-foot-long hoagies bought at Roy's in Bangor and drinking beer from a cooler.

Sierra shook her head. "I didn't receive an invitation."

Matt stared at her for a moment and then started to laugh.

"What's so funny?" Sierra glanced around to see if they were attracting any attention.

"Sierra, no one received an actual invitation. There wasn't time to have them made and then mailed."

"So what did Norah and Ned do, call everyone?"

"The out-of-town relatives and friends, yes." He didn't see what the problem was. "Word of mouth spread it to everyone in town."

"So the three hundred guests everyone has been telling me about is, what, an estimate? No one RSVPed?" she asked, horrified.

"There was nothing to RSVP to, and three hundred is a pretty good estimate, in my opinion. Ned's a very likable guy. Everyone will want to be there." He reached across the table and covered one of her hands with his. "I would very much like to officially invite you and Austin to come to the wedding, as my date and guest."

Sierra looked at him. "First off, what's wrong with Norah? Isn't she likable?"

"Norah's very likable." He chuckled. "But she and her mother just moved here in June. I know a few of her coworkers at the newspaper are coming." He trailed a fingertip across Sierra's wrist.

"What happens if more than three hundred people show up? Or less?" Sierra turned over her hand and lightly teased the palm of his hand with one of her fingers.

"We'll make room for them somehow, and if there's food left over, the Methodist church knows which families in town could use it the most and will make sure it's delivered."

"It's that simple?" Sierra looked unconvinced.

"It's that simple. I've been to other spur-of-the-moment weddings, Sierra. It all works out." He captured her wayward finger because it was driving him nuts. "Relax, and tell me Austin and you will be coming with me." That way if someone tried hitting on her, he'd be in the right to bash some heads. The outfit she was wearing was going to cause a heart attack, and it just might be his.

"I would love to come with you, Matt." Her eyes glittered with secrets. "But Austin won't be here."

"Why not? Where's he going?" Sierra and Austin were inseparable. This was the first time Matt and Sierra had been out alone together.

"Jake is flying into Boston for business on Wednesday morning. Jake's sister lives in Boston, so he invited us down so he could spend a few days with his son. I think it's important that Jake and Austin spend the time together, but they don't need me. So I'm staying right here in Misty Harbor."

"How's Austin getting there?"

"I'm meeting Jake halfway, along Interstate 95 on Wednesday afternoon. Then I'll meet him there again Sunday afternoon to pick Austin back up." There were secrets in Sierra's eyes that were teasing him, tempting him.

"It's all worked out?" Four nights Sierra would be alone in the Alberts' home. Somewhere outside on the patio a band started to play a slow, soft melody, perfect for dancing under the stars. It was a real shame his hormones had already started to dance to some fiery Latin beat.

Sierra looked at Matt and knew exactly what he was thinking. The same thing she was: Wednesday couldn't get here soon enough. "Oh, just so you know, I won't be wearing this to Ned and Norah's wedding." She had no idea why he had asked, but it had seemed important to him.

"Why not? It's gorgeous and you look fantastic in it."

"Matt"—she tried not to roll her eyes—"I'm wearing it tonight."

"So?"

She did roll her eyes this time. "Forget it. It's a woman thing," she said as their waiter approached their table. Men were so clueless about certain things.

After the waiter left with their order, she glanced around the room in wonder. She had seen shabbier five-star hotels. From what she had been able to see of Cliffside Manor, it had been painstakingly restored. "I thought you said you were a carpenter."

"I am." Matt looked amused.

"Carpenters build houses and bookcases, things like that." She had seen and met many carpenters over the years. They had come in many shapes and sizes, but not a one of them had looked like Matt. She would have remembered.

"I can build a house, and I have built my fair share of bookcases." Matt smiled. "I specialize in restoration. It matches my love of history and my obsession for detail."

"Brain with the brawn?" She liked that in a guy. She'd never dated a carpenter before or any other guy who made his living with his hands. Her dates tended to be businessmen, smart, savvy men who got their brawn from a gym. She doubted very much that was where Matt got his.

Matt chuckled. "I'll take that as a compliment."

"It was meant as one." She glanced around the room. "Exactly how much of this room did you do?"

"The entire window wall. A previous owner had lined the whole wall with patio doors but was smart enough to save the original windows in the carriage house. I restored the old windows and replaced them exactly how they were originally." Matt nodded across the room where a massive fireplace took up half the wall. "The interior of the fireplace had to be completely redone, but thankfully the marble mantle was in great shape. I replaced a couple of rotten floorboards, and sanded and revarnished this room and three others."

"What about the crown molding?" Sierra stared up at the ceiling. The intricate molding had to be ten inches wide and hand carved.

"I only had to duplicate an eight-foot section. From the rest I stripped off eight layers of paint before giving it a fresh white coat."

She twisted and turned in her seat as she studied every foot of the crown molding. She couldn't spot the new piece. "I'm impressed." The red and gold silk wall covering looked elegant and old. "Tell me you hung the wallpaper." If he said yes, she'd offer him a job with the Randall Corporation and pay him a fortune. It would be worth every penny.

"Afraid I can't take credit for that one. There's a company in Bangor that specializes in walls. They did the plastering and hung the silk. I prefer to work with wood, and sometimes stone, brick, or slate."

"With all this talent"—her arm swept the room—
"why stay here in Misty Harbor? Why not move to a big
city? I have a feeling work this good is in great demand
and you would be able to practically name your price."
She didn't have a feeling about it; she knew. She had ne-
gotiated with *craftsmen* before. A good *craftsman* was
worth his weight in gold. Matthew Porter wasn't a carpenter, he was a *craftsman*.

"Misty Harbor is my home, Sierra. It's where my heart
is." Matt's gaze held sincerity. "It's where my dream is."

"What's your dream, Matt?" What did a man like Matt
dream about? She had a feeling his dream didn't concern making money or retiring at fifty.

"Living in Misty Harbor's lighthouse." Matt watched
her closely, waiting for a reaction.

She blinked. "Where?"

"The lighthouse where I saw you and Austin that first
morning. It's been my dream since I was eight years old
to live in it."

"You want to live in a lighthouse? There's not enough
room inside, is there?" She was confused. Didn't a
woman named Millicent Wyndham own the lighthouse?

Matt chuckled. "When I was eight, it didn't matter.
Now that I'm older, I agree. That's why I want to build a
replica of the original lighthouse keeper's house that at
one time was right next to it. It was struck by lightning
and burned to the ground before it could be saved."

"When was this?" She hadn't even known there had
been a house at one time.

"In 1940. For my twenty-fifth birthday my brothers and
parents went around town and got every old picture of the
place they could lay their hands on. It turned out to be
only three old black and whites. Between them and what
passed for blueprints back when it was originally built,

which Ned had found for me, I can build a replica with all the modern conveniences—like indoor plumbing."

"Indoor plumbing is good." Her heart sank. Matt wanted the lighthouse. The same lighthouse that the Randall Corporation would be incorporating into its newest hotel, set right on the coast of Maine. Twenty acres of prime real estate was about to go onto the market, and her father was seriously thinking about buying it. That was why she was in Misty Harbor.

She and Austin had been sent here by her father to scope out the town and the surrounding area. Millicent Wyndham, the woman who owned the property now, wasn't too sure that a hundred-room, high-end hotel would be in the town's best interest. From what her father told her, Ms. Wyndham was the town's matriarch, and what she said went. One of Sierra's jobs was to find out if Ms. Wyndham was telling the truth about the town or she was trying to jack up the price by playing hardball.

"So when do you start building?" she asked. Her mind was whirling with all kinds of possibilities. Could Matt really outbid the Randall Corporation? Seemed unlikely, but she had learned a long time ago never to judge a book by its cover.

"I don't." Matt moved his glass of wine out of the waiter's way as he set their plates down in front of them. "Thank you."

She mustered up a smile for the young man. "Thank you. It looks delicious." When he left, she asked Matt, "Why not?"

"Millicent, the woman who owns the property now, gave me the heads-up a couple weeks ago. A fancy hotel chain has contacted her, expressing its desire to buy the lighthouse and the twenty acres it sits on."

She cringed. *Hotel chain!?* Holiday Inn was a hotel

chain. Randall Hotels were individually built with the finest materials to fit into the surrounding area. Her father considered the words "hotel chain" blasphemy.

Matt cut into his steak with a little more force than necessary. "There is no way I can compete financially with that kind of money."

"So your dream is gone?" She'd never considered that by building and running hotels, her father could be hurting people. That she could be hurting people. She didn't want to kill Matt's or anyone else's dream.

"No." Matt grinned. "Not yet. Nothing has been signed and until I see bulldozers up there digging a foundation, I will continue to consider the lighthouse up for grabs."

"Well, that's good." *Until you find out who I am, and then you'll hate me.* With that depressing thought, she looked at her meal and suddenly lost her appetite.

Matt held Sierra close and slowly swayed to the music. He wasn't really dancing; Sierra didn't seem to be in the mood. An older couple was kicking up the dance floor and having a ball. Or to be more accurate, they were kicking up the slate patio of Cliffside Manor. It had taken him a couple tries to talk Sierra into dancing. Something seemed to be bothering her.

He leaned down and whispered in her ear, "Are you feeling okay?"

She nestled closer. "I feel fine, Matt."

"You're not cold?" The breeze blowing in off the ocean was on the chilly side, and the outfit she was wearing left her arms bare.

Sierra's cheek was pressed against his collarbone. "In your arms? How could I be cold?"

"I like the sound of that." Matt held her closer and

turned so his back was to the wind. Something wasn't right. He could feel it. Sierra had been her normal talkative self before dinner, but afterward she had barely said a word. "You miss Austin, don't you?" He'd finally figured it out.

"I always miss Austin when he's not with me."

He relaxed. It wasn't him. "Are you ready to go get Austin?"

"Yes." Sierra glanced up and smiled.

He brushed his thumb over the curve of her lip. "Next time just tell me you miss him." His mouth brushed the same path as his thumb. Since neither of their cell phones had rung during dinner, he knew Austin was fine and was probably handling the separation better than his mother. "I kind of miss the little guy myself."

"Thank you. It's just that he's never gone over to a friend's house before."

Matt shrugged out of his suit jacket and draped it across her shoulders. "What are you going to do when he stays for sleepovers at his friends'?"

"He's only four." Sierra huddled in the jacket and frowned up at him.

"Tyler, Hunter, and Morgan do it all the time. They sleep over at each other's houses, my parents, Ned's, and last month I had the three of them at my place for a night."

"That's different."

"Why?" They started walking along a well-lit path that took them around the side of Cliffside Manor and toward the parking lot.

"Because you're family. Austin has only spent the night with me, or his father, or with Rosemary, his nanny."

"Hasn't he ever spent the night with your father?"

Matt's father spoiled the kids every chance he got. Even Jill's and Kay's parents took them overnight.

Sierra laughed. "The last time Austin spent more than five minutes alone with my father, he was trying to teach him who was on which denomination of money, and which was more valuable."

"How old was Austin?" He held her elbow as the path became uneven.

"Two." Sierra rolled her eyes as they reached her rental SUV.

He had no idea what to say about that one. Sierra's father sounded a little uptight to him. "My father can make a quarter magically appear from his ear."

Sierra leaned against the car and laughed. "That's what families are supposed to have, sleepovers and magic quarters."

He crowded her close. "Families come in all shapes and sizes, Sierra. They are all different." He couldn't imagine being an only child, with no brothers to pound on once in a while. No brothers to lean on. "Large families have their drawbacks, magic quarters and all."

Her smile tugged at his heart. "I imagine they do."

"Did I tell you how beautiful you look tonight?"

"Three times, but who's counting?" Sierra's arms wrapped around his neck.

"Your smile is breathtaking." He bent his head and captured her mouth.

Sierra stood on her toes and melted into his arms. His jacket slipped from her shoulders, but it was a long time before either of them noticed.

Juliet stood at the rail of the boat and felt the cold sea spray against her face. She had taken Gordon's advice and worn a windbreaker and a sweatshirt underneath. Even in August, it was darn cold out on the ocean. It was even colder barreling across the waves as if a tidal wave was about to overtake them and send them all into the abyss.

She didn't have to worry about drowning, though. She was frozen solid. She would float like an iceberg.

Juliet cringed at the sound of the poor screaming engine. The engine backfired, and a billow of black smoke filled the air behind them. Lawrence Blake was a maniac behind the wheel, or whatever was being used to steer the boat. Her hand gripped the rail tighter as they hit another wave.

"Bend your knees a little, and they will act as shock absorbers. Don't lock them." Steven Blake joined her at the front railing.

She managed a small smile and wondered how he knew her knees were locked in terror beneath her jeans. She didn't want to become an iceberg. "Does your uncle usually go this fast?"

"Believe it or not, he's actually going slower than normal."

She rolled her eyes behind her sunglasses and hoped he couldn't see. Lawrence was his uncle, after all. "How can you tell?"

"I asked him to, plus it's our last run of the day. There's no hurry now." Steve leaned against the metal rail and faced the back of the boat. "I'm glad you finally decided to come. I was beginning to think I would have to go looking for you."

"It's only Tuesday." Juliet told herself she was only imagining Steve singling her out, but she had a feeling she was lying to herself. Steve did seem interested in her. Amazing. "You only gave me the ticket on Thursday."

"Ah, you were playing hard to get?" Steve looked intrigued by the possibility.

She laughed. She'd never played hard to get in her life; she wouldn't know how. "What I was playing was shop-keeper, designer, and janitor."

"I heard that Gordon's shop is now a smoke-free bookstore, with just a little area designated for tobacco products." Steven chuckled at the idea. "How did you talk him into that one? The place usually reeks like the bottom of an ashtray."

"I didn't talk him into anything. Gordon made up his own mind and hung the NO SMOKING signs himself." No one had been more stunned than she, when she had walked into the shop on Friday and saw the orange and black signs.

"So you haven't been avoiding me?" Steve looked pleased.

"No, I've been busy." The shop had been cleaned from top to bottom, the books were now arranged by subject matter, and there was even a little kids' table and chair set for the younger customers. The antique hand-knotted wool rug that was burned and singed beyond redemption had been given a proper burial in the Dumpster out back. There was still a hint of smoke in the shop, but at least she could now breathe.

By the number of customers coming in and out all day long, they had appreciated the changes too. Gordon was even complaining about having to work twice as hard now, but there had been a gleam in his eye when he had said it.

"Hold whatever thought you have that's making you smile like that." Steve flashed her a quick smile and then pulled the portable microphone out of his windbreaker. He used his binoculars for a moment and grinned.

Steve turned on the mike. "Ladies and gentlemen"—the other passengers quieted down—"if you all would look off the port side of the boat, which is the left side"—Steve waved his arm to the sea—"we are about to pass Sammy, a harbor seal."

Juliet stared off into the calm sea. She didn't see a seal.

"He's a little hard to see just yet, but I wanted to give everyone ample time to find a good spot if they wanted to see him." Steve pressed in closer to her as a bunch of tourists flocked to the front of the boat. "We named him Sammy, because we're not sure if he's a Sam or a Samantha."

Steve waved to his uncle in the wheelhouse, and there was a noticeable slowing of the boat. "Sammy likes to hang out in this part of the sea and can be spotted on most of our tours. The engines catch his attention, and he likes to stick his head out to investigate."

Steve looked over his shoulder at the water. "The little bump in the calm water is his head, which you'll see better as we pass."

Juliet smiled as the bump indeed turned into a seal's head. Sammy was gray with a few black markings and big black shiny eyes. The other tourists on the boat waved, yelled, and took a hundred photos. Sammy stared back with a total lack of interest.

Steve leaned in close. "What do you think he's thinking?"

"That we're the ones putting on the show, not him."

Steve laughed. "Right you are."

Steve turned the mike back on as Sammy was left behind and the engines once again screamed and billowed the occasional cloud of smoke. "As I said before we started, it takes awhile before we make it out to the whale feeding grounds. They are about twenty-five miles off-shore. We have about another forty minutes before we reach them. Keep your eyes out for whales, even though they only rarely come in this close, but they have been known to in the past. If you have any questions, please come find me and I'll be more than happy to answer them."

"Impressive. How many times a day do you do this?"

"Two to three times a day, every day, seven days a week." Steve gave her a long look. "The schedule is hell on my social life."

"I can imagine." What would she know about having a social life? She didn't have one unless one counted parent-teacher conferences as a social event.

Steve looked as though he wanted to ask her another question, but they became surrounded by a group of giggling ten-year-old girls and a harried, green-looking mother. As Steve patiently started to answer their hundred and one questions, Juliet slid to her left and away from the group. It wouldn't be fair to the other passengers if she hogged all of Steve's time.

Thirty-five minutes later, the boat suddenly slowed down. Hurricane-force winds stopped blowing her hair and the windbreaker felt funny not being plastered to her chest. She could finally breathe normally and relax her death grip on the railing.

She heard Steve's voice come over the speaker. "We have reached the feeding grounds. This is where everyone has to help and be my eyes. I need you all to search the water for anything unusual. Sometimes you can actually see the blow, which is the water vapor being exhaled through the whales' blowholes. The whales we usually spot along here only need to breathe anywhere from five to fifteen minutes, but they can hold their breath for up to forty minutes. Sometimes they surface so fast you will see only the fin, and other times you might see their flukes, which are their tail fins, come out of the water. So you need to be quick and ready with the cameras."

Juliet chuckled as she scanned the calm sea. Some tourist she'd make. She hadn't brought a camera.

Someone shouted on the port side of the boat, and everyone ran toward that side. She stayed where she was and gripped the railing as the boat shifted its balance. Steve's voice crackled over the loudspeakers. "Easy, it's nothing. No whale yet."

A man by the front of the boat shouted. Twenty-five passengers stampeded toward the front as the boat slowly moved through the water.

Juliet stood by the back of the boat, casually scanning the water and enjoying the sun on her face, now that it was thawing out. She unzipped her jacket and thought about taking it off. There were seven false alarms before an actual sighting was made, far off the port side.

The boat turned in that direction as Steve, who had binoculars trained on that area, began to speak. "It's a fin whale, and a pretty big one at that." Steve looked up at Lawrence and pointed in the direction he wanted the boat to go. "He didn't dive deep, so he'll probably be up for air in about seven minutes or so."

Juliet joined the crowd on the port side of the boat. If they hadn't capsized yet, she didn't think her weight would tip them over the edge. Everyone grew quiet and waited.

It took eleven minutes for the fin whale to make his reappearance, but by the *oohs, ahs,* and the clicking of the cameras it had been worth the wait. She stood there in awe as the long, dark whale barely broke the water with his head. He arched his back and she had a clear view of his ridiculously little fin, considering his size, and part of his tail as he went back under. The amazing part was, he had been about forty feet away from the boat, and if she wasn't mistaken, he had been bigger than the boat.

"There he goes, folks. I estimate him to be about seventy-five feet long. Fin whales can get to about eighty feet in length. He's a baleen whale, which means he doesn't have teeth. He has hundreds of thin plates in his mouth, which are called baleen, that he uses to screen his food. He can be found in all the oceans, not just off the coast of Maine."

"What does he eat?" asked one of the girls, who thankfully no longer was giggling and annoying everyone on board.

"Mainly plankton, which are drifting masses of tiny animals and plants, but a fin whale also eats anchovies, herring, and other small fish."

"Do they eat people?" asked a little boy around eight. The boy looked hopeful.

"No," said Steve, chuckling. He glanced up from the crowd of kids surrounding him, half a boat length away, and smiled right at Juliet.

She felt that smile clear to her knees.

Steve's hair once again was pulled back in a ponytail, and he was wearing the same windbreaker he had the other morning in the shop. When she had walked down the gangplank to get onto the boat, he had been there collecting tickets, but his back had been toward her. He hadn't seen her until he turned to take her ticket. First surprise, then joy as he recognized her had been in his golden, light brown eyes. There had been no way for him to fake that look. Steven Blake had been very happy to see her.

Juliet felt her heart give a little jolt of awareness as she slowly smiled back. She had no idea where this was going because she had to head back to Boston in another week. She had a third-grade classroom to pull together and report in to her mother. Victoria Carlyle wanted a complete report on Gordon Hanley. Their nightly phone calls no longer were satisfying her mother.

Chapter Eleven

Matt felt funny driving Sierra's rental SUV everywhere, but there was no help for it. Austin needed the safety seat, and there was no way the bulky seat and two adults could fit in his pickup truck. He glanced in the rearview mirror and smiled at Austin. "You doing okay back there, buddy?"

Austin grinned. "Super-duper."

He chuckled. Austin had picked up that particular saying from Tyler. "We're almost there." He was taking Austin to his place while Sierra, Norah, and Norah's mom headed into Bangor to firm up some orders for the wedding and do some shopping. Austin would have been bored out of his mind, so Matthew volunteered to show him his shop and where he lived. It was one and the same.

He rented the old garage with an apartment above it for two reasons. One, it had everything he needed, even though he had outgrown the shop space three years ago. Two, and more important, it was cheap. He had better use for his money than paying rent. He had a dream to buy. Lately, it looked as though that dream would never be fulfilled, but he hadn't given up total hope. His brothers didn't call him the dreamer of the family for nothing.

Millicent Wyndham knew how important the lighthouse was to him. Hadn't she given him the heads-up about the hotel chain sniffing around looking to buy the property? Millicent had been truthful and up-front with him. At seventy-four, she claimed she wasn't getting any younger. Considering the steel trap of a mind that she still possessed, he had his doubts. Millicent would probably outlive them all. Since she had no heirs to leave her belongings to, she was looking for ways to help the town.

Millicent had married Jefferson Wyndham when she was eighteen. Jefferson was the son and only heir of the Wyndham fortune. The Wyndhams had made their money and had employed most of the town building ships at a time when wooden ships had ruled the seas. The Wyndhams' legacy was Misty Harbor, and Millicent was carrying on that tradition.

Millicent would make sure her "baby" was taken care of into the future, no matter whom it hurt or how many toes she had to step on. If Millicent thought it would be in the town's best interest to have a major hotel built next to the lighthouse, he would wager everything he had in the bank that the hotel would be built. Money mattered to the feisty old matriarch—she wasn't stupid by any stretch of the imagination—but the town's welfare mattered more.

Matt considered himself a reasonable man, one who could look at both sides of an argument. The major hotel would generate more tourists, which in turn would generate more money being spent in town. Businesses would prosper. The town would prosper. The hundred-room hotel also would bring a lot of jobs to the locals.

Businesses would pop up all over the place to cater to the guests. It seemed like a win-win situation.

Until he thought about the history.

Misty Harbor was founded on fishing, lumber, and eventually one of the largest shipbuilding operations on the East Coast. There was a lot of history in the town. The lighthouse was packed full of history—important history to him and every other resident in town. His family had Carrie's Hill. Edna and Bill McCain had gotten married in front of the lighthouse wearing flowers in their hair and no shoes back in the late sixties. He could name at least four kids who had been conceived while their parents played in the tall grass under the summer moon.

All to be bulldozed for the sake of what some called progress. It was enough to break a man's heart.

"Are we there yet?" asked Austin as he playfully kicked the back of the driver's seat.

Matt wondered if he had picked up that bad habit off of Tyler or he had been doing it before now. "This is my street." The road they were on was close to Sunset Cove but had none of the views. From his second-floor apartment he had a wonderful view of trees. Valley Road was just as its name claimed, in a valley. It was the main reason rent was so cheap. Who wanted to live on the coast of Maine and see nothing?

"See the big white building up ahead? That's it." It didn't even look like a house. It looked like a big white square with two huge metal garage doors and wooden steps going up the side of the building. Thankfully his one-bedroom apartment had a more welcoming appearance—once guests were inside.

Austin looked out the window as Matt pulled into the parking lot. "Where's your house?"

"Upstairs." Matt shut off the SUV and opened his door. At least in the valley you could still smell the sea. He opened Austin's door and released the boy from his seat.

Austin stood in the parking lot frowning at the building.

"What do you want to see first, the apartment or where I keep all my tools?" If he understood little boys as much as he thought he did, he knew which Austin would pick.

"Tools." Austin continued to frown at the building, unsure where the door was located.

Bingo! "Follow me, and I'll show you the side entrance."

Austin followed him around the side of the building. Instead of going up the stairs to the apartment, Matt unlocked a door behind the steps.

He reached in, hit the light switch, then pressed the automatic garage-door openers that raised both metal doors. Without any air circulating, the shop tended to get warm.

Austin's eyes grew wide as a cooling breeze and light flooded the shop. "Wow!"

There was nothing wrong with the boy's Y chromosome. "I say that exact same thing some days." He loved his shop, even though it was more than a bit crowded. It was a woodworker's paradise and the envy of all his brothers. He spared no expense when it came to his tools.

"Please don't touch anything, and I'll give you a tour." He wasn't afraid Austin would damage anything, he was more worried about him getting hurt or cut on something sharp. Sierra would have his head on a platter if something happened to her son on his watch.

Austin stepped into the shop. "Do you make things?"

"Sure do. That's what all these tools do." He stepped over to the table saw. "This cuts big pieces of wood"—he pointed to a nearby chop saw—"and that one cuts little pieces."

"Do you make houses?" Austin's little head was bobbing and moving all around. He didn't seem to know what to look at first. "What's that?" he pointed to a piece of equipment that took up nearly an entire wall.

"It's a lathe. It cuts wood by turning it." Matt reached for one of the porch posts he was making for Paul's house in his spare time. Since Ned and Norah had announced their wedding date, he hadn't had five minutes of spare time. In fact, Sunday night he had been up till one in the morning cutting all the fancy ends to the pieces of the arbor. Thankfully, he didn't have neighbors too close by.

"See how the wood goes in and out? It's not just straight."

Austin's little fingers followed the curves the lathe had cut into the solid piece of wood. "Super-duper."

"Yes, it is, and no, I don't build houses."

"Hotels?"

"No, I don't build them either," he said, chuckling.

"Cars?"

"No, they're not made from wood."

"Airplanes?" Austin's forehead had a crease in it from thinking so hard.

"No, they aren't made from wood either." He was trying to think what he had made that would impress a four-year-old. "I made a toy box for Tyler, and a dollhouse for Morgan."

"What did you make for Hunter?"

"A sailboat sandbox, and before you ask, I haven't made anything for baby Amanda yet, because her parents haven't told me what they would like for her. She's still too little to play."

"Oh." Austin continued to eye every piece of equipment in the shop. "What's this?"

"It's a plane, and no, it doesn't fly. It's for smoothing a wood surface." He had an entire shelf neatly lined with antique planes that he used in his work. They were his pride and joy, along with a case of hand-carving tools from the nineteenth century. The plane Austin was looking at was a new one.

Matt followed Austin around and automatically answered his hundred and one questions before saying, "I have an idea." Anything had to be better than explaining for the fifth time why there was sawdust all over the floor. "Since your mom is going to be a while yet, how about you and I make something." The ladies had gone shopping, and he figured the mall closed by ten, so they'd be lucky to see Sierra by eleven.

"What? A sandbox?"

"No, that's too big for you to carry home." Besides, he wasn't even sure where Austin's home was. He glanced around the shop and prayed for inspiration. What could they make that would be easy, quick, and small enough for Austin to manage? Since a brilliant idea didn't whack him in the head, he went with an old standby. Thankfully, Austin was young enough not to know it was an old standby. "We can build a birdhouse."

"A birdhouse?" Austin looked unsure.

"Sure. You hang it from a tree and put bird food in it. That way you get to see all kinds of birds." He walked over to a huge bin filled with little pieces of scrap wood. "If we make it quick enough, I have some extra paint just sitting around. I think you're old enough to give it a coat or two of paint."

"Really?"

"Really." Matt held up a piece of wood about twelve

inches by ten inches. "Come on." Matt showed him the wood. "We need a couple more pieces of wood about this size. Think you can help me find some in this mess?"

"Yeah." Austin dug into the wood bin without being asked twice.

"Easy there. You don't want to get a splinter." He helped Austin select a few more pieces of wood and then they carried them over to his work table.

"First thing we need is a plan." Matt laid out the pieces of wood, picked up Austin, and sat him on a stool.

Austin looked at the wood and nodded. In a serious tone, he said, "We need a plan."

Matt bit the inside of his cheek to keep from laughing. "I'll do all the cutting, but you have to sand and hammer in the nails."

Austin smiled. "I know how to play in sand."

This time he couldn't contain his laughter. "It's sandpaper, not sand." He reached up on the pegboard and pulled down two pairs of safety goggles. He tightened the elastic band on the small pair and slid them onto Austin. "Safety first."

The high-impact safety glasses took up a good portion of Austin's face. "Can you see okay?"

Austin nodded.

Matt put on his pair. "It's going to get loud in here when I cut the wood to the right size. Are you afraid of loud noises?"

Austin shook his head.

Matt didn't know if he should believe him or not. Tyler loved the sound of the equipment running. The louder the better. Hunter, on the other hand, was scared. He reached for a pair of ear protectors and fitted them to Austin's small head and over his ears. Better to be safe than sorry. "I want you to sit right here, and don't move, okay?"

"Okay," shouted Austin.

Matt walked over to the table saw and turned it on. He glanced at Austin, who waved back. He slowly cut the wood, keeping a careful eye on Austin. The little boy didn't seem to mind the noise at all. Matt made quick work of the rest of the wood and then drilled a big hole through the center of one piece. He carried them over and joined Austin at the work table.

He plucked the ear protectors off the boy. "Ready to sand? No more loud noises."

"Yes."

Matt handed him some medium-grit sandpaper and showed him how to sand the edges of the pieces of cut wood. Austin went to work. Matt got the rest of the tools together as he watched the boy concentrate on the job. Austin's little tongue was sticking out the side of his mouth. Figuring the boy had had enough sanding time, he placed the rest of their equipment on the table. "Ready to hammer in some nails?"

Austin nodded, which caused his safety goggles to wiggle farther down his nose. Matt tightened the elastic strap. "If I hold the nail for you, promise not to whack my fingers?"

"Promise."

Matt tried not to cringe. He had heard that promise before, right before Tyler had smashed his thumb black and blue. Matt held the first nail. Amazingly Austin hit the nail and not Matt's fingers.

He wasn't so lucky on the second swing of the hammer.

Or the third, fourth, sixth, and tenth.

Twenty minutes later the birdhouse was nailed together. Matt's fingers might turn black and blue, and there was a blood blister forming under his thumbnail, but at least none of the bones were broken. It was worth every agonizing whack just to see the look of pride and wonder on Austin's face as the birdhouse came together.

"You did it, kid." He studied the slightly crooked and out-of-plumb birdhouse. "You're going to have all kinds of birds coming to this house. This is great. In fact, I think it's the best one I ever saw."

Austin beamed. "Can I paint it now?"

"Sure can." He spread a couple sheets of old newspaper on top of the table and placed the house in the middle. "I have red, green, yellow, and blue paint." He had more than that, but he didn't want to explain what sage, celery, or ivory was to a four-year-old. He pulled down the four small cans and hunted down a cheap toss-away brush.

"You can take off the glasses. I don't think you'll get paint in your eyes." He had been more worried about a chip of wood or a bouncing nail. "We need one more thing." He reached into a drawer and pulled out one of his old T-shirts he kept handy for really messy jobs. "You need to put this on, Austin. Your mother would have a cow if you ruin your clothes."

Austin giggled. "What would Mom do with a cow?"

Matt shrugged. "Milk it, I guess."

Austin's giggles turned into laughter.

Four hours later Sierra climbed the wooden steps to Matt's apartment. Norah and her mom had just dropped her off out front and left. She had placed all her shopping bags in the back of the SUV. Thankfully Matt had turned on the outside lights so she wouldn't trip and break her neck climbing the stairs. With his love of history and preservation, this wasn't the kind of place she expected to see Matt living in. She had pictured some quaint carriage house with his shop in the bottom part and an apartment upstairs.

The only things wood on this place were the steps; everything else was cinder block and metal. She reached the landing and knocked on the door.

She heard Austin's voice before the door swung open. She was about to lecture her son on opening doors alone when she saw Matt standing there. "Hi." How was it possible for him to look better than he had nearly five hours ago?

"Hi, yourself." Matt stepped back so she could enter. "We didn't expect you this early."

"It's only a little after nine." Austin's bedtime was nine-thirty. It looked like he was going to miss it, but she had found the perfect outfit to wear to Norah's wedding. It was going to knock Matt's socks off.

"Mom, Mom, come see what I made." Austin ran to the kitchen table. "Matt let me use his shop."

"He did?" She looked at the brightly colored, ummmmm . . . thing for a full minute before she figured out what it was supposed to be. "It's a birdhouse!" The large hole in the center gave it away. "You made this all by yourself?" She knew he couldn't have possibly, but she wanted to hear what he said.

"Naw, I let Matt help. He cut the wood, but he doesn't hold nails very good."

She bit her lower lip as Matt rolled his eyes. "I see." She studied the birdhouse more closely. There was a half inch gap on one end where the roof came together. "Did you paint this all by yourself?"

"Yep." Austin pointed to the hole in the front. "See, that's where birds go in to sleep. Can we hang it in our tree at home?"

Sierra felt her heart sink. They didn't have a real home.

"We can hang it in one of the Alberts' trees tomorrow morning." Little boys needed a place to hang their birdhouses.

"Okay." Austin scrambled off the kitchen chair he had climbed up on. "Come see Matt's TV. It's big." Austin ran toward the living room, where she could hear a baseball game being broadcast.

She glanced around Matt's kitchen. It was small but clean. The cabinets were natural wood, and the countertops were made of one-inch-square blue and green glass tile. "Tell me you didn't make the cabinets."

Matt shrugged. "I got a great deal on some maple."

"Is there anything you can't make out of wood?" The birdhouse didn't count. She knew he had allowed Austin to do as much of it as possible. She thought it was the sweetest thing anyone had ever done with her son.

"A boat. My brothers and I tried to build one about twenty years ago. We got about a hundred yards out in Frenchman's Bay before it sank." Matt grinned. "Haven't had a reason to try it again. One day I might, though."

She shook her head. "Your poor mother." What Peggy Porter must have lived through raising the four Porter boys. "It's amazing she's still sane."

Matt laughed. "Who do you think christened the boat with a bottle of Coke and pushed us out?"

Sierra closed her eyes and tried not to laugh. Peggy was just as bad as her sons. "Your whole family is certifiable."

She couldn't imagine having a parent shoving her off into the bay to see if the boat she was in was seaworthy. When she was younger and they were staying at a hotel on water, her father would send her off with one of the staff for a boat ride. One of the uppity-ups from the staff would accompany her and point out all the trees, plants, and waterfowl. It was boring and they had always

strapped so many flotation devices to her that she had resembled an orange marshmallow.

She had preferred to sneak into the kitchen and beg
the chef for a big bowl of ice cream. She would then
wolf it down so fast that she ended up with a brain
freeze. At least that was an interesting way to spend an
afternoon.

"Some say that." Matt leaned forward and gave her a
quick kiss since Austin was out of the room. "I know
I'm crazy about you."

She smiled. "How crazy?" She liked the sound of that.
Something special was happening between them. Matt
thought he was falling in love with her. Was it possible
for her to be falling right back? If she was, what was
going to happen come Labor Day weekend when she
was supposed to be heading back? What would Matt say
when he found out she was a Randall, and it was her
father who had contacted Millicent about the lighthouse
and the surrounding acreage?

So many questions. So little time.

Matt pulled her into his arms and kissed her like she
wanted him to.

Sierra blocked everything out of her mind but the feel,
the taste, and the scent of Matt. Warm desire rushed
through her body. She wanted more. So much more. Her
tongue traced his lower lip, and she felt him shiver. She
smiled against his mouth and her palm cupped his rough
jaw. Matt needed to shave twice a day. When, not if, they
made love he was going to leave behind his mark.

Her shiver matched his.

"Mom, come see!" Austin shouted from the other
room.

Sierra broke the kiss.

"Crazy enough to know I shouldn't be kissing you with

Austin in the next room." Matt whispered against her mouth. "But crazy enough not to care." He slowly released her.

"I'll be right there, hon." Sierra watched the emotions swirling in Matt's gaze. His light blue eyes had darkened with desire and his unsteady breathing matched hers. They both wanted the same thing.

They both were going to have to wait until tomorrow night.

Juliet looked at the two men sitting at the kitchen table and laughed. "I cooked, so I'm not cleaning up." Gordon and Steven Blake both sat back, contented, full, and testing her. She wasn't going to cave. "I spent three hours in this kitchen roasting that chicken and fixing that meal you two just devoured."

It was true. There was hardly a thing left. Two lone rolls and a spoonful of peas. That was it. The chicken had been picked clean as if vultures had attacked it and the mashed potatoes had been inhaled. Gordon and Steve ate like her brothers. Were all men such bottomless pits?

Gordon patted his nonexistent stomach and grinned. "'There is no love sincerer than the love of food.'"

"Don't you quote Shaw to me." She put her hands on her hips and glared at the man who was her father. "Wash the dishes."

"I'll dry," Steve said in a rush and with a grin. "Masterful women scare me." Steve stood up and stretched. "Besides, any woman who can quote Shaw terrifies me."

"'Courage mounteth with occasion.'" She couldn't help quoting back.

Steve cringed in fake horror. "Shakespeare too! There's no stopping her now, Gordon."

Gordon roared with laughter. "I've only been able to stump her once, Steve. She's darn good."

"*Pudd'nhead Wilson* doesn't count," she griped. Nothing had surprised or delighted her more than when Steve joined in Gordon's game of quotes. Steven was a bookworm, along with having a master's degree in biochemistry and a love for the sea. She had been halfway in lust with him on looks alone. This new development pushed it over the edge.

She was enjoying herself way too much.

"She doesn't know *Pudd'nhead*?"

"Of course I know Twain. I just never heard that particular quote about temptation." She looked at her father. "I seem to remember you stumbling over one the other day."

"Steinem? You expected me to know Gloria Steinem?"

"Why not? You expect me to know Keats, Shaw, Shakespeare, Dylan Thomas, Thoreau, Wilde . . ." She started to tick the men off, one finger at a time.

"Okay, I get the point." Gordon looked at Steve and grinned. "Feisty, isn't she?"

Juliet was taken aback. No one had ever called her feisty before. She was the quiet, calm, and cool Carlyle. With Gordon she was different. Back at home if she started sprouting Shakespeare or Wilde, her brothers would make fun of her and call her "egghead" and then go into some silly routine about it only being a flesh wound. With Gordon she had to use every ounce of her functioning brain, and then some. He kept her on her toes. She liked that.

She also liked Steve.

At the end of the wild whale-watching ride she had screwed up her courage and asked a man to dinner for the first time in her life. The fact that he seemed to be friends with Gordon had helped matters, along with the fact she wouldn't be sitting across from him in some restaurant racking her brain for something intelligent and interesting to say. She would be doing the cooking.

She didn't consider herself a gourmet chef, but she knew the basics and could prepare roast beef, meatloaf, chicken, and even the occasional seafood dish. She could make a cake from a box, brownies from scratch, and Christmas cookies by the batch. Christmas at the Carlyles' wouldn't be the same unless she spent three solid days in the kitchen baking cookies. Her brothers had become so spoiled that in October they were now mailing her pictures of cookies that they wanted her to bake.

She wondered if Gordon liked cookies.

Gordon started to fill the sink with soap and water. Steve picked up the dirty dishes and carried them over to the sink. She wrapped up the two rolls but scraped the peas into the garbage, along with the chicken bones.

Five minutes later she was wiping down the table when Steve brought up a subject she and Gordon had been avoiding.

"Gordon, you said Juliet was the daughter of a dear friend."

"Yes, Victoria Carlyle." Gordon gave Juliet a meaningful look before placing the next plate into the drainer.

"Is this Victoria any relationship to you, Gordon?" Steve glanced between her and Gordon.

She knew it looked a little strange with her first hanging around Gordon's shop every day and redoing the place. Then they'd really started tongues wagging in town when she had moved out of the bed-and-breakfast and into Gordon's guest room. Her moving into his apartment solved a couple problems, the first being that she felt strange with him paying for her room at a local bed-and-breakfast. She didn't ask, and Gordon didn't say, but she had a feeling he wasn't very wealthy. The other reason was, with her doing so much work on the interior of the shop, running back and forth to the B&B was wearing her out.

She had come to Misty Harbor to meet and possibly get to know Gordon Hanley. What better way to get to know someone than to move in with him? Of course, that action had caused a lot of speculation.

"No relation. Victoria is someone I met years ago." Gordon continued to wash the next plate. "Why do you ask?"

Steve dried a plate and placed it into the cabinet. "I can't help noticing a remarkable resemblance between you and Juliet. You two could be related. Are you sure you're not brother and sister separated at birth?" Steve laughed at his own joke.

Gordon gave a fake chuckle that didn't fool her. By Steve's expression, it didn't fool him either.

She knew Gordon was leaving it up to her, if or when the town would know she was his daughter. It was sweet of him, but it was an awkward situation. How do you blurt out that Gordon had a daughter no one ever knew about, and guess what, it's me? Surprise!

Juliet took a deep breath. She didn't think she would ever get a better opportunity. "Speaking of being separated at birth . . ."

Gordon spun around in shock. Soap bubbles and water went flying.

Steve looked from Gordon to Juliet with confusion in his face.

"Steve, there's no easy way to say this, so I'll just come right out and say it. I'm Gordon's daughter. My mother and Gordon had a relationship, and she never told Gordon she was carrying his child. Mom married a great guy named Ken Carlyle, and he raised me as his own." There it was, out in the open, and it felt good.

Steve blinked in surprise.

Gordon looked astounded. "Juliet, you didn't have to say anything."

She thought she saw tears in Gordon's eyes but didn't want to embarrass him. "Yes, I did. That busybody Priscilla Patterson and her skinny sidekick were in here this morning while you were at the post office. Priscilla started lecturing me on living in sin and wicked ways."

Steve laughed. Gordon sputtered in outrage. "She didn't!"

"Sure, she did." Juliet winked. "Don't worry, I straightened her out."

"What did you tell her?"

"I told her I was just using you until someone richer came along."

Gordon looked appalled. "Juliet, that is going to be all over town by now. People will think you're a gold digger, if not worse."

She took a step closer and kissed Gordon's cheek. "Relax, Gordon." She still couldn't bring herself to call him "Dad." "Imagine how silly she's going to look when it becomes known I'm your daughter." She took hold of his wet hands and squeezed. "This past week with you has shown me many things. It also explains a lot."

"Such as?" Gordon looked so happy.

"Well, I finally figured out why I never seemed to fit in with the rest of the Carlyle gang. Why I have two left feet and couldn't hit a basket with a ball if my life depended on it. Why I prefer Shakespeare over the Three Stooges, and why I have really dark hair."

There was no mistaking the tears in Gordon's eyes

now. "Hey, I can shoot a basket, as long as I can stand in one spot and not have to run around while doing it." Gordon's hand reached out and cupped her cheek. "You're the most beautiful daughter a man could ever hope for."

"Thank you." She leaned into the warmth of his palm. "You make a pretty cool dad." There, she'd finally said it.

Gordon sniffed and wiped his eyes. "Hey, Steve, why don't you take my daughter out for an evening stroll? Buy her a double-dip French vanilla ice cream cone down at Bailey's. It's her favorite."

Gordon pushed them both to the top of the steps leading down into the shop and grabbed the towel out of Steve's hands. "I know you're an adult, Juliet. But seeing as I'm new at this dad stuff, I'll be waiting up."

He then eyed Steve. "Is this where I get to threaten you?"

"Gordon!" She grabbed Steve's arm. "Come on, before he changes his mind and gives me a curfew." She tugged a laughing Steve down the stairs and out into the night.

Chapter Twelve

Sierra drove back into Misty Harbor in the early evening. Austin was safe with his father, and they had already reached Aunt Jean's place hours ago. While Jake had driven directly to his sister's house, she had taken the scenic route back to town. She had gotten off Interstate 95 in Brunswick and traveled north on Route 1 through Rockland, Camden, Belfast, and up into Ellsworth. There had been plenty of stops along the way.

She had even taken Route 176 south into Blue Hill and then continued along the coast into Sedgwick searching for that perfect place. She had seen many beautiful and scenic pieces of property, but none had been for sale. Matt had called her once and she told him she was shopping and that she would meet him over at his parents' after dinner.

It was the truth.

She was shopping for a parcel of land, right on the coast, that was big enough to meet her father's requirements, and then some. If she told her father, Jake, and the rest of the board that Misty Harbor wasn't the right town to build their hotel in, she'd better have an alternate site in mind, one that would knock their socks off.

Millicent Wyndham hadn't been pulling her father's leg or trying to up the price. A fancy resort hotel like her father planned would in fact change quaint and relatively quiet Misty Harbor. Sure, she didn't know of one business in town that wouldn't appreciate the extra tourist dollars. The hotel would create jobs and add to the tax base. Other hotels would follow, all wanting a piece of the action.

Property values would start to soar, which would also increase the residents' taxes. Community services would have to be added too, both in employees and budgets. Traffic would start becoming a problem. Driving on Route 1 through Camden had been a challenge, and her one trip into Bar Harbor had been a nightmare. Austin complained about how far they'd had to park away from anything and all the walking he had to do. The main streets had restaurant after bar after gift shop after bar after hiking-gear shop. Austin and she had left after dinner and some shopping, but she could see the signs of the partygoers starting to come out for the evening.

There was nothing wrong with having a good time while on vacation. She vaguely remembered a three-night stay in New Orleans with Jake when they first had been married. "Vaguely" being the crucial word.

Misty Harbor was the quaint coastal fishing village that everyone wanted to see when they came to Maine. It was a working town, with working families. People like the Porters were raising their children there. It was home, not a fancy hotel with a concierge.

The town didn't need an elegant hotel to bring in the tourist dollars. There were plenty of towns in the surrounding area that had, or could handle, a large resort hotel. If Misty Harbor did some promotional advertising for its shops, restaurants, and whale-watching tours, then the town could benefit from nearby hotels. People coming to the coast of Maine for a vacation didn't want to sit in their hotel rooms all day. They needed places to go and things to see and do. Misty Harbor was more than equipped to handle a couple hours' worth of sight-seeing without changing the structure of the town.

Once the hotels started going up, the tourists would come, and come, and come until all the quaintness had been squeezed right out of the town.

Sierra parked the SUV in the Alberts' driveway. She knew from experience the traffic jam of pickup trucks and SUVs over at Matt's parents' house. She would walk over and see how it was going. Matt had said they were painting the arbor and hanging some lights tonight. Tomorrow all the rose bushes would be delivered. It was Wednesday evening, and the weather forecast for Saturday looked perfect. Not a rain cloud in sight.

Ten minutes later she had changed into jeans and was approaching Matt's parents' house. It sounded like a party was going on in the backyards—a very noisy party. She stepped between the two yards and shook her head in amazement.

The arbor was gorgeous. How did they build that in less than a week? It was already painted white, and Norah and Ned were both standing on stepladders stringing lights on it. Paul was cutting his parents' grass, while John was cutting Norah's mother's grass. Flower gardens were packed with blooming plants and a fresh layer of mulch. Joanna and her new husband were stringing lights on her back porch, and Kay and Jill, with the help of the kids, were raking up the grass. The one person she didn't see was Matt.

"Hi, Sierra," called Kay. "How's it looking?"

"Absolutely fabulous." It was the truth. The gardens looked like they had been there for years.

"Where's Austin?" called Hunter.

"Where's Austin?" asked Tyler, who had stopped raking and was looking for his new friend.

"Sorry, guys, he's visiting with his dad. He'll be back Sunday night." It felt so good to hear other kids asking for her son. When she had left Austin with Jake, he had been talking his dad's ear off about all his new friends, and Matt, and the birdhouse he built, and the whales. Jake had noticed the change in their son right away. Austin was more outgoing and talkative.

It was a good change, one that made her more determined than ever to settle down somewhere and make a home with her son. A real home, with excellent schools nearby, lots of friends for Austin, and maybe even a dog. Austin loved animals.

"Hey, Kay, where's Matt?" She still wasn't able to see him, but his truck had been parked out front.

"In the garage." Kay pointed to the Porters' garage.

She chuckled as the sound of a power tool reached her ears. "Figures." Matt was never far away from the tools. She headed for the garage.

Standing in the shadows of the wooden garage doors that opened outward instead of up, she watched Matt. She had no idea what he was making, but it was big. Every time he moved it around to get a better angle, the muscles in his shoulders and back flexed and strained beneath his T-shirt. She wondered if they were as hard as they looked.

Matt made one more cut and then turned off the saw. He glanced up and gave her a smile that was pure wickedness. "Hi. I didn't see you standing there."

"I didn't want to startle you when you were playing with a saw." She had been more than willing to stand there well into the night watching the play of muscles beneath his shirt. She stepped into the garage, away from prying eyes, and closer to him. She missed Austin already, but there was something tantalizingly naughty about not having him underfoot right at this moment. "I didn't want you to cut off anything"—she gave him a teasing smile—"important."

Matt brushed off some of the sawdust coating the front of his shirt and jeans as he rounded the object he was building. Desire burned in his gaze. He wiggled his fingers. "Got all ten fingers"—he shuffled his feet—"all ten toes"—he grinned—"and anything else you might deem important."

She leaned against a shelving unit holding all sorts of tools and junk. "Austin wanted me to tell you goodbye again."

Matt closed the space between them and chuckled. "He said goodbye three times last night before he went to bed." The tips of Matt's fingers traced the curve of her jaw. "I missed you today."

"You were on my mind a lot today, too." Half the time she had been worried about his reaction once he found out who she was, and what her father's company was after. The other half of the time she was thinking about tonight. She was a thirty-one-year-old woman who knew what she wanted.

She wanted Matt. It was as plain and as complicated as that.

Her arms circled his neck and she tugged him closer. Austin was going to be away for only four nights. She intended to make the most of them. "What did you miss most about me?"

Matt chuckled as his arms slid around her back. "That's a no-win question." His lips teased her ear. "No matter what I answer, you'll twist it around to make it sound like I don't like what I didn't say."

She playfully nipped at the lobe of his ear. "In a strange way, that made sense." With the tip of her tongue she traced where her teeth had bitten. "Can I tell you what I missed most about you?" One of her hands was buried in the thick hair at the back of his head. The other was stroking his back and the muscles she had been admiring earlier.

"You can tell me anything you want." Matt's mouth was skimming her jaw.

"Your mouth." She turned her head, and this time she playfully nipped at his lower lip. "I love how your mouth makes me go all hot inside."

Matt groaned and kissed her.

The shelf behind her shook as her weight shifted. One of Matt's hands steadied the shelf while the other cupped her bottom and brought her in contact with the growing evidence of his desire. The hot feeling she had told him about exploded into molten desire. This was passion, need, and want all rolled up into one powerful kiss.

But was it love?

She didn't know, and at this particular moment, she didn't care. Her tongue mated with his in a rhythm that matched the tempo of her body.

The shelving unit shook as Matt's hand lost its grip.

"Aw, jeez, would you two get a room," groused Paul with a laugh. "There are kids around."

She jumped back so fast, her head whacked into one of the metal shelves.

Matt moved in the other direction and nearly fell onto a green fertilizer spreader. Matt glared at his brother's retreating back. "Paybacks are hell, Paul." He quickly gathered her into his arms and gently rubbed the back of her head. "Are you okay?"

"I'm fine." She looked at the lawn mower sitting in front of the garage doors. Paul had finished cutting the grass and was returning the mower to the garage. She hadn't even heard him. "I'm also embarrassed." Thankfully it hadn't been one of the kids who had found them kissing.

"You're embarrassed because you were caught kissing me?" Matt cupped her chin and tilted up her face.

"No." She knew her cheeks were roughly the same color as the lawn mower sitting eight feet away from them: candy-apple red. "We were doing a bit more than kissing." She had been melting in his arms and on the verge of being totally seduced. More important, she hadn't cared where they were. That in itself was a first.

"No, we weren't." Matt took a deep breath. "Don't be embarrassed. Paul's not going to say anything to anyone."

"How do you know?" Okay, maybe she was making this into a bigger deal than it really was. This was the twenty-first century. People kissed all the time. That was all it had been, too. Their clothes were still in place, with nothing undone. Hands had been visible.

"Because I caught him doing a lot more than kissing once." Matt grinned and gave her a quick kiss.

"I'm sure Jill appreciates you keeping your mouth closed on the matter." She didn't even want to think about that one.

"Jill doesn't know." Matt grinned.

Her eyes widened in shock. "It wasn't Jill?" Paul and Jill had seemed so in love. How could he do that to his wife and mother of his children? How could Matt smile about something like that?

"Relax, Sierra." Matt glanced around to make sure they weren't being overheard. "Paul was eighteen at the time, and Jill was nowhere in the picture. Our parents were out at sea and had left John in charge. John had a date, so he left Paul in charge of me and our younger brother, Ned. Paul, being Paul, invited a girl over to our house and then promptly gave me the keys to his truck and told me I could have it for the night if I took Ned along. Considering I had gotten my license the month before and I still didn't have a car, we were out of there before I even thought about grabbing my wallet. Needless to say, half an hour later we were getting low on gas, and I needed some cash."

"So you went back home." She tried not to laugh. "And walked in on Paul and his date."

"Oh, yeah." Matt tugged her over to the project he had been working on. "I've been hanging it over his head since the day he met Jill."

"Why? I'm sure she'd understand if he was only eighteen at the time."

Matt slowly shook his head. "Jill's not that under-standing." Matt planted a loud kiss on her lips. "Have you ever used a sander before?" He handed her a power tool.

She knew it was a power tool, because it was plugged in. "No, but how hard can it be?" She could tell Matt was trying really hard not to roll his eyes.

Matt's eyes twitched. "Okay, it's pretty easy." Matt got behind her. "Put your hands here and here." His hands covered hers as he placed them on the sander. "All we need to do is smooth the wood a little before I paint it. You're going to move the sander back and forth over the sides."

"Okay, but what is it?" It looked like a rectangular box that stood four feet high, about seven feet long, and two feet wide. The sides were plywood, but there was a nice piece of pine across the top.

Matt looked at her and blinked. "What is it?"

"Yeah." Why was he building a box when there was a wedding to get ready for?

Matt took the sander out of her hand and tugged her around to the other side of the box. "Now do you know?"

The back of the box was open, and it had three shelves built in. "It's a bar!" She smiled in amazement. "You built the bar. Just like that?"

"We needed one." Matt handed her a pair of safety goggles and the sander. "Now get to work. We need to prime it tonight."

She pulled on the plastic glasses and was about to turn on the sander when Tyler came running into the garage.

Tyler looked at her, then at Matt. "What'ya doing?"

She held up the sander and grinned. "Matt's letting me sand the bar." She never used a power tool before, unless a blow-dryer counted as one. "Want to watch?"

"Nah." Tyler looked unimpressed. The little boy turned around and walked out of the garage.

Matt shrugged.

She cringed and glared at Matt when she heard Tyler yell, "You're fibbing, Uncle Paul. They weren't kissing."

Matt held the door open as Sierra climbed into his truck. His gaze admired the view of her jean-clad bottom while his mind was conjuring up all kinds of scenarios on how this evening was going to end. He felt eighteen all over again.

"Thanks." Sierra gave him a wide smile as she snapped her seat belt.

"No problem." He closed her door and walked around

to the front of his truck. It was close to nine o'clock, and his brothers were packing up their kids. He could hear Tyler giving his father an argument about something. Baby Amanda, who had been a real sweetheart all night long, had chosen this moment to voice her objections. He climbed behind the wheel and closed his door. He and Sierra both watched as his brother John tried to reason with his daughter about something.

"Is she always that stubborn?" Sierra chuckled as Morgan crossed her arms and shook her head.

"From the day she was born." Matt was enjoying himself watching his brothers trying to corral their kids. It was like herding kittens. Hunter was doing somersaults on the grass while Paul and Jill were passing baby Amanda back and forth trying to calm her down enough to get her into the car seat.

Sierra frowned at her hands and swiped at a lock of her hair that had escaped her ponytail. "I need a shower. I've got paint everywhere."

He wasn't about to tell her that next time she shouldn't invite a five-year-old to help her paint. Tyler was more a Picasso than a Renoir. Thankfully she had put plastic down on the driveway before painting, and no one was going to see the back of the bar but the bartenders. "I don't know, I think the white goes well with your tan." He didn't want to think about her in a shower.

"I still need a shower, Matt."

"So do I." He had finished up a job at an inn in Southwest Harbor around three. He had gone directly to his parents' house and started working on the bar. First thing tomorrow morning he was putting the final coat of paint on the bar, and then Joanna was putting on some fancier finishing touches. He was dirty, tired, and practically sitting on the edge of his seat in anticipation.

Sierra had been sending him signals all evening. Strong, unmistakable signals. Neither of them would be sleeping alone tonight.

He watched as Ned and Norah pulled away. Then John and his family. Paul and his family were the last to disappear down the street. He turned the key in the ignition but didn't put the truck in gear. "So whose place do we go to first? Yours or mine?"

"Yours." Sierra pulled her tote-size pocketbook onto her lap and started to search through it. A moment later she pulled out her cell phone and checked for messages.

"Okay." He started to drive as she punched a couple numbers into the phone. His place wasn't too bad. If he remembered correctly his breakfast dishes were still in the sink and the bed was unmade, but everything else was pretty neat and clean.

"Hi, Jean. Can I speak to Austin?" Sierra smiled at him as she waited a moment. "Hi, sweetie. How are you doing?"

He couldn't hear Austin's comments, but from Sierra's replies he guessed her son was telling her all about his day. In minute detail.

"Really? Yuck." Sierra scrunched up her face. "Who cleaned it up?" Sierra laughed. "That I would've loved to have seen."

He made a mental note to ask about that one later.

"Austin, you knew your daddy was there on business, so that means he has to attend meetings." Sierra rolled her eyes. "Well, you should have eaten the squash anyway."

Matt bit his lip to keep from laughing. He wouldn't have touched the squash either.

"If it was yellow and gooey, I'm just guessing it was

squash. Now if it had chunks in it, my guess would have been creamed corn."

He definitely didn't want to go there. What were they feeding that poor kid if he didn't even know what it was?

"So Aunt Jean gave you your bath and helped you get into your pajamas?" Sierra was silent for a moment. "No, you may not have another snack. One slice of chocolate cake before bed is enough. So you go hop into bed and be a good boy for your daddy and Aunt Jean." Sierra made kissy sounds into the phone. "Now give your dad the phone and get to bed. I'll call you in the morning."

So Jake was there. Why didn't he give his son his bath? Probably didn't want to get all wet. Sissy. He knew Sierra had said she and Jake were friends, but in his opinion Jake had to be a jerk. No sane man would divorce Sierra. The guy had to have more than a couple screws loose, but Matt was eternally grateful to him for setting Sierra free.

"Hi, Jake. So how's Austin behaving? Having any problems?" Sierra flashed Matt a killer smile. "Of course he wanted two slices of cake—he's four, Jake.

"I know it's hard to say no, but if you would have given in, he would have been up all night with a tummy ache." She chuckled. "Meaning you would have been up all night too."

Sierra's smile grew. "Yes, I have plans for the next several days."

His foot pressed the accelerator a little harder. By the tone of her voice, there was no doubt what those plans were.

"Of course I'm behaving. When have you known me not to?" Sierra laughed. "That didn't count."

Okay, he was not going to ask, no matter how much it bugged him. Sierra had been married, and she was a mother, for goodness' sake. Austin hadn't appeared under a cabbage leaf.

"Yes, you can reach me anytime, day or night. I always have my phone on. Bye."

Sierra clicked the phone closed. "Austin's fine."

"So I heard." Jake sounded fine too. Where was this streak of jealousy coming from? He shook his head as he turned onto his street. "You won't mind waiting for me while I clean up?"

"I won't mind." Sierra looked off into the night. "It's so peaceful here. I like that."

"I wouldn't live anywhere else." He turned in to his parking lot. "If you think it's quiet now, you should see the winter months. There's nothing quite like it."

"I can imagine." Sierra unfastened her seat belt and opened the door.

Matt met her at the front of the truck and took her hand. "Be careful on the steps. I forgot to leave the light on."

Sierra's hand felt small and soft within his. "Well, if I fall"—her hand squeezed his—"I'm taking you with me."

He held tighter. "There's no way I'm letting you go." He wasn't just talking about climbing the stairs either. He wanted Sierra in Misty Harbor. Somehow. Some way.

He unlocked the door and flipped on the lights. "You'll have to excuse the mess. I usually don't have company."

Sierra glanced around the kitchen. "Is that what I am, company?"

Matt closed the door and backed her up against it. The tip of his finger traced a smudge of white paint on her cheek. "You're more than company. Much more."

Sierra's eyes darkened to a deep gray with a touch of green. They were the same color as the sea during a storm. "I'm glad." Sierra turned her head and captured his fingertip with her lips.

He groaned as he watched her lips close around his finger. He'd never seen a more erotic sight. The tip of her tongue lightly stroked his skin before she released him.

Sierra's eyes reminded him of the sea, but there was a fire burning in them. A fire that matched his own. "Matt, I want you."

A shudder racked his body. If he kissed her now, they would never make it out of his kitchen. He didn't want to make love to Sierra smelling of paint and sawdust. He wanted it perfect. She deserved for it to be perfect. With a step back he gained his control. "Can you keep that thought for five minutes?"

A small chuckle escaped her tempting lips as Sierra glanced down at herself. "I think we might have to wait more than five minutes."

Matt took another few steps back and dug deep for some more control. "I'll hurry." He could do this. He was thirty years old. He sprinted for the bathroom, pulling his shirt over his head as he ran.

Sierra watched as Matt disappeared into his bedroom. The tempting display of his bare back was enough to make her drool. *Saints have mercy!* All those muscles she had been thinking about were real. Here she stood with her tongue hanging out of her mouth while the man whose bones she wanted to pounce on was getting naked in the next room.

A refined lady would sit her butt in a kitchen chair, demurely cross her legs, and wait until Matt was ready to do the ravaging. She glanced at the paint smear on her forearm and decided she wasn't a refined lady tonight. She didn't want to wait. And whoever said that men had to do all the ravaging?

She heard the shower start as she locked the front door and headed for his bedroom. Matt had a thing for the color brown. The living room had beige carpeting, a brown leather couch and chair, and wood tables. The huge television was the main focus of the room, but there were crowded bookshelves on either side of it.

His bedroom was just as colorless. The room had beige carpeting and a dark rustic bedroom set that would have been more at home in a cabin in the woods than an apartment on the coast. A huge framed photo of a moose was above the bed. She frowned at the picture and wondered who had been crazy enough to get that close to the animal. The moose wasn't smiling.

She dropped her tote on the unmade bed. The tan sheets were rumpled, the brown plaid comforter was kicked to the bottom of the bed, and a pillow was on the floor. Either Matt was a slob, or he had spent the same restless time in bed last night as she had. Before she lost her nerve, she kicked off her sneakers and started to undress.

Two minutes later she pulled back the shower curtain and joined Matt in the shower. By Matt's startled expression she wasn't sure if she'd just committed a major faux pas. "Need any help washing your back?"

His wicked smile eliminated her fear. Shampoo was running down the side of Matt's face and he was semi-aroused. His gaze was skimming every inch of her body. "Only if I can return the favor."

Matt's voice was deep, unsteady, and threaded with a roughness that caused her nipples to harden. Or maybe that was the heat of his gaze. "It's been awhile since anyone has washed my back." She hoped Matt would get her meaning and know she didn't make a habit of joining men in the shower. They hadn't known each other for three weeks, and here she was standing before him naked and willing.

Matt's gaze softened as he pulled her under the warm water with him. "I figured that one out a long time ago." He ducked his head back under the spray and rinsed the rest of the shampoo out of his hair.

When he was done, she went under the water and soaked her hair. She hadn't bothered to look into a mirror, but she knew there was paint in it. "Could I use your shampoo?"

"Sure." Matt put a bottle into her hand and started to wash himself. "I'm sure it's not what you're used to, but it will get the paint out."

She closed her eyes and lathered it up. "Thanks." A moment later she was rinsing the suds from her hair when she felt Matt's work-roughened hands start to rub her back. She leaned into his hands.

When she thought all the suds were rinsed from her hair she turned to face him. There was nothing "semi" about his arousal now. It was strong and thick, and nudging her stomach. She smiled as Matt's hands never missed a stroke.

"You wear an awfully small bathing suit." Matt's voice was a low growl as his hands cupped her breasts.

She swiped at some bubbles that were on her belly and smeared them onto his chest. Dark hair teased her fingertips. "You work outside without your shirt a lot." His chest was as tan as his arms and face.

"Sierra," Matt's voice broke, "you're killing me here."

"No, I'm not." She backed up under the spray and smiled as the bubbles slid down her body and into the drain. She tugged him closer. "I still have paint on my arms." The areas Matt had been soaping had never had paint on to begin with. She took the soap out of Matt's hands and started to scrub her face and arms. Hopefully she would get most if not all of the white paint off. Making love to Matt while looking like a reject from the Ringling Bros. circus wasn't what she had in mind.

She had just finished rinsing the suds from her arms when Matt grabbed the bar of soap and put it in the dish. "That's it. You're clean enough." He turned off the water and pushed open the shower curtain and grabbed for a towel.

She chuckled as she reached for the other towel. "Is 'you're clean enough' considered foreplay?" She bent over and wrapped the towel around her soaking-wet hair.

A shrill yell escaped her as Matt lightly smacked her on the bottom and then threw her over his damp shoulder. "I'll show you foreplay."

Her hair was still wrapped in the towel, but the rest of her was still wet. "Matthew Porter, if you throw me onto that bed wet, I'm not sleeping in it." She tried to sound stern and not giggle. There was no way in hell she would be spending an entire night in a damp bed.

Matt grabbed another towel off a shelf on his way out of the bathroom. He lowered her to her feet next to the bed and started to slowly, and quite thoroughly, dry every inch of her skin.

She grabbed his shoulder with her hand as the soft towel caressed her inner thigh for the third time. "I think you dried that part"—her voice hitched when the towel disappeared and warm fingers took its place—"already."

Matt's mouth replaced his fingers. "You still seem to be wet there."

Her eyes crossed and her knees buckled as his towel stroked higher. "Okay, enough of the foreplay, Matt." She fell back onto the bed. She was about to climax, and they hadn't even gotten to the good part yet.

Matt chuckled as he stood up and slowly unwrapped the towel around his waist. "Lord, you are beautiful."

Her gaze skimmed his chest and rested on his penis. His desire for her was obvious. It was at full attention and quivering with need. "You're, ummm . . ." *handsome* wasn't the word she was looking for.

"I'm what?" Matt looked down and rolled his eyes. "Desperate? Horny?"

She shook her head. "Those aren't the adjectives going through my mind."

"Aroused? Easy?"

Sierra scooted back farther onto the bed, kicking the comforter and her tote bag onto the floor. "I was thinking more along the lines of, big."

Matt burst out laughing as he joined her on the bed. "Is it any wonder that I'm falling in love with you?"

She gazed into his eyes. Matt was serious. No candlelight dinners, no champagne, and no red roses. Straight-up and honest, he meant every word he was saying. She reached up and cupped his jaw. "Oh, Matt." There was so much she needed to tell him, but this wasn't the time or the place. She needed answers first.

"You don't have to say anything, Sierra." Matt turned his head and placed a kiss in the center of her palm. "This is enough"—his lips slid to her wrist—"for now."

"You're special, Matt." She pulled her hand away from his mouth and placed it around his neck. "What we have here, right now, right here, is very special. I don't want to lose that, Matt."

"We won't." Matt's thumb grazed her lower lip.

"It's complicated, Matt. Oh, so very complicated. There are things you don't know about." She didn't want to lie, but if she spoke the truth they wouldn't have these few days together.

Matt's gaze burned into hers. "Is there someone else?"

"No." She gave him a slow smile. "Unless you mean Austin."

Matt shook his head and relaxed. "Then we have time to work it out, Sierra." He leaned down and kissed her.

The heat of his mouth burned away the concerns plaguing her mind. There was only here and now. There was only Matt.

Chapter Thirteen

Sierra woke to the sensation of Matt's mouth trailing its way down her spine. The man was insatiable. She smiled into the pillow.

"I know you're awake." Matt blew on a spot his tongue had just caressed.

She shivered. "How do you know?" she muttered into the cotton pillowcase. As far as she knew she hadn't moved a muscle or made a sound. She wasn't too sure her body could move after last night. Matt Porter was a thorough lover. He had not only found her G-spot, but her H-spot, I-spot, J-spot, and every other letter of the alphabet.

"You groaned when I did this." Matt's fingers traced the tan line her very tiny bathing suit bottom had left behind.

She felt her groan vibrate in her throat and tried to suppress it. She wiggled her bottom in an attempt to get his hands off it. "Stop that." She didn't have the energy to swat him. Matt had awakened her in the middle of the night for round two.

Or maybe it had been she who had awakened him. Either way, instead of falling asleep after spending nearly an hour making slow, sweet love, Matt had been energized and hungry. For the first time in her life she'd had milk and cookies in bed. There were now chocolate chip cookie crumbs everywhere.

Matt's hands held her hips still. "Wiggling that sweet ass of yours is not the way to get me to stop." Matt chuckled as his tongue swept up a crumb from the back of her thigh. "How many calories are there in a serving of Sierra?" Matt playfully teased the sensitive area on the back of her knee with his mouth.

"Are you always this cheerful in the morning?" Without raising her head, she grabbed the pillow he had used last night and threw it at him.

He chuckled as he dodged the pillow. "I was going to wake you up to go see the sunrise out at the lighthouse with me, but you looked like an angel sleeping in my bed." One of Matt's hands was spread across the small of her back, holding her in place while his warm, searching lips traveled up the back of her thigh.

"Matt, what are you doing?" Her eyes crossed when his tongue outlined the curve of her bottom.

"Searching for more crumbs." Matt took a teasing nip of flesh.

"Matt!" She tried to roll over, but Matt's hand kept her in place. At five feet ten inches, she wasn't a little woman to hold down so easily.

Matt laughed. "If I have to tell you what I'm doing, Sierra, I'm doing it all wrong." He removed his hand from the small of her back.

Sierra rolled onto her back and smiled at him. Matt's hair was all rumpled from sleep, but there was nothing sleepy about his light blue eyes. They burned with a fire all their own. The light sprinkling of hair scattered across his chest made her want to sink her fingers into it once again. She ran the sole of her foot up the back of his thigh. With Matt's height, he was almost halfway off the bed. "You weren't doing it wrong. You're just too far away."

Matt scooted up onto the bed, directly on top of her. His elbows took most of his weight. "Better?" Matt's mouth skimmed her chin and teased her lower lip.

She wiggled her hips as Matt nestled deeper between her thighs. She could feel the head of his erection against her opening. "Tell me you have a condom on."

Matt's lips nibbled their way down her throat and across her collarbone. "It's been on for the last ten minutes." With one hand he cupped a breast and gently sucked her hardened nipple into his mouth.

Sierra wrapped her legs around his thighs and urged him deeper.

Matt's tongue bathed her nipple as he slowly entered her about an inch.

She arched her hips and tried to take more of him. Matt wasn't cooperating. "More, Matt." She was so close to the edge. Her hands stroked down his back until they cupped his hard, tight ass. She tugged him closer as her stomach clenched and her breath hitched in anticipation. The edge was falling away.

Matt gently bit her nipple.

She screamed as Matt plunged and the orgasm that had been building erupted.

Matt shouted something against her breast as he joined her in a release that had him shaking.

Sierra stood in the late afternoon sun and tuned the real estate agent's voice out. Mr. Biggs was full not only of himself, but hot air too. She had christened him Mr.

Bigshot two properties ago. As any good Realtor would do, he had saved the best for last.

Over one hundred acres of prime real estate right on the coast of Maine. The view was fantastic, even though it wasn't of the Atlantic Ocean. It was Frenchman's Bay, and way off in the distance, on the other side of the bay, was the town of Bar Harbor. The property was situated along Route 186 between West Gouldsboro and South Gouldsboro.

"As you can see, there's easy access to the bay," Mr. Bigshot went on. And on. And on about the stupid, plain-as-the-nose-on-his-face characteristics of the land.

Yes, she'd figured they were mature pine trees by their sheer size. Oh, there were fish and other wildlife in the bay—amazing. Seals too—imagine that. If Mr. Bigshot pointed at the setting sun and told her that way was west, she was giving him a mighty shove and watching him roll down the hill into the bay.

He probably would tell her it was wet.

"If you continue down Route 186, there is the town of Winter Harbor. It has a Navy base, but I understand that it will be closing soon."

Cliffside Manor, the restaurant Matt had taken her to, had been right outside of Winter Harbor. "Where are the nearest golf courses?" Her father and Jake both loved golf. With this amount of land, they could build an eighteen-hole course right on the coast of Maine. Talk about a perk.

"Oh, you play? There's one in Winter Harbor, but it's only a nine-hole course."

"Occasionally." She'd learned and perfected her game at an early age because she'd figured out if she wanted to spend time with Daddy, she had to do it on his schedule. She had eaten more meals at clubhouses than at home. "Any others?"

"There's a couple of really fancy ones on Mount Desert Island. There's Kebo Valley Golf Club, right outside of Bar Harbor. I think there's also one in Northeast Harbor and another in Southwest Harbor."

"That's nice." It was always nice to size up possible competition. She had her homework cut out for her if she was going to impress her father and Jake. She looked out over the bay and saw a couple boats. Not much water traffic at all. "What about boats?"

"What about them?"

"Would I be allowed to put in a dock?"

"I don't see why not. What size boat do you own?"

"I don't own one yet."

Mr. Biggs gave her a long look as if he wasn't sure whether to believe her or not. He looked as though he was calculating how much time he had just wasted this afternoon by showing her four properties. "Are you planning on buying one, Ms. Morley?"

"I will if I'm living on the coast of Maine." Of course she wasn't thinking about a boat that would require a dock or even an engine. She was thinking more along the lines of getting Austin a little rowboat for Sunset Cove.

Mr. Biggs had no idea who she was or who she represented. As far as the agent knew she was a single mom looking for a place to build, who might or might not have money. She was playing her cards close to her chest for a couple reasons. Matt was the main one. She didn't want it getting back to him who she really was until she'd had the opportunity to tell him first.

She carefully walked downhill to the edge of the bay as the agent's phone rang. After Matt had dropped her off at her place this morning, she had taken a shower and worked the phone. By ten o'clock she had a meeting set up with a real estate agent in Trenton and an appointment with Mr. Biggs for two in Ashville. The first appointment had been a bust, but she had hit pay dirt with Mr. Bigshot. He just didn't know it yet.

Something special had happened between her and Matt last night. Special enough that she wasn't willing to walk away from it. It hadn't just been the sex. She had had sex before. She wasn't a virgin, for goodness' sake. What they had shared went deeper than sex. It had gone straight to her heart.

She was in love with Matt Porter.

Mr. Biggs was out of breath by the time he reached the edge of the bay. "So what do you think about this piece of property, Ms. Morley?"

"Not bad." She continued to look out into the bay. "What's the asking price?" She had given Mr. Bigshot a short list of needs, such as acreage and waterfront. When he had questioned her about price, she had told him they would discuss it later. She hadn't even bothered asking the price on the other three pieces of property; they hadn't met her requirements.

Mr. Biggs quoted a price that made her flinch. "I'm taking it that there will be room for negotiating that amount?" She knew what Millicent Wyndham was thinking about asking for her twenty acres, including the lighthouse. The only thing built on this piece of property were a couple of birds' nests, and the asking amount was way more than five times Millicent's price.

Mr. Biggs looked startled for a moment. His greedy little eyes narrowed in thought. "I'm sure Mr. Jefferies might come down a little. Not a whole lot, mind you, just a digit or two."

Sierra turned and started to climb back up the hill. It wasn't easy in dress sandals, but Mr. Biggs was having a harder time. "How long has it been on the market?" She had seen the faded and weathered FOR SALE sign by the main road. It took months out in the elements for that kind of damage.

Mr. Biggs was sucking in oxygen. "Not long at all. It's a prime piece of real estate, so it won't last long. They aren't making any more oceanfront properties." He wheezed and laughed at his own joke.

She reached the top of the incline and waited for him. "I could ask around." She didn't have time for dillydallying. Her father and Jake knew she was up to something. Both were eager for a report. "Besides, the property is not oceanfront, but it is right on the bay."

"About nine months." Mr. Biggs didn't look happy with that admission.

She figured that probably meant closer to a year. "Any particular reason it hasn't sold yet, besides the sticker shock?" The price was indeed too high, but she'd let her father and Jake worry about that detail.

"Truth?"

"Yes, please." What did he expect her to say, no, I prefer lies and bullcrap?

"Jefferies is a stubborn old coot who refuses to budge one dollar on that amount." Mr. Bigshot looked as if he'd just lost a new Cadillac in commission.

She smiled. Her father and Jake were going to love tangling with Jefferies. "Just as long as there is nothing wrong with the property."

Juliet walked along the sidewalk in Bar Harbor holding Steve's hand and peering into display windows.

"People actually buy this stuff and lug it back home with them?" The table lamp on the other side of the glass was made of used lobster buoys and old fishing net.

Steve chuckled at a five-foot stuffed moose and a clock made out of starfish. "I guess so. Why else would they keep selling it year after year?" Steve gave her hand a tug. "Come on. Let's go in."

She shook her head but followed him inside the gift shop anyway. Bar Harbor wasn't quite what she had expected. She'd thought the coastal town would be along the same lines as Misty Harbor, only bigger. It was bigger all right, and crowded with tourists of all shapes and sizes. Baby strollers and cranky toddlers jammed the sidewalks, along with pushy adults and obnoxious teens. Oh, there were plenty of great tourists, but it was always the bad ones who stood out and demanded attention.

She missed the slow, leisurely walks down the streets of Misty Harbor. There she could walk along the dockside, eating a double scoop of French vanilla ice cream, and not worry about someone running into her. Tuesday night Steve had taken her out for ice cream and a walk. He had also managed to steal a few innocent kisses in the shadows.

The streets of Bar Harbor didn't have shadows. Everything was lit up like the Fourth of July. But they did have wonderful restaurants overflowing with some of the best seafood she had ever tasted. Steve had even gotten her to try one of the local beers to help wash down her lobster. Dinner had been great, overlooking the water and watching the parade of boats coming in for the night.

It had been romantic.

Steve held up a twelve-inch red plastic lobster with black wire antennae, a sneer, and claws the size of frying pans. "Are you sure you can't use one of these back home?" he teased.

"No." She nodded to the back of the store, where a selection of children's books was displayed. "But that looks interesting."

Steve tugged her over to the books and grinned as he opened up a pop-up book and a seal sprang up. "Now this is cool." The next page was a huge humpback whale. Steve was like a little kid discovering Christmas morning.

"I was thinking more along this line." Juliet reached out and picked up a storybook on catching lobsters, and another on harbor seals. "My kids will love these."

Her classroom always had more books than the other classes because she couldn't resist supplementing what little the school district supplied. Other teachers had families to support, while she had only herself, and no one had ever accused her of being high maintenance. School budgets were notoriously stingy.

"You buy books for your classroom?" Steve picked up another pop-up book. This one had birds springing out every time he flipped a page.

"Of course. Most teachers do. We never seem to have enough to satisfy the kids' appetite for learning." She squatted down, making sure her skirt wasn't dragging on the floor. "You're the marine biologist; come help me pick out a couple more books on marine life. Kids are fascinated by all kinds of animals."

"So are adults." Steve squatted down next to her. "How many do you want?" He frowned at the array of books before him. "There must be a book on every sea creature imaginable here."

"I doubt that." Juliet pulled down a couple more books. "Since you know so much about whales, you pick out a couple whale books. How many kinds of seals are there in the Gulf of Maine?"

"Five." Steve was looking at a picture book on baleen whales. "Harbor seals can be found all year-round, but sometimes they migrate south for the winter. Then there are hooded seals, harp seals, grey seals, and ringed seals, which have all been sighted in the gulf. Why?"

"Just curious." She had the harbor seal book in her hand along with another book on seals in general. "What about fish?"

"What about them?" Steve chose two whale books and put the rest back. "You want a book on fish?"

"I want to do a lesson on things that live in the Gulf of Maine. Since I teach right outside of Boston, most of the kids have seen the ocean." She pointed over to the wall of bins holding plastic and rubber animals. There were also bins overflowing with shells. "After we pick out a dozen or so books, we get to go find the matching animals, that way it will be fun and hands-on for the kids. Most learn better that way, and I can usually hold their attention through an entire lesson."

Steve's amber-colored eyes glowed with pride. "Why didn't I have a teacher like you in third grade?"

"Because I was only in kindergarten at the time." She wrinkled her nose and pushed a stray lock of hair out of her face. Tonight she had left it down, put in her contacts, and even added a few touches of makeup. The way Steve was looking at her tonight, she didn't feel like the awkward or klutzy Carlyle. She felt beautiful and special.

"I'll help you match the animals, on one condition." Steve leaned forward and stole a quick kiss from her surprised mouth.

"What's that?" She could think of a lot of conditions that she would be more than willing to comply with when it came to Steve. His kisses were tantalizingly quick, and she had only six more nights in Misty Harbor before she had to return home.

"I'm paying for the animals. You can buy the books."

"Why would you do that?" It was a very sweet gesture, one that could cost him a small fortune if he wasn't careful what he picked out.

"Because if kids had more teachers who cared like you do, there might be more marine biologists, more scientists, and more people looking for answers to the world's problems. The ocean's ecology is a mess, and we need answers. Soon." A faint blush swept up Steve's cheeks as he stood back up. "I'm sorry, I'll get off my soapbox now."

Juliet stood and gave him a quick kiss in return. "It's a wonderful soapbox, Steve." She meant it. It was wonderful to meet and talk to someone who cared about the world around him. "My class and I would be very grateful and pleased with any animals you wish to purchase."

Steve's eyes gleamed with excitement. "Really?" His hands reached out and pulled another book off the shelf and placed it on the pile already in her hands. "You can't teach about the ecosystem of the gulf without first learning about plankton."

She laughed at the book on top of the pile she had already selected. Its title was *Plankton Soup* and there were two cartoon whales holding forks in their fins and wearing napkins tied around their necks. "I'm sure it will be a hit."

She handed Steve the pile of books. "You can go start matching animals to books while I keep looking here to see if there's anything else interesting."

"Okay." Steve headed for the wall of bins.

She glanced around the book section in wonder. It wasn't a very big space, but it was crammed with all kinds of goodies for the mind. Gordon really needed to improve and expand his children's section of the bookstore. Maybe he could even get in some rubber fish to go along with the picture books, or at least a stuffed animal or two. Something a little more manageable than the five-foot moose in the window. Kids would be begging to go inside, and mothers, once they saw how Gordon was changing the shop, would be taking them there more often. A child couldn't have too many books.

Forty minutes later she and Steve left the shop. Each of them was carrying two bags. She had ended up buying a total of fifteen books. Two were for her own personal use: one on whales, and one on the environmental impact people were having on the world's oceans. The rest of the books were for her classroom.

Steve's bags held thirty-five animals, countless shells and starfish, and a coffee mug he had purchased for her. The cup had a whale on the front with "Maine" written under it. He claimed it was to remind her of their first semi-informal date, their afternoon aboard the whale-watching cruise, when she was back in Boston teaching her class.

She didn't want to think about next Wednesday morning when she had to head back home. It was less than a week away, and there still was so much she wanted to know about Gordon and his life in Misty Harbor.

Then there was Steven Blake.

If Sierra was having a hard time believing Friday night was already here and halfway gone, all she had to do was look around Norah and her mother's cottage. Total chaos reigned. Norah appeared to be in shock. Joanna was giving Zsa Zsa, the Pomeranian, a bath in the kitchen sink. Chelsea Dennison, Norah's college roommate who was going to be the maid of honor, had brought five suitcases for a three-day stay in Misty Harbor.

One of the suitcases had contained the pink dress she was going to wear for the ceremony. The dress was now hanging on the coat-closet door in an attempt to get the wrinkles to fall out of it. It was never going to happen. Sierra had never seen so much frill, netting, and puffiness sewn onto one dress before. It was hideous. Norah's perfect wedding was about to be ruined by a pink nightmare. The only thing missing was the matching parasol.

Kay had taken one look at the dress and fled out back to consult with Jill and her mother-in-law. Sierra had no idea what they were consulting about. Short of setting it on fire, there wasn't much anyone could do at this late date. Norah had looked at the dress and without saying a word reached for a bottle of wine and a glass. Norah was now sitting alone in the far corner of the dining room muttering to the half-full glass.

Norah had seemed so happy when she and Chelsea had driven up an hour ago. Norah had picked up her best friend at the airport, and they had been talking nonstop, until the dress that was dipped in Pepto Bismol came out of the suitcase.

"What can I do to help?" asked Chelsea.

Sierra realized she and Chelsea were the only ones standing there in the living room. She had been abandoned by the Porters. "I could use some help making bows for the centerpieces." Thirty vases sat on the coffee table along with four different-colored ribbons.

"Great." Chelsea sat on the floor, ready for her instructions.

Sierra sat on the couch. "I thought they would be pretty if we used four colors of ribbon in each bow. Norah wanted some color, but nothing too bright. More on the pastel level." She glanced over her shoulder at the dress and tried not to shudder. Where did Norah get the idea that Chelsea's gown was a calm, almost pale pink?

Chelsea's gaze followed hers and she bit her lower lip. "Norah said it would be fine."

"She did? When?" She had seen the look on Norah's face as the first fifty yards of netting spilled out of the suitcase. Norah hadn't said a word.

"On the phone." Chelsea toyed with a roll of ribbon. "When Norah called and said she was getting married in less than three weeks and wanted me to be her maid of honor, I was so happy and thrilled for her. We talked about dresses, but since there wasn't any time, and I had just been in my sister's wedding in June, Norah told me to wear that gown. She said she could work with pink."

"I see." Well, at least now it all was making some sense, except why would her sister make Chelsea wear such an ugly garment? "You sent her the shawl made out of the netting, didn't you?" That would explain the pink netting Norah had been showing everyone.

"I sent her netting, yes, but it wasn't a shawl." Chelsea cringed. "My sister made us wear that as a bow pinned to the back of our heads. It looked like every member of the wedding party was being attacked by mammoth butterflies." Chelsea looked ready to cry. "Please tell me Norah won't make me do that again. Two little kids laughed at us as we marched down the aisle in the church. It was humiliating."

"Don't worry about that one." Sierra glanced into the dining room, where Norah was still muttering to a now-filled wine glass. "So Norah said okay to the gown without seeing it first?"

"She said she knew my sister's taste in clothing and whatever she had picked out for her own wedding would be perfect." Chelsea nervously tied a knot into the ribbon.

"I think Norah was just so happy that I had something to wear. It was another problem checked off her to-do list."

Sierra studied the young woman before her. Chelsea seemed like a nice, reasonable young lady. One she could see being best friends with Norah and dropping everything to fly to Maine to be in the wedding. Chelsea was a couple years younger than she, and quite pretty. "Did Norah happen to mention that there are quite a few single guys in Misty Harbor?" She winked. "I also hear that a lot of them will be at the wedding."

Chelsea grinned. "So Norah tells me." Her smile fell as she looked across at the dress that was obstructing the entire closet door and half the wall. "Fat lot of good that's going to do me. I look like a pregnant marshmallow pig dressed in that."

Sierra remembered her manners and didn't comment on that. "Can I let you in on a little secret?" She moved closer so they wouldn't be overheard. "There are some brides, and no, Norah is not one of them, who purposely pick the ugliest dresses they can find for their bridesmaids and maid of honor."

"Why would they do that?" Chelsea had moved closer to the table.

"Well, I'm not sure how to put this delicately, because I may be talking about your sister, but some brides want and demand to be the center of attention. How would they look, not only on their special day, but in all the pictures, if certain members of their wedding party outshone them?" It was a nice way of saying her sister was self-absorbed, self-conscious, and insecure.

Chelsea looked at her, and then at the dress as if it all suddenly started to make sense. "So she humiliated us on purpose?"

"No, she probably did it subconsciously." She didn't

want to start a fight between sisters. What was done in the past was done and over with. They had a more serious problem right now.

"What do I do now? The wedding's tomorrow afternoon." This time there were actual tears in Chelsea's eyes.

"I have an idea." Sierra glanced at her watch as she pulled her cell phone out of her tote. There was still time to pull off a fast miracle. It took her a moment longer to find what she was looking for.

She smiled as she read the card and punched in the number. "Claire, hi, it's Sierra Morley, and we have an emergency. Can you stay open for an extra half hour? We'll be right there." A moment later she said, "Thanks, I owe you one," and closed the phone.

"Norah," she yelled as she stepped into the dining room and removed the glass from the bride-to-be's hand. "Get your shoes back on, we're heading out."

"Where? Why?" Norah jammed her feet back into her sandals.

Chelsea was already waiting at the door with her purse in hand. Sierra tugged Norah through the living room. "I'm driving." She didn't know how full that bottle had been when Norah had started. Norah stuck her tongue out at the dress as they went by and out the front door.

Matt followed Sierra into the Alberts' house and closed and locked the door behind them. "Want to tell me again how Norah got drunk while buying a dress?"

"Norah wasn't drunk. She was happy." Sierra didn't bother to turn on any lights as she walked through the house. The hallway light was always on, and it gave off enough light to see. She walked directly into the bedroom and tossed her tote onto the chair.

Matt carefully hung his rental tux on the closet door. "She was singing that song about 'I'm getting married in the morning.'"

"See, she was happy that she and Chelsea found a dress they both liked." Sierra kicked off her shoes and congratulated herself on making that call. Not only had Claire stayed open for them for a whole extra hour, she had pulled out a bottle of white zinfandel to celebrate.

"Ned wasn't too happy that you went out and got Norah loaded." Matt kicked off his shoes and chuckled. "And I never realized how off-key she sang until tonight."

"I did no such thing, and it was Ned, who was singing along with her, who was off-key. He's only upset because he can't have his wicked way with her tonight because she is staying with Chelsea at the cottage. It's bad luck for the groom to see the bride before the ceremony." She unbuttoned her blouse and tossed it on the chair.

"That's a dumb rule." Matt's shirt landed on top of hers but his gaze was glued to the front of her bra.

"So's dancing in the end zone after scoring a touchdown, but guys do it." She slowly released the button on her slacks and twitched her hips as she allowed them to slide down her legs. Teasing Matt was fun. Their first night together, everything had been new. Last night they had christened her bed with wild sex and a midnight snack of Jolene's chocolate éclairs. She would never look at cream filling the same way again.

Matt groaned as his fingers fumbled for the snap on his jeans. "Can I ask another question?"

Her fingers teased the front clasp of her bra. "Ask away."

Matt's jeans hit the floor. His erection was at full mast and tenting the front of his boxers. His underwear had screwdrivers printed all over them. She wasn't sure if that was a carpenter gag, or if it referred to what they would be doing in a few minutes. At the foot of the bed was a duffle bag Matt had packed the day before and a couple of his items were in the bathroom next to hers.

"Why were Norah and her friend allowing Zsa Zsa to rip up that dress?"

"Therapy." The front clasp released and her breasts bounced free. "It's a girl thing. You wouldn't understand." Even Kay, Jill, and Peggy Porter had understood.

Matt stopped breathing as her bra hit the floor.

She smiled. "I'm heading for the shower. Care to join me?" She turned and started to walk to the bathroom.

"Sierra," choked Matt, "did you have those panties on all night?"

She figured they would get a reaction from him. She glanced down at the tiny purple satin thong she had picked up in Victoria's Secret in Bangor the other night. Norah and she had been having a competition to see who could buy the tiniest pair.

It turned out that Joanna, Norah's mom, won the game.

Sierra hooked her thumbs into the thin elastic that passed as a waistband, even though it didn't go anywhere near her waist, and gracefully stepped out of the thong. "No, Matt." She kicked them to the side and smiled. "I haven't been wearing them all night." She continued into the bathroom.

Before the shower could even heat up, Matt joined her. There wasn't a screwdriver in sight.

Chapter Fourteen

Sierra grabbed one of the last remaining seats just as the guitarist started to play a slow, romantic melody on his acoustic guitar. Norah had opted out of the traditional bridal march in favor of a local resident who had a Spanish flair.

She glanced up at the arbor where Ned, Matt, and the minister stood. The arbor had turned out better than the photo Norah had ripped out of the magazine. The Porter boys indeed could build anything. From where she was sitting it was impossible to tell which were the real roses and which were silk. Hundreds of pink, white, burgundy, and purple blooms cascaded over the white arbor. Behind the smiling minister stood four six-foot-tall brass candelabras, each holding six lighted burgundy candles.

The thousand miniature lights that Ned and Norah had painstakingly strung the other night were lit, but at four in the afternoon, it wasn't close to being dark enough to appreciate them yet. Norah's mom had decided that more plants were needed and had gone out and purchased a dozen indoor trees and had them all potted in huge white ceramic pots. Two six-foot palms stood on either side of the arbor. Another palm stood next to the bar and four weeping figs, strung with lights, were in the corners of the tent where the dance floor and DJ were set up. The rest were over by the tent housing the buffet.

Dozens of terra-cotta pots overflowing with colorful flowers were spread between both properties. Sometime last night, while she was out with Norah and Chelsea, a five-foot-tall bare-breasted mermaid fountain appeared, along with two wooden benches. Someone obviously hadn't been thinking when they stocked the fountain with goldfish. Eight seagulls were perched on top of the white buffet tent eyeing the treat.

All in all, it was the most gorgeous outdoor wedding Sierra had ever seen. She made a mental note to take plenty of pictures and send them to Lianna, who always had her eye out for different weddings with a traditional touch. She also needed to send Lianna a thank-you present for all her help in pulling this together from three thousand miles away. Hours of phone calls and e-mails deserved something extra-special.

Tears filled her eyes as Chelsea stepped out of the cottage wearing a gorgeous pale pink gown that she and Norah had decided on last night at Claire's. The low-cut, tight gown wasn't your traditional maid of honor's outfit, but by the murmurs going through the guests, the men appreciated the choice. Chelsea was definitely not going to be without a dance partner later on.

Sierra turned back to look at Matt to see if he was appreciating their mad dash to Claire's. Ned had his gaze glued to the back door of the cottage waiting for Norah to make her appearance. Matt was staring at her as Chelsea slowly made her way to the arbor. She tried not to blush as a few guests turned in their seats to see whom Matt was looking at. Three hundred white chairs had been placed in a semicircle facing the arbor. All but four were taken.

Another murmur went through the guests as Norah, who was holding on to Karl James, her new stepfather, stepped out of the house. She looked like a fairy princess. Not a fairy-tale princess with long blond hair and sparkling blue eyes, but a fairy princess. Norah had dyed her short spiky hair a darker red that almost matched the burgundy roses she was carrying. She had highlighted the height of her cheekbones and the tilt to her green eyes, giving her a more fey appearance. The sparkle of a dozen earrings in her ears competed with the gleam of happiness in her eyes.

Sierra turned in her seat to see if Matt was appreciating this gorgeous fey woman who was about to become family. Ned looked as if he had stopped breathing. Matt was still staring at her. She blushed and glanced away. Didn't Matt know not to stare at a woman during a wedding ceremony? Every guest there was now probably thinking there would be another Porter wedding in the near future.

A group of ten cheerleaders and their moms was standing by the food tent watching the wedding. They had taken the catering job seriously. Every one of them was wearing either black pants or a skirt with a white blouse neatly tucked in. If one took the dreamy expressions off their youthful faces, they would almost look professional.

The music stopped and the minister started to speak. Sierra turned her attention to the ceremony.

Matt couldn't believe that the ceremony only took ten minutes. It had taken his younger brother Ned twenty-seven years to find Norah, and only six hundred seconds to make her his for life.

He held out his elbow for the maid of honor and then followed Ned and Norah back down the makeshift aisle. Everyone was talking at once and the sound of cameras clicking was driving him nuts. He glanced over at Sierra and winked. He hadn't had a chance to talk to her in hours. Everything had seemed to be last-minute and rush, rush, rush.

Matt had spent the morning setting up chairs and moving plants. He then had showered and changed in his parents' house and kept Ned from going nuts until it was time for them to take their places in the arbor. His last sight of Sierra had been of her lying naked and satisfied in her warm bed this morning, teasing him to come back. She hadn't been done with him yet.

It had taken every ounce of willpower he possessed to walk out the door. As it was, he had been a half hour late with the helping and his mother had scolded him, while his brothers had nudged each other knowingly.

Sierra was amazing, and he was in love.

He smiled as someone took his and Chelsea's picture. At least he thought her name was Chelsea. He was having trouble concentrating because he had no idea what he would do if Sierra and Austin went back to San Diego. Sierra was hiding something from him and he had been racking his brain trying to figure out what it was. She had sworn there wasn't anyone else in her life, and he believed her.

So why was she holding back?

"Hey, Matt, you're supposed to be happy for me." Ned gave him a light punch in the arm. "Smile, will you?"

"Sorry." He gave his brother a genuine smile. This was Ned and Norah's day and he would not ruin it with gloomy thoughts. Besides, Sierra was here and Austin was still with his father in Boston. He had one more night in her bed. One more night to convince her how perfect they were together.

"We need to get some pictures now," said Norah's mom. "We need everyone back to the arbor."

Matt took the opportunity to make a detour over to Sierra on his way to the arbor. All the men were taking the chairs and placing them at the tables that had already been set up. The line at the bar was six deep and the two bartenders appeared to be working their butts off. The cheerleading squad was scattered throughout the crowd with trays of hors d'oeuvres and perky smiles.

He snagged a stuffed mushroom as he reached Sierra. "You are the most beautiful woman here." He gave her a quick kiss and popped the mushroom into his mouth. The green dress she was wearing outlined her every curve and was a bit more low-cut than he was comfortable with. Oh, he loved the gentle swell of her breasts, but he just didn't want anyone else enjoying them. He had recently discovered this jealous streak where Sierra was concerned.

It was unsettling, to say the least.

Sierra smiled up at him and straightened his tie. Her gaze held a devilish gleam. "My, oh my, what you do to a tux, Matthew Porter, should be outlawed in three states." Her pink fingernails slowly teased their way down the front of his shirt.

He chuckled as he caught her hand. "Just as long as one of them isn't Maine." The black tux felt like a monkey suit to him, but by the gleam in Sierra's hungry gaze, she seemed to appreciate it. He hated ties. He always felt as if he was being choked to death.

"You'd better get going. I think they're waiting for

you." Sierra nodded toward the arbor where everyone was standing around and Norah's mom was giving orders.

"Come with me." He reached for her hand.

"Scared?" she teased as she tried to avoid his hand.

"Yes, of someone stealing you away." He pulled her closer and had the insane urge to hang a TAKEN sign around her neck.

Sierra laughed and kissed him on the cheek. "No one is going to steal me." Her fingertip was warm as it wiped away the lipstick mark she had left behind. "Now go get your picture taken, and smile nice."

"Yes, ma'am." He left Sierra in the crowd, but he glanced back once to see that Steven Blake, Gordon, and his friend, Juliet, had joined her. He wasn't sure what was with Gordon and Juliet, but there was a rumor going around that Juliet was actually Gordon's daughter. Considering how closely they resembled each other, Matt had a feeling it was more than just a rumor.

Gordon had never felt more proud in his life. His daughter was beautiful, gracious, and extremely intelligent. She was also on the shy side, but she had made friends with Steven Blake pretty fast. Part of him was a little worried that their growing relationship would take his newly found daughter away from him. The other, greedier part was hoping that his daughter would fall head-over-heels in love with Steve and stay in Misty Harbor permanently.

He was going to miss Juliet something awful come Wednesday morning when she had to go back home. She had turned his entire life and shop upside down in the short time she had been there, and he'd never been happier.

"Sierra, you remember Juliet." Gordon introduced his daughter.

"Yes, of course." Sierra gave Gordon, Juliet, and Steve Blake a warm smile. "Steve, the whale man, as my son likes to call you."

"Where is the little fellow?" Steve looked around the crowded yard.

"I'm afraid he's not here." Sierra looked a little overwhelmed by the crush of people.

"How about if you sit with us, since I believe your date has to sit at the head table with the wedding party?" Gordon, and anyone else in town with two good working eyes, knew that Matt and Sierra were an item. Since Sierra was an out-of-towner, he wasn't sure if she knew anyone else at the wedding.

"Thank you, I'd be delighted."

"Great." Gordon now wouldn't feel like a third wheel with Juliet and Steve. His date for the event had deserted him for a younger man. "Steve, why don't you and I go fight the crowd around the bar and get the ladies a drink?"

"Sure." Steve looked at Juliet. "What would you like?"

"White wine would be fine if they have it." Juliet gave Steve a smile that gave Gordon hope that his daughter just might stay in town.

"Sierra?" Gordon asked.

"The same." Sierra glanced at the crowd. Some guests were already making their way to the tables. "Why don't Juliet and I go get our seats?"

"That's a good idea." Gordon noticed that Steve's hand was still on the small of Juliet's back. "We'll find you there." He turned to go and said over his shoulder, "You coming, Steve?"

Steve gave Juliet's waist a squeeze and then hurried after her father.

Matt carried a chair over to Sierra's table and wedged it in between her and Gordon Hanley. "There, my obligation is now complete. The toast has been given, the meal eaten, and the music is about to start any minute now." The past hour had seemed like three without Sierra with him. Every time he had glanced in her direction she was laughing, talking, and totally enjoying herself with her new friends.

Sierra's cheeks were flushed, and he had to wonder if it was from the sun or the wine. "Matt, did you know Olivia is three days overdue?"

Matt glanced at Olivia Wycliffe and had no idea what to say. Was he supposed to offer condolences or encouragement at a time like this? "Ah, hang in there, Olivia. Won't be long now."

Olivia chuckled while her husband, Ethan, seemed to grow pale. "Thank you, Matt. That's very sweet," Olivia said.

The dress Olivia was wearing was stretched across her enormous stomach. She was sitting so far back from the table, he had no idea how she had reached her plate to eat. He honestly didn't remember either Jill or Kay getting that big while carrying his nieces and nephews. Maybe there was more than one little Wycliffe in there.

Sierra kicked him under the table. "Ethan's a little concerned, Matt."

"Why?" Short of Olivia exploding in front of them, he didn't see a problem. Olivia looked radiant, but there were traces of dark circles beneath her eyes. Maybe she hadn't been sleeping well, but who could blame her for that one? He wouldn't be able to sleep in that condition either. It would take Rusty Miller's crane to get her out of bed once she was lying down.

"Look at her, Matt," demanded Ethan. "You don't see a problem?"

Olivia frowned at her husband. "Are you saying I'm fat?"

"No." Ethan rolled his eyes. "But, hon, you can barely walk."

"Yeah, well, now I want to dance." Olivia pointed to the tent set up in the other yard. The DJ had started to play dance music for those who had already finished eating. "Unless you think I'm too fat to dance with." Olivia smiled sweetly across the table at Gordon. "I'm sure someone won't mind whirling this old cow across the dance floor."

Gordon bowed his head. "I would be delighted."

Olivia's eyes went wide and her hand flew to her stomach. A soft "oh," tumbled from her lips.

"What's wrong?" cried Ethan.

"Nothing. Your kid kicked me." Olivia rolled her eyes.

Ethan threw up his hands in defeat. "She's been doing that all day long. She's driving me nuts."

Matt shrugged. Olivia looked healthy to him, and she sure sounded feisty enough to deliver twins. He looked at Sierra, who was looking at the soon-to-be mother with speculation. "Ethan, why don't you take your wife dancing? I'm sure she knows what she can and can't do." Both his sisters-in-law had beaten the fact that pregnancy did not make them stupid into every male Porter's head.

Ethan looked at his wife with love and sympathy in his eyes. "Would you really like to dance?"

Olivia beamed with happiness. "Yes, as long as it's a

slow one. I don't think I'm up for anything more strenuous than a slow shuffle."

Ethan looked at his wife as if she had just lost her mind, but he was smart enough to keep his mouth shut. "Of course." He stood up and held out his hand so he could help Olivia out of her chair.

It took Olivia a moment to get the right momentum, but she managed to stand using Ethan and the table for leverage. Matt wanted to cheer at the feat. Olivia Wycliffe did not look like a woman who could walk, let alone dance. Ethan's arms were never going to fit around her.

Olivia's eyes shot wide open as she grabbed for her stomach with both hands. "Ethan!"

"What?" Ethan looked at his wife in alarm.

"I think my water just broke," Olivia said in awe.

Every ounce of color drained from Ethan's face. "You think?"

Olivia tried to see over her bulging stomach. "You look. I haven't seen my feet in three months."

Sierra chuckled.

Matt felt the blood leave his own face. Holy hell, Olivia was going to have the baby right now. Right here! "I'll get Doc Sydney." He had just seen Sydney Olsen with her husband, Erik, and their infant daughter over by the fountain. He jumped up and hurried away. The last place he wanted to be was anywhere near Olivia. Someone might make him do something he didn't want to do.

Sierra saw that they were starting to attract a bunch of interest from nearby tables. "Ethan, why don't you help your wife to your car?"

Ethan gently held Olivia's elbow. "Can you walk?"

Olivia, who knew Sierra had a son, looked at her, rolled her eyes, and silently mouthed the word "men."

"Ethan, sweetheart, light of my life, I'm having a

baby, not knee replacement surgery." Olivia started to slowly waddle her way across the yard with Ethan matching her steps and lecturing her about something the entire way.

A moment later, she saw Matt and a woman follow. She assumed that the brown-haired woman was Doc Sydney.

"Well, that's an interesting development," said Gordon, who looked a little dazed by the turn of events.

"I guess that means she's not going to get to dance after all," said Juliet.

Everyone was laughing when Matt rejoined them. "Doc's going with them to the hospital."

"Problems?" Sierra asked.

"No," said Matt, chuckling as he shook his head. "Doc just didn't trust Ethan to drive."

Juliet loved being in Steve's arms. "For a guy who spends most of his time out on a boat, you sure can dance."

Steve chuckled and pulled her closer. "I can do all kinds of things."

"I bet you can." She laid her head against his shoulder. The wooden dance floor was crowded with couples enjoying the reception. The DJ had a lamp next to his equipment, giving him plenty of light to see by. Four huge weeping figs were strung with hundreds of miniature lights that lit the interior of the tent nicely without blinding anyone. The low lighting gave everything a romantic glow.

Steve kissed the top of her head. "When are you coming back?"

She knew what he was asking. "Gordon invited me

to spend Thanksgiving with him." It was the first long break of the school year.

"That's three months away." Steve's feet were barely moving to the music. "I don't know if I can last three months without seeing you."

"Well"—she took a deep breath and screwed up her courage—"you could always come to Boston for a few days."

"Is that an invitation?" Steve stopped dancing and gently tilted up her chin so he could see her face.

"Yes." She wondered if she had the same look of hope in her eyes as Steve had in his. "The last couple of weeks have been an emotional roller coaster ride for me, with meeting and then getting to know Gordon. His being my father has answered a lot of my questions about myself and why I was always so different from my brothers and sister. But there are still a ton of questions left to be asked."

"I can imagine." Steve ran his thumb over her lower lip. "Meeting me hasn't helped, has it?"

She smiled against his thumb. "I need to spend time with Gordon, to get to know him, but I want to spend time with you. I'm being torn in two very different directions. I expected Gordon—whom I didn't expect was you."

"If I come to Boston for a visit?"

"There will be only you and me. I won't have to worry about Gordon staying up at night until I get in." She laughed. "It's a little strange, to say the least, but I can sympathize with his confusion about this whole father-daughter relationship."

Steve relaxed, pulled her back into his arms, and started the slow shuffling of feet. "So I'm not the only one who thinks there's something special happening here and that we should explore it?"

She smiled against the lapel of his suit jacket. Her tawny marine biologist looked scrumptious in a suit and tie. "I think we'd be fools not to."

Sierra sat on the bench and kicked off her shoes. Wearing new shoes to dance in wasn't the smartest decision she had ever made. The soft bubbling of the fountain next to her helped drown out some of the noise coming from the dance floor. It was after ten o'clock at night and the reception was still going in high gear. She was exhausted. Matt and his brothers had sneaked around front to decorate Ned's pickup truck. She didn't even want to think about what they were doing to it.

The wedding and reception had been perfect. No one could have asked for a better day. The only incidents to mark the day were Olivia's water breaking, and two seagulls that dive-bombed the fountain, causing quite a stir among the children. It had taken five hulking men and a kitchen strainer to rescue the goldfish and put them in the house where they were safe.

Sierra tilted back her head and closed her eyes. Matt wasn't allowing her to sleep very much at night. She smiled at the memories.

"May I join you?"

Sierra opened her eyes and smiled. "Please do, Ms. Wyndham." She had been introduced to Millicent Wyndham earlier. The matriarch of Misty Harbor was just as she had pictured her: a true lady.

"Thank you, Ms. Morley." Millicent sat. "Or should I call you by your maiden name, Miss Randall?"

The lady had steel beneath that elegant facade. Sierra had had a feeling that Millicent knew who she really was when they had been introduced. "Please call me Sierra."

What was that old saying, "the jig is up"? "How did you find out?"

"I knew Lucas Randall would be sending someone to scope out the property and the town. I just wasn't expecting his daughter. The Internet is a wonderful invention. It's full of all kinds of information." Millicent glanced down at Sierra's sandals. "Nice shoes, by the way."

"Thanks." The older woman hadn't sat down to discuss shoes. "When I first came here, no one informed me that someone else was interested in the lighthouse property. Being told by that person over a nice romantic dinner put a damper on my evening."

"I see." Millicent gazed off in the direction of the dancing. "So you had no idea Matt wanted the property when you met him?"

Sierra followed Millicent's gaze. Chelsea, the maid of honor, was leading the bunny hop and having the time of her life. Considering the stir Chelsea was causing with all the single men of Misty Harbor, it was going to take a crowbar to pry the girl out of town.

"None at all," she answered, "which is causing quite a dilemma now. I didn't want anyone in town to know who I was, because I wanted a fresh, unvarnished perspective. I didn't want any of the town's residents to try to sway my view in one direction or the other. It was you, after all, who told my father you weren't sure if a hotel would be in the town's best interest."

"Has Matt tried to sway your view?"

"Matt doesn't know I work for the Randall Corporation, or that Lucas Randall is my father."

Millicent frowned. "You haven't told him?"

"The moment just never seemed right." She felt that sick, twisted feeling in the bottom of her stomach. "I made my decision concerning the property before I became involved with Matt." Before she had fallen in love. "While the property and the lighthouse are quite charming, they don't meet our needs."

"I see." There was a smile playing at the corner of Millicent's mouth. "So why haven't you told Matt who you are? From what I've seen, the boy obviously has some strong feelings for you."

Only Millicent could get away with calling Matt a "boy." "It's complicated."

Millicent chuckled. "Life usually is."

Wasn't that the truth? "My mother was a very fragile woman, both physically and emotionally. My father loved her dearly and used his money, power, and strength to protect her from the world. She died when I was seven."

"I'm sorry to hear that. Growing up without a mother must have been hard."

"It's even harder when every time your father looks at you, he sees his beloved wife. I inherited my father's height, but I look just like my mother. My father makes the mistake of thinking I'm just like her, that I need protecting from the realities of life. He believes women are frail and delicate creatures, and we have no place in the cutthroat business world."

Millicent snorted. "Please."

"Yeah, tell me about it. I've been trying to prove something to him since I graduated from college and joined the business. So far I've impressed him twice: once by marrying his heir apparent to the business, Jake Morley, and once by giving him a grandson."

"Ouch."

"Oh, I know he loves me, and I'm not complaining. Just once I want to do something in the business that will knock his socks off and make him realize I am not my mother. I don't want to inherit the business. I want a life. Whoever runs the Randall Corporation will not have a life. I want to be part of Austin's life."

"What does Jake Morley think about all this?"

"Jake thinks I should demand the business and that I'm not assertive enough with my father."

"So where does Matt fit into all this?" Millicent asked.

"I'm not sure, but I do know if he finds out who I really am, his first reaction is going to be the same as yours and everyone else's—that I was using him." She watched as the cheerleaders and their mothers went back and forth between the house and the buffet tables. They were holding up their end of the deal by doing the cleanup work. "I'm not sure if what Matt and I have now is strong enough to survive that first reaction."

"If it doesn't, maybe it wasn't meant to be. But what if it does? What then?"

"I want to knock his socks off too." Sierra smiled. "I believe I have it all worked out where I not only impress my father and Jake, but Matt too. Being a business-woman is who I am. Matt has to understand that."

Millicent nodded. "Teddy's property."

"Excuse me?"

"Teddy Jefferies' piece of land out on Route 186."

"How do you know about that?" Here she had thought she had been low-key about the whole business.

Millicent chuckled. "I keep my ear close to the ground when it comes to Misty Harbor."

"The Jefferies property is twenty miles away."

"Practically right around the corner." Millicent leaned back into the bench and relaxed. "Just because the Randall Corporation doesn't want the lighthouse prop-erty doesn't mean that another hotel or business won't.

The value of the land is considerable, and the taxes I pay on it go a long way to fill the town's budget. If I donate the land to the town, it will lose the tax revenue, and they're having trouble meeting their expenditures now, which means they would raise everyone's property taxes. I also sincerely doubt Matt would be able to afford the piece of ground at its current value." Millicent gave a weary sigh. "As you said, it's complicated."

"Life usually is." Sierra quoted back Millicent's words.

Millicent laughed. "I like you, Sierra Morley, even though I still think you're making a mistake with Matt. Tell him the truth."

"I haven't lied to him." She had just been awfully careful to make sure the subject never came up in their conversations.

"He's not going to see it that way." Millicent laughed as the three Porter boys came sneaking back around the side of the house. "Now there's trouble if ever I saw it."

Sierra laughed with Millicent. John, Paul, and Matt all looked so proud of themselves. "How much money do you want to wager that they tied more than tin cans to the back bumper of Ned's truck?"

"I'm a betting woman, Sierra, but I won't bet on that. I've seen the Porter boys in action since the time they could walk."

"Well, the town's still standing." How bad could they have been? They all had grown into remarkable men.

Millicent snorted as Matt started walking toward them. "No thanks to them."

"How are my two favorite ladies?" Matt sat down between them and spread his arms wide on the back of the bench.

"I was just about to tell Sierra about the time I caught you up on my roof," Millicent said.

Matt shrugged. "Lost baseball."

"The night Paul and you dug up six of my prize rose bushes and replaced them with six dead ones?"

Sierra cringed at that one.

"It was a dare we had to do so we would be allowed to get into the clubhouse." Matt looked guilty for that one.

"What about the time I caught you behind Bailey's ice cream shop playing tonsil hockey with that girl? What was her name?"

Matt sat up straight as a flush swept up his cheeks. "Gee, look at that fountain, Sierra. I wonder who picked it out?"

Sierra giggled. "You're cute when you blush."

"Guys don't blush." Matt glared at Millicent.

Millicent smiled serenely as she looked around Matt to the bare-breasted mermaid pouring water out of a shell. "I'd say from the size of her bosom, your father, Matt."

Matt's eyes opened wide. "What do you know about my father and his preferences in the female form?"

"What, you think he married your mother for her cooking?" Millicent laughed with delight.

Matt groaned and buried his face in his hands.

Sierra patted Matt on the back. She could sympathize with him. Children should never have to think about their parents having sex.

The music from the tent unexpectedly stopped in the middle of a song. "Excuse me, everyone, I need to make an announcement." John Porter took the DJ's mike. "Ethan and Olivia Wycliffe have just become the proud parents of a baby boy. Olivia and son are doing exceptionally well, and from all accounts, Ethan managed to pull through it without too many complications."

Someone shouted a question that Sierra couldn't hear.

"The baby weighs eight pounds, four ounces, is twenty-one inches long, and no name has been given to the little tyke yet. Olivia and Ethan are still discussing it."

Cheers erupted, and somewhere over by the bar another champagne cork popped. The music was turned back on and more people crowded their way onto the dance floor.

"Ah, that's the fourth baby born this year." Millicent beamed with pride. "We're going to need another teacher or two soon." Millicent looked at Sierra. "You wouldn't happen to know any teachers, would you?"

Considering she'd just had dinner with one, it was an easy question to answer. "Gordon's daughter, Juliet, teaches third grade."

Chapter Fifteen

Juliet stood in the doorway of the bookstore and looked across the street to where Gordon stood in conversation with Harvey Krup, the owner of Krup's General Store. Both men were puffing away on their pipes and more than likely discussing yesterday's wedding. Sunday mornings in Misty Harbor were quiet and peaceful.

A few residents had stopped in earlier. Most wanted to gossip about who had drunk too much at the reception and who had danced with whom. Some had even placed bets with Gordon on whether Chelsea, the maid of honor, would be going back to Philadelphia.

Seemed Chelsea had partaken a little too freely of the nectar of the gods and had declared she wanted to become the mayor of Misty Harbor. Someone had tacked up a VOTE FOR CHELSEA poster on the door of Buddy's Bait Shop down at the docks. In the middle of the poster was a blown-up digital photo of Chelsea at the wedding. She looked like Miss America. The only thing missing had been the crown and sash. A petition was already circulating throughout town to put Chelsea's name on the November ballot.

Gordon had signed the petition without blinking an eye.

Juliet didn't know what shocked her more, the fact that what appeared to be normal, sane residents were taking Chelsea seriously, or that Juliet's father was running a booking operation out of the shop.

Juliet had placed five bucks on Chelsea waking this morning with a killer hangover and regretting her impromptu speech about a lobster in every pot and a Johnson outboard engine in every garage. Juliet had missed the speech but had heard the highlights from Gordon this morning over coffee. That's what she got for leaving the reception early with Steve to go strolling down by the docks. They had missed all the politics.

"Hey, you're scaring all the customers away with all this fresh air." Gordon knocked the ash out of his pipe and into the ashtray filled with sand next to the front door. A NO SMOKING sign had been taped to each front door. "It's still a little chilly out."

"No, it's not." Juliet moved away from the doors but kept them open. A breeze was ruffling a couple pages of the magazines. Gordon had opened the shop while she had slept in. Once he had filled her in on the local gossip, she had kicked him out front for his morning smoke. "It's a beautiful morning. The fresh air will do you good—clear out those lungs."

Gordon raised his sunglasses to the top of his head, snorted, and placed his now-empty pipe next to the cash register. "You got in awfully late last night."

"I thought you weren't going to wait up." It had barely been after one in the morning, and she knew for a fact she'd hardly made a sound when she had come in. She had even avoided the squeaky step on the stairway. "I discovered something last night."

Gordon frowned. "Do I need to buy a shotgun?"

Juliet laughed and tried not to blush. Although no home runs had been scored last night, a couple of the bases had been tagged. "I was referring to you."

"Me?" Gordon looked intrigued. "What about me?"

"I discovered why all the kids seem to be afraid of you." Juliet sat on the stool behind the counter and grinned. "That question has been bothering me since the first day I got here."

"Why didn't you ask?" Gordon laughed. "It's no secret."

"I realize that, but the adults had the good manners not to believe it or bring it up in normal conversation, and the little kids were avoiding me too. I was guilty by association."

"Who let the cat out of the bag?"

"Don't you mean the bat out of the belfry?" Juliet was enjoying herself. "What I don't understand is why in the world you let the kids think you're a vampire." She had put two and two together and couldn't believe the four she came up with, but it all made sense. When she expressed her suspicions to Steve, he had come clean and admitted that even he had been scared of Gordon as a little boy.

It seemed Gordon played a very convincing vampire when he wanted to.

Gordon shrugged. "Winters get kind of boring here. The kids need something to inspire their imagination. Lord knows they don't get it from most of the crap they have to read in school nowadays." Gordon wrapped his arm across his nose and mouth and in a deep Hungarian accent said, "I vant to bite your neck."

"Isn't it a little too early for Halloween, Gordon?"

Juliet almost fell off the stool. "Mom!" Victoria Carlyle was standing in the doorway of the shop with her gaze glued to Gordon's back.

Gordon slowly turned around and dropped his arm. "Vicki?" He couldn't believe that Victoria was standing in his shop. Twenty-seven years since he had last seen her, and she hadn't really changed that much. Her blond hair was now streaked with gray and cut short. Designer glasses were perched on her nose and her eyes were just as blue as he remembered. Her mouth was just as luscious. Brown leather sandals, well-worn jeans, and a sleeveless top with lots of embroidery clothed her still-trim body. Chunky wooden bracelets encircled both of her wrists.

No, Vicki hadn't changed much over the years. She was still the most beautiful woman he had ever laid eyes on.

"Hello, Gordon."

His brain froze and he forgot how to talk. All he could do was stare at Vicki and sink into the past.

Victoria flushed when he didn't say anything in return and then turned to her daughter. "Juliet, you look wonderful." Victoria walked over to her daughter and pulled her up off the stool. "Whatever you have been doing, it agrees with you."

"Thanks, Mom." Juliet kissed her mother's cheek. "What brings you here?"

"Can I say I was in the neighborhood?" Victoria nervously glanced around the shop. She felt like an idiot. She shouldn't have come, or at least she should have called first. Gordon hadn't even returned her hello. He was standing there staring at her as if a ghost of Hamlet's father had just walked into the bookstore.

Maybe it was Halloween after all, or at least the opening act of a great tragedy.

"I don't think that one will cut it, Mom." Juliet glanced

over at Gordon, then back to her mom. "Misty Harbor's a good five-hour drive, and that's pushing it with no breaks. What time did you leave home, anyway? It's only ten-thirty."

"I spent the night at a small bed-and-breakfast outside of Camden." She had found the place by pure luck late yesterday afternoon and decided to stop there for the night. She needed the time to build up her courage. Facing Gordon after all these years was going to take a heap more courage than she usually possessed. Besides, she had known that Gordon and Juliet were attending some wedding yesterday and wouldn't be there anyway.

Seeing Gordon for the first time in more than two decades after driving for nearly six hours wasn't what she wanted to do. She wanted to be well rested, fresh, and looking her best. She wanted to impress the hell out of him. Instead, he had gone totally speechless.

She didn't consider that a good sign.

Gordon had every right to toss her tush back out on the street. She hadn't told him he had a daughter for fifteen years. Then out of the blue she had dropped that bombshell by sending him not only a picture of Juliet but also a letter begging him not to have contact with her, and saying that Juliet was being raised by a loving man she thought was her real father.

She never should have come.

Juliet looked wonderful. There was color in her cheeks and her eyes were sparkling. Her daughter was not only fine, she seemed to have blossomed. The nightly phone calls home hadn't been telling the whole story. "I've been worried about you." It was the truth. Her quiet, shy, sweet Juliet had done something so out of character by coming to Maine all by herself. What mother wouldn't have been worried?

No matter how many times Juliet had reassured her that everything was fine, she was fine, and that Gordon seemed very happy to have her there, she still had to come to Maine to see for herself. She was dying of curiosity to see and meet Juliet's version of her Gordy, the man she had fallen in love with more than twenty-seven years ago. The man who had fathered her first child.

Juliet gave her a hug. "Mom, I'm fine. I told you everything was okay."

Victoria hugged her daughter back and felt tears come to her eyes. "I know you did." She turned her head and looked at Gordon through the tears.

Professor Gordon Hanley had been every college girl's dream. He had been twenty-nine, six-foot-two, thin, with long, flowing black hair and hazel eyes that were either dreamy or sparkling with intelligence. They had been, until they made love, then his eyes turned a deeper green and filled with fire and love. At least she had thought it was love. Gordon had looked at her as if she were the only woman in the world. He had once called her his Juliet.

Their affair had started before Christmas, and by Easter break Gordon had shattered her heart and her dreams. She didn't remember all the words he had spoken to her that night so long ago, but she did remember how much it had hurt, and that their relationship was over.

Eight weeks later, back at her parents' house, she had discovered Gordon had left her with more than a broken heart. He'd left her carrying their child.

She had been so scared back then. If Gordon didn't love her, how could he love their child? He wouldn't. She had run to her old high school sweetheart and friend, Ken Carlyle, and cried her heart out. Ken had held her, comforted her, and promised her that everything would work out. And it had.

By July she and Ken were married, and no one had guessed that the bulge under the empire waist of her wedding gown was not Ken's child. Ken had gently held Juliet the minute after her birth, and there had been nothing but pride and love on his face.

Juliet had been Ken's firstborn child—his little dark-haired bookworm, as he liked to call her.

Ken had been a wonderful husband and father to all four of their children. She had fallen in love with him, but it was a sweet love, one that grew every year, until nine months shy of their twenty-fifth wedding anniversary. One night while driving home from work he had been killed by a drunken driver.

That time, when she cried her eyes and heart out, she had been surrounded by their four children. That time it had been she who had held them and promised that everything would be okay. That everything would work out. And it had. Life went on and eventually the joy and the smiles came back into their lives. But Ken Carlyle had left a big void in all their lives.

"Victoria, you're here!" Gordon seemed to snap out of his daze.

She stepped away from Juliet and straightened her top. If her daughter had found the courage to face the man who fathered her, so could she. "Hello again, Gordon." His hair was still dark and flowing, but now it was streaked with gray. The angles of his face seemed sharper.

Gordon looked at Juliet, as if seeking her help. Whatever message passed between father and daughter, Juliet caught it.

"Mom, come, I'll give you the nickel tour of Gordon's shop." Juliet grabbed her mother's hand and tugged her over to a bookshelf. "You wouldn't believe all the great books I've found here."

Victoria let herself be led around the shop and listened as her daughter went on and on about the different sections of books and how she had convinced Gordon to make a separate section for children.

Although the books were interesting, Victoria liked the small selection of elegant stationery and the pens. Who would spend that kind of money on a platinum fountain pen?

"Come look at these, Mom." Juliet tugged her away from the pens and over to a case filled with fancy containers.

"What are they?" Some looked like crystal, some wood, and some silver. Most looked like antiques.

"Gordon, why don't you explain the tobacco humidors to my mom?" Juliet shot a look across the shop that dared Gordon to argue with her. "I think I'll run upstairs and see what we have to make for lunch."

"No," she blurted out a little too fast. "I mean, it's not even eleven o'clock. What's the rush?" She didn't want her daughter to leave her alone with Gordon. She didn't know what to say to him.

"Your mother's right, Juliet. There's no rush." Gordon walked across the shop and joined them by the display cases. "It's good to see you, Victoria." Gordon bowed. "'She walks in beauty, like the night.'"

"Lord Byron. Very good." She smiled at the memory of the quote game they used to play—a game she had taught their daughter. "'Whenever a man's friends begin to compliment him about looking young, he may be sure that they think he is growing old.'"

Gordon raised a brow. "Washington Irving. Really, Vicki, I expected better from you."

Juliet's laughter filled the room.

Victoria faked an indignant glare. "'It were not best that we should all think alike; it is difference of opinion that makes horse races.'"

Gordon's laughter joined Juliet's. "Twain's *Pudd'n-head Wilson*?" It took Gordon a moment to catch his breath. "I now know where Juliet gets it from."

"Not everyone believes the English language rises and falls with Shakespeare." She remembered nights lying in Gordon's bed as he read Shakespeare to her.

"Careful, Gordon, I've heard her quote Janis Joplin once when she was really mad."

"Janis Joplin?" Gordon looked impressed.

Victoria blushed a brilliant red and confessed, "It wasn't Joplin. I lied. The quote was all mine. I yelled something I shouldn't have, and at the time figured it sounded like something Janis would have sung about."

Her daughter looked at her in awe. "Wow, Mom, I never would have put a tequila bottle and that particular body part together like that."

Gordon's laughter was contagious. The awkwardness had passed. It didn't look like he was going to toss her tush back out on the street. At least not yet.

"It was very sweet of you to take us to dinner, Matt." Sierra reached up and brushed a kiss across his cheek while Austin wasn't looking.

"I told you Tony's makes the best pizza around." Matt waved to Austin as the merry-go-round he was riding made another rotation.

Sierra waved too. Austin was really enjoying himself, and she had missed his smile horribly these past couple of days. She had met Jake at the same restaurant along Interstate 95, near lunchtime, and retrieved their son. Austin had talked her ear off on the first hour of the drive back to Misty Harbor, but then he had fallen asleep. Jake and Aunt Jean had obviously catered to his every whim for the past five days and spoiled him. Jake had ended up buying another suitcase for all the clothes and toys they had bought Austin during his stay in Boston.

Matt had met them at the Alberts', and she suggested a relaxing evening at home with some hamburgers on the grill. Matt suggested that they go into Sullivan for pizza and the amusements to celebrate Austin's return. Her son had very vocally seconded that suggestion. She had been outvoted by a bunch of men.

Austin's only complaint so far had been that Tyler hadn't joined them. Tonight she wanted her son all to herself and Matt. She wanted to pretend that they were a family.

Sierra felt Matt wrap his arms around her waist and tug her against the front of him. She relaxed in his arms as she watched her son tighten his grip on the pole with both hands and continued to ride the white wooden horse like a pro. Austin was growing up so fast. He didn't even need her to ride the merry-go-round with him any longer.

Soon he would be in school all day and then college. Then he'd be getting married and starting his own family. She sighed as the years flashed before her eyes.

"What's the matter—tired?" Matt tightened his hold.

She wasn't just tired, she was exhausted. She was burning the candle on both ends and doing a very fine balancing act. It was just a matter of time before all those balls came tumbling down on top of her head. "I was just thinking about how fast he's growing up."

Matt chuckled. "He's only four."

"Old enough for nursery school this fall." If that wasn't enough to make her want to cry.

"Come on, Sierra, think of all the friends he's going to make."

How could she think that when she had absolutely no idea where or if her son would be attending a nursery school?

Matt chuckled as Austin did another rotation. This time when he went by Austin didn't even wave. Her son was too busy talking to the little girl on the horse next to him. "He's going to be a ladies' man, I can see it now," Matt said.

She could feel the vibrations of Matt's laughter against her back. She didn't even want to think about that one. Her son couldn't even take his own shower yet. "Then he'd better learn that soap is his friend."

Matt was still laughing when the ride came to an end. "I'll get him," Matt said as he hurried around the barricade and up onto the ride. A crowd of parents rushed the merry-go-round, all anxious to get to their kids before the little guys tried to dismount on their own.

She watched as Matt swept Austin off his horse and up into his arms. The smile and trust on Austin's face said it all.

"Mom, Matt says I have to ask you if I can ride the horse again." Austin held out his arms to her.

She took her son out of Matt's arms. "You just had two really big slices of pizza." She really would rather have the pizza stay in his little tummy. "We'll come back some other time and you can ride it then." She made a mental note to squeeze in some time for another trip to Sullivan with Austin. If she could find a way to buy a couple more hours in every day, all those titanium credit cards in her wallet might actually do her some good.

"Hey, they have Skee-Ball," Matt said, distracting her son from the horses.

Austin's gaze followed Matt's finger to a row of Skee-Ball machines. "I don't know how to play."

"Don't worry, I'll teach you." Matt hurried over to the row of machines and grabbed a spot that had three lanes open next to each other. "I'm a pro at this."

Austin eyed the short wooden lanes and then he gazed at the red and white–striped cart near the entrance to the amusements. "Can I get some of that?" He pointed to a towering swirl of blue cotton candy on a stick the vendor was handing to a little boy.

She shuddered at the thought of all that sugar. "No, but if you're still hungry after we're done playing, then I'll think about getting you a snow cone."

"A blue one?"

"Can I get a brown one?" Matt asked with a little-boy look on his face.

She chuckled as she shook her head at both of them. "Only if you both behave."

She stood at the end of her Skee-Ball lane and tried to remember how to play. She looked over at Matt, who was dropping quarters into Austin's machine and showing him how to hold the ball.

Her heart didn't know whether to sing or sink. They weren't pretending, they did look like a typical family out for a good time.

Two hours later Matt carried a sleeping Austin into his bedroom while she hauled the giant tiger Matt had won him by shooting a basketball into a hoop three times in a row. She had no idea what they were going to do with a four-foot tiger that Austin had already named Tony, in honor of either the pizza shop or the cereal tiger. She wasn't sure which.

Matt laid Austin on his bed. "What do you want me to do with him?" There was a chuckle in Matt's voice. Austin was out for the night and hadn't so much as fluttered an eyelid since being removed from the car.

"Take his shoes and socks off; I'll get the rest." She sat Tony in the corner of the room and then hunted down a clean pair of pajamas. Thankfully she had taken Austin into the ladies' room and cleaned up most of the mess that the blue snow cone had left.

Within five minutes Austin was in clean pajamas and tucked in for the night. He never woke up. "Come on, I could use a glass of wine." She pushed Matt out of her son's bedroom and shut off the light.

"Sounds good to me." Matt followed her into the kitchen. "Does he always go to sleep that fast?"

"No, Jake and his aunt must have kept him very busy for the last few days. He even took an hour nap on the way back to Misty Harbor this afternoon." She went to the refrigerator and pulled out a bottle of wine. "I picked up some beer today in case you would rather have one."

Matt gave her a look that curled her toes. "You bought me beer?"

The way he said it, one would think she had bought him season tickets to the New England Patriots' home games. "You seem to like it more than wine." She reached into a cabinet for a wine glass.

"I wasn't sure what kind to get; there are so many to choose from." Three-quarters of the aisle at the food store had been beer. The other remaining shelf space had been wine and liquor. The only conclusion she could make from that was that the people of Maine must really like their beer. "I let Austin make the final decision. He picked the one with the moose on the label."

Matt chuckled as he opened the door and pulled out a cold bottle of beer. "Smart boy. Remind me to buy him a tricycle or something."

"Hey, I'm the one who paid for it."

Matt set the bottle on the counter and then swung her up and sat her next to it. "So you are." His mouth nuzzled her neck. "Does that mean you like me?"

"Some people would think that," she teased. She loved the way Matt made her feel—like a woman. A very desirable woman.

"You taste like heaven." Matt's mouth nibbled its way over to her mouth for a long, slow kiss.

She melted under the onslaught of his mouth. Matt made her want things she'd never known she wanted. She wrapped her legs around his waist and her arms around his neck and hung on as he carried her into the bedroom. Neither one broke their kiss.

Austin was in the next room, but nothing short of a nightmare or a bathroom call would wake her son now. Just to be on the safe side, she whispered against Matt's mouth, "Lock the door."

Matt fumbled with the lock. "Are you sure it's okay?"

"Yes." No, she wasn't sure if it was okay or not. No one had ever handed her a mommy booklet when she gave birth to Austin four years ago. And she was sure as hell that no one mailed her "The Single Mom's Guide to Sex Without Scarring Your Child for Life" pamphlet when her divorce was final. But this was Matt. This was the man she had fallen in love with.

This was the man she wanted.

Matt lowered her to the bed and followed her down. "I missed you today. I should have gone with you to pick up Austin. That was a long distance for you to drive alone." Matt's hands were undoing the front of her blouse.

She tugged his shirt over his head without bothering to unbutton it. "Your brothers needed your help in breaking down the wedding and returning the tents and tables." She wanted Jake to meet Matt, the man she was hoping would become a very important person in their son's life. But they would be meeting soon enough. Her father, Jake, and two other executives were flying in a week from Wednesday. She had nine days to prepare to knock their socks off.

Nine days to get up the courage to tell Matt who she really was.

With Matt's mouth working its way down to the zipper of her jeans, nine days seemed like a lifetime away.

Matt couldn't sleep. He lay with Sierra in his arms and wondered what she was hiding. She kept putting him off every time he mentioned the future. Their future. Time was running out, and so was Sierra. She and Austin would be leaving the day after Labor Day. Yet she was stonewalling him at every turn.

Why?

He glanced down at Sierra and gently brushed her hair away from her face. She was beautiful. She was also exhausted. He could see it in her face. She had been running herself ragged for the past couple of weeks. It wasn't just the wedding either. She was up to something, but for the life of him he couldn't figure out what.

He carefully eased Sierra out of his arms and got out of bed. He didn't think they had locked the front door or turned off the living room lights. He stepped into his jeans and headed for the kitchen. It was only ten-thirty at night.

He chuckled as he put the wine and beer back into the refrigerator and got himself a glass of milk. Sierra and he had been so distracted that neither bottle had been opened. A distant low-sounding beep caught his attention. He followed the sound into the den.

He turned on the light and shook his head as a fax machine spit out a few pages. The businesswoman strikes again. He walked over to the Alberts' desk, which Sierra had obviously overtaken. A fancy laptop was in the center of the desk and a portable printer/fax machine was sitting by its side. The machine had enough bells and whistles on it that it could probably contact the space station. Sierra took her work seriously.

He glanced at the page that had just come out of the fax, and he frowned. The letterhead was from the Randall Corporation, the hotel company that was trying to buy the lighthouse and its surrounding acreage. What would they be faxing Sierra?

He placed his glass of milk on the desk and picked up the page. It took a moment for his heart to understand what his brain was relaying. The signature that was sprawled across the bottom of the legal document said it all: Sierra Randall-Morley, vice president of the Randall Corporation.

Anger, hurt, and betrayal made it nearly impossible to breathe. He had to get out of there before he said or did something he would regret. He now knew what Sierra had been hiding.

Sierra woke alone at dawn. She stretched and yawned. Matt must have gotten up and left, knowing that Austin would be getting up soon. Matt and she hadn't had time to discuss the logistics of the physical aspect of their relationship.

She didn't want to spend her nights alone, but she didn't want her son to see Matt coming out of her bedroom in the morning either. How would she explain that one to a four-year-old? She couldn't.

A frown pulled at her mouth as she stared up at the ceiling. How did other single mothers handle situations like this? Did lovers sneak in and out in the dead of night, or was she supposed to take a vow of chastity now that she was a mother and single? She'd have to talk about it with Matt tonight.

She kicked off the blanket and got out of bed. There were a hundred things that she had to do, and hopefully the San Diego office had faxed her those documents she was waiting on. She pulled on her robe and hurried to the den. Hopefully she'd be able to get in an hour or two of work before Austin got up.

Sierra knew something was wrong as soon as she stepped into the hallway. The den light was on. It hadn't been on last night when they had returned from Sullivan. Curious, she walked down the hall and peered inside. The sight of the half-drank glass of milk caused her to close her eyes and pray that she was still sleeping and that this was a nightmare.

A nightmare she would be waking up from very soon.

She opened her eyes and knew her prayers hadn't been answered. The glass was still sitting there on the desk. With a heavy sigh she walked over to the desk and stared down. Someone in the legal department at the main office in San Diego had been on the ball, for a Sunday evening. The documents had been faxed.

Only one page had been moved. The page with her official company signature: Sierra Randall-Morley.

Matt had taken a look at the letterhead and her signature and added two plus two and came up with four. The only problem was, she was now on six, not four.

She slowly sank into the chair and looked at the desk. She had been so careful not to leave any paperwork out in the open. She hadn't wanted Matt to find out this way.

Millicent had warned her.

Matt hadn't even given her an opportunity to explain. He had just walked out of the house and her life without saying a word. She couldn't blame him. The evidence had been incriminating.

Tears filled her eyes as she thought about her next step. She had two choices. One, she could pack up Austin and fly back to San Diego an emotional wreck and blow this one chance for true happiness. Let someone else from the company come out to Maine and complete her assignment.

She could prove to her father that he had been right all along, that emotions and business could never mix. That when the tough choices had to be made, the woman would make them from the heart, not with her head. And then she would drive herself sick wondering if she had made the right choice. She would become her mother all over again.

She wasn't her mother. She was stronger than that.

Or, number two, she could stay in Misty Harbor and fight for what she wanted. She wanted her father's respect and an acknowledgment that she was just as good as the other executives of the corporation. The other, all male, executives.

She wanted her father to see once and for all she wasn't her mother. She could be a woman, a mother, and a businessperson without falling apart.

She wanted a home for Austin. A real home, with good friends for them both that had nothing to do with the Randall Corporation or how big her bank account was or what her last name happened to be.

But most important, she wanted Matt. She wanted the man she had fallen in love with.

Chapter Sixteen

Wednesday morning was damp and overcast, but that didn't stop the tourists from lining up to buy whale-watching tickets. Juliet knew Steve had to get going, but she didn't want to stop kissing him. "I'll call you tonight, okay?"

"Please drive safely." Steve kissed her again for good measure. "You have my number, right?"

"Your home number, your cell phone number, and your e-mail address." Juliet hugged Steve tighter. They were in Gordon's apartment, while her mother and Gordon were downstairs giving them some privacy. "I'll see you at the beginning of October." October was a whole month away.

"If I can last that long without kissing you." Steve kissed her again. "It might be the end of September."

She laughed. It beat crying. "Okay, get going. I'll talk to you tonight." For the past three days it had been nearly impossible to get a moment alone with Steve.

Her mother had ruined her love life by arriving in Misty Harbor. Gordon at least gave her and Steve some space and time. Her mother was clinging tighter to her than Saran Wrap. At first she thought it was because her mother really had missed her. Then she realized the real reason. Victoria Carlyle was using her as a shield against Gordon.

Gordon was doing the same thing. Neither one wanted to be alone with the other. Juliet didn't think it had to do with anger, resentment, or being mad at each other. She thought her parents still had feelings for each other. Only a blind man wouldn't be able to see the looks they gave each other when they thought the other wasn't looking.

It was cute. It was also embarrassing having your parents make cow eyes at each other. They should get a room.

Juliet frowned. Her mother had been sharing Gordon's guest room with her for the past several days. Her mother wasn't packed, nor did she show any signs of leaving today, which meant her mother and Gordon were going to be alone in the shop, and in the apartment.

She really didn't want to think about that one too closely.

"Come on, Steve, you're going to be late for the boat." She tugged him toward the stairs. "Your uncle doesn't strike me as the most reasonable man."

"Lawrence is a marshmallow behind that wall of steel." Steve gave her another quick kiss before starting down the stairs. "You should meet his wife."

Five minutes later Gordon placed Juliet's suitcase in the trunk of her car. "Are you sure you have everything?"

"If I don't, I'll get it at Thanksgiving."

"So you're definitely coming then?" Gordon seemed thrilled by the prospect.

"Wouldn't miss it for the world." Juliet kissed his cheek. "You take care of the shop. I'll be inspecting for dust when I get back."

Gordon chuckled. "I don't know who you'll be coming to see, Steve or me."

"Both." She wasn't going to get into that argument.

"Hmmm . . ." Gordon's brow raised behind his sunglasses, but there was a smile playing on his lips.

Juliet glanced at her mother, who was nervously pacing in front of the shop. She lowered her voice and leaned in closer to Gordon. "I'm going to be very disappointed in you if you upset my mother."

Gordon frowned. "I asked her to stay an extra day or so, so we can talk. She said yes."

"As long as it's just *talking*," she teased.

Gordon snorted.

"Do I need to buy a shotgun?" Juliet repeated Gordon's words back to him.

"You're twenty-seven years too late on that one." Gordon was serious.

Juliet laughed. She had a somewhat better understanding of the situation. There was enough blame and heartache to go around.

"What's so funny?" Victoria walked over to them.

"Nothing, Mom. I was just lecturing Gordon on the virtues of a dust-free shop. It increases the profits, and he just might be able to afford that return trip to Venice he's been talking about."

"Venice?" Her mother seemed intrigued.

She kissed her mother's cheek and thought about how much her mother would love to travel overseas again. Ken Carlyle had been a "see America first" kind of guy. She doubted her mother had used her passport once in their entire marriage. "I'm sure Gordon will tell you all about it. Gordon loves to travel. It's what he does in the off-season."

She walked around to the driver's side of her car and got in. "I'll call your cell phone, Mom, as soon as I'm home."

"Drive carefully."

"Will do, and both of you behave. Try not to get into any more trouble." She put the car in gear and drove down the street with a huge smile on her face. Neither parent appreciated her last comment.

Victoria watched as her daughter's car turned the corner and disappeared from sight. Without looking at Gordon she walked back into the shop. Now the hard part was about to begin, the part she had been dreading for days.

How did she apologize for not telling Gordon she had been pregnant with his child twenty-seven years ago? Then to hide the fact he had a daughter for fifteen years, and then to send him a picture of her along with a letter begging him not to contact her, that some other man was raising her.

She was a horrible person. Seeing it from his perspective, sending him that picture and letter had to be the cruelest thing she had ever done. Gordon was never going to forgive her, and she didn't blame him.

Tears swam in her eyes as she wrapped her arms around herself. Maybe it would have been best if she had left with Juliet.

Gordon entered the shop and closed the door behind him. The OPEN sign was hanging in the window, but it was just too cool to keep the doors open.

She glanced over her shoulder at Gordon. Twenty-seven years, one wonderful marriage, and four children later and she still had feelings for him. Watching the interaction between Juliet and her father these past few days had been heartbreaking. They had practically finished each other's sentences. They had not only been on the same page, but also had been in the same paragraph.

As the old saying went, they were two peas in a pod. They should have been given the opportunity to know and love each other these past twenty-six years. "Gordon, I'm so sorry." Tears overflowed her eyes.

"Vicki, I need to say something before you continue any further." Gordon took a step closer but didn't touch her. He never touched her.

"First, there's nothing to apologize for. I was the one to break off our affair. I told you it was over. I was the one to tell you that I did not love you anymore." Gordon looked at her with love in his eyes. "I lied, Vicki."

"Why?" She closed her eyes and thought back to that night. "Why would you have said such a thing?"

"The board of trustees at the university found out about our affair. They suggested quite strongly that I end it immediately. To my lifelong shame, I did. I lied and hurt the woman I loved to save my precious job. When you didn't return to the campus in the fall, I made some discreet inquiries and learned that you had gotten married over the summer. I tendered my resignation and left the university halfway through that year."

"Oh, Gordon," she cried. "You loved teaching."

"'For of all sad words of tongue or pen. The saddest are these: "It might have been!"'"

She was crying in earnest now. He had loved her back then. "I don't know who said that." She didn't even think she could remember all the names of her children.

"John Greenleaf Whittier." Gordon took another step closer. "I want to thank you and Ken Carlyle for doing such a wonderful job raising my daughter, Vicki. Juliet is perfect, and for that I have you to thank."

She gave a very unladylike sniff. "You forgive me?" How could he when the guilt was smothering her?

"There's absolutely nothing to forgive you for." Gordon opened his arms and she flew into them.

Gordon's arms tightened around her like he was never going to let her go.

After a moment he pressed his lips to the top of her head. "Would you like to hear about Venice?"

With those words she knew she had been granted a new beginning. A different beginning. A better beginning. "I would love to."

Matt couldn't believe Millicent Wyndham had talked him into coming. Okay, she hadn't talked, she'd threatened. Millicent had asked him nicely to attend a meeting Sierra was holding with the board members of the Randall Corporation concerning a possible hotel on the coast of Maine. He had politely refused. He did not want to attend any business meeting concerning the lighthouse, and he sure as hell didn't want to face Sierra and her betrayal.

Millicent hadn't taken no for an answer and had threatened to use the one person guaranteed to get his butt there: his mother. The wrath of Peggy Porter thinking one of her sons had been impolite to Millicent would be unimaginable. He would rather swim with a great white shark than suffer the ire of his mother. At least with a seventeen-foot killer shark he stood a chance.

Matt parked his truck and slammed the door for good measure. Not only had Millicent insisted he be there, but she'd had the gall to hold the meeting at her house as well. He stomped his way up to the front door and rang the bell. It was two o'clock on a Friday afternoon and he'd had to leave a job in Ellsworth to make this meeting. There was no way he was getting into a monkey suit for it.

For more than a week he had been avoiding everyone and everything. He had even taken three days off and gone hiking alone up in the woods. The peace and solitude hadn't improved his mood. At the end of the three days he couldn't even stand himself.

"Hello, Matt. Glad you could make it." Millicent answered the door and welcomed him into her home. "Please come in."

"Thank you." He knew he was five minutes late. He would like to think he had done it on purpose, but he hadn't. Time had gotten away from him and there was a lot of traffic pouring into the area for the holiday weekend.

"We're meeting in the dining room." Millicent led the way.

Millicent had the grandest house in Misty Harbor. It screamed history, antiques, and money. Lots of money. Last year he had done a small renovation job in one of the bedrooms upstairs after a nasty storm had caused a leak in her roof. The formal rooms downstairs weren't for show. Every square inch of the large house had the same attention to detail.

Matt heard the murmur of voices before he entered the room. Millicent had pulled out all the stops for the meeting. One of the hand-carved mahogany servers was loaded with silver plates with fancy little cookies and cakes. She had even pulled out the antique sterling coffeepot and her great grandmom's china from France. He was impressed.

At the long table that could easily seat twelve, if not more, sat four men and Sierra. Austin was down at the other end all by himself coloring in a book. Austin glanced up, smiled, and waved.

He waved back. He had missed the little tyke.

"Would you care for something to eat or a cup of coffee before we begin?" Millicent was always a proper hostess.

"No, thank you." Matt walked to where Austin was sitting and took the seat next to him.

Without missing a beat, Millicent picked up her cup and sat on Austin's other side. "I believe we're ready, Sierra."

Sierra shuffled some papers. She was sitting at the head of the table with two big easels behind her. She hadn't once looked at him.

Matt leaned back in the chair and studied her. She was gorgeous, as always, but he could tell she had taken extra care with her appearance. She was wearing makeup and her hair was piled on top of her head in a neat, orderly twist that looked totally professional. Even her earrings were tiny and so un-Sierra-like. Today she was wearing a navy business suit with a white silk blouse. He didn't like this Sierra at all.

"First, I believe introductions are in order." Sierra nodded to a neatly dressed man in his sixties. "This is my father and the president of the Randall Corporation, Lucas Randall. The man next to him is our CEO, Jake Morley. Sitting across from them are Bob Turner and Mike Resnick." Each man nodded as his name was mentioned.

Sierra looked at Millicent. "Millicent Wyndham has graciously offered the use of her home for this meeting. She not only owns the lighthouse and the twenty acres it is sitting on, but she's Misty Harbor's town-appointed matriarch. Then there's Austin, whom you all know, and Matthew Porter. Millicent requested Matt attend this meeting for a couple reasons. He's also interested in buying the lighthouse property, and since he is a lifelong resident of the town, Millicent feels he has a vested interest in this meeting. I agree."

Matt sat there and frowned. Sierra hadn't looked at him. Oh, she made a good show of looking in his direction, but her gaze had been over his head and at the curtains behind him.

He leaned over and helped Austin select the right color of green for the frog.

"The Randall Corporation has a long tradition of building hotels that cater to our clientele's needs and wishes. They demand the best, and we supply them with it. It's my recommendation that the Randall Corporation build their next hotel on the coast of Maine. It's beautiful and majestic, with scenery that is unparalleled. We couldn't ask for a better location.

"That being said, the property Ms. Wyndham is considering selling, which includes twenty acres and a very charming, quaint, and historical lighthouse that would add that 'special touch' the Randall Corporation is known for, is not right for the company."

The green crayon snapped in half between Matt's fingers. Matt slowly raised his head and looked at Sierra. She had her back to the room as she flipped back the top sheet on the first easel.

Matt cringed when he saw the pencil drawing. Whoever the artist was, he or she was good. It was the subject matter that appeared all wrong.

"As you can see, to incorporate the lighthouse into a hotel that contained seventy-five rooms, as this one does, doesn't work. The structure overshadows the lighthouse. Every ounce of quaintness and charm has disappeared. Twenty coastal acres is not nearly enough land for the hotel, the lighthouse, the parking, the landscaping, or anything else. There is also no easy way down the cliff to the water below. Lighthouses were built to warn ships away from the rocks and shore. As you can see, there are plenty of rocks, which is all nice and scenic, but there's no way to access any kind of water recreation. The view is spectacular, but you might as well be landlocked."

Matt tried to remember to breathe. Sierra didn't want the lighthouse and the property?

Austin tugged on his sleeve. "Matt?"

"What's the matter?"

"You broke my crayon." Austin looked upset.

"I'm sorry, buddy. I'll buy you a new box." Matt trimmed some of the paper around the tip of the crayon. "See, you can still color the frog." He showed Austin that the crayon still worked.

Sierra went over to the other easel and flipped back the top page. "Since I believe it would be in the best interest of the Randall Corporation to build in Maine, I went looking for a more suitable piece of ground."

She stepped away from the easel so everyone could see the picture. This one was also in pencil and expertly drawn, but instead of cringing, Matt appreciated the historical feel of the hotel.

"This piece of property is about twenty miles from here and consists of a little bit over one hundred acres. There will be plenty of room, enough to build an eighteen-hole golf course right on the coast." Sierra turned the page and a drawing of the golf course appeared.

"There's thirty acres right on the coast." Sierra flipped to the next page. "As you can see there will be plenty of room to build a dock. Some of our clientele might prefer sailing into our resort instead of driving. We might also consider purchasing a few boats for some of our guests to rent."

Sierra turned another page. "My opinion, gentlemen,

the one you have paid me to have, is to build a coastal resort with all the amenities that our clientele expect."

Matt sat there stunned as Sierra's father, ex-husband, and the other executives started firing off questions in rapid succession. He could barely process a question by the time Sierra was firing back answers. Sierra was fielding every question with expertise that made him proud.

This was the businesswoman side of her she had told him about. He had seen bits and pieces of it during the planning of the wedding. But this was exceptional. That Sierra could put together such a presentation in such a short amount of time was a testimony to her drive, ambition, and talent. He could see the admiration in the men's eyes and knew the resort hotel would be built exactly where Sierra was recommending.

The questions finally started to die down.

"Excuse me, gentlemen," Sierra said. "There's more."

A murmur went through the table.

"I realize that this is hardly the time or the place, but I'm going to do it anyway. I want to be in charge of the planning and construction phase of the hotel. Then once the resort is ready to be opened, I want to manage the actual day-to-day operation of it.

"Furthermore, if the job is not offered to me by the end of today, I will be handing in my resignation, effective immediately. Austin and I will be living in Misty Harbor. No more hotel rooms, room service, and flying around the country on a moment's notice. I have already registered Austin for nursery school, which begins Tuesday, the day after Labor Day."

Bob and Mike started firing off more questions.

Sierra's father and ex-husband looked directly at Matt.

Matt felt the world shift beneath his feet. Sierra and Austin were staying. Sierra's father was giving him a speculative look. Jake Morley smiled at him and gave him the thumbs-up sign. He wondered if Jake knew he hadn't talked to Sierra in more than a week. He was a fool.

Just because Sierra was staying didn't mean he had won the lighthouse. He still couldn't afford his dream. Some other hotel chain would eventually snap up the property. If a hotel had to go up there, he would have rather it been Sierra's. Why hadn't he stayed that night and talked to Sierra? Why hadn't he stayed around to hear her side of the story? Why had his first and only reaction been one of betrayal?

Matt felt the pounding of a headache. Austin was tugging on his shirt and Sierra still hadn't looked at him.

Sierra watched Matt walk out of the dining room. A moment later she heard his truck start up out front and he drove away. *Well, that didn't go as planned.* She had been expecting some kind of reaction out of Matt. Instead, all she had received was silence.

Her father and Jake were looking at her with sympathy, but she took heart in Millicent's smile. Maybe it wasn't as bad as she feared.

"Sierra, the job is yours, if you still want it." Lucas Randall looked at her with love in his eyes. "You did a bang-up job on this proposal. Now tell us the downside."

A smile tugged at her mouth. Her father did in fact know her very well. "One person's downside is another person's challenge."

"Oh, Lucas, we're in for it now. I've seen that look before," teased Jake. "Spit it out, Sierra. Bob and Mike have a six o'clock plane to catch. They deserve to spend time with their families this holiday weekend."

"Did you two get settled in the bed-and-breakfast

okay?" She had made reservations for her father and Jake for the long weekend. She had hoped both men would be dying to see the property and the surrounding area and would spend some time with Austin.

"You're stalling, Sierra," Lucas said.

"Okay, the property is for sale, and just as I described, but there's a catch. The owner is asking a ridiculous amount."

Jake smiled that barracuda smile that perfectly matched her father's when they were on the scent of a challenge. "How long has it been on the market?"

"Eleven months"—she handed out packets to each of the men—"this time."

Her father raised a brow and opened his folder. "This time?"

"Mr. Jefferies has put that particular piece of property on the market three times in the past twenty years. Each time the asking price has been overpriced."

"Teddy's an unreasonable, stubborn old coot at times." Millicent chuckled as if her words were an understatement. "But there are ways around him."

"And you would know these ways?" Lucas Randall flashed Millicent a charming smile.

"For a price." Millicent didn't bat an eyelash.

Sierra wasn't positive, but there might have been a flush to her father's cheek. Was he trying to flirt with Millicent, or was it the other way around?

"I would love to discuss that price, say, over dinner tonight?"

"Of course." Millicent smiled. "Sierra warned me that you can be a charmer, Mr. Randall. I see that she was correct on that one."

Her father flashed her a quick look before turning his attention back to Millicent.

"The price I will be asking concerns all of you, and your future hotel. For my knowledge of—let's not call them secrets, let's say insights—into the workings of Teddy Jefferies's mind, I would like the four of you, and Sierra, to put your thinking caps on. Misty Harbor could use the influx of more tourists. I want you to try to figure out ways to promote our quaint little town to your clientele."

Jake chuckled. "You want us to go into the advertising business?"

"Not exactly." Millicent moved her now-empty cup so it was sitting perfectly in the center of the saucer. "People vacation in Maine for various reasons. There are lots of activities of interest in the area, from fishing, boating, and hiking, to sitting in our restaurants eating lobster and clam chowder. One of the main draws of the coast is our quaint fishing villages."

"You want us to promote your village to our guests."

Millicent smiled. "Exactly. Competition for those tourist dollars is getting tougher. We're not Bar Harbor, Camden, Boothbay Harbor, or any other major tourist town. We're one of the thousand 'cute, little, and quaint villages' that line the entire coastline."

"Are you trying to blackmail me, Ms. Wyndham?" Lucas asked incredulously.

"Not at all." Millicent looked offended at the mere suggestion. "You're free to go negotiate with Mr. Jefferies on the price of the property." Millicent neatly folded her linen napkin. "All I am saying is, once you're tired of beating your head and wallet against Teddy's stubbornness, we'll talk."

Lucas Randall threw back his head and roared with laughter. "By God, woman, I don't know if I should offer you a job or kiss you."

* * *

Sierra parked her rental SUV next to Matt's truck. She knew she would find him here at the lighthouse. She got out of the car and looked at him sitting on Carrie's Hill staring out over the ocean. She had come this far; she wasn't going to chicken out now. She took off the prim and proper suit jacket, tossed it onto the passenger seat, and untucked the white silk blouse. The earrings had come off during the short drive to the lighthouse. With quick fingers, from years of experience, she plucked the pins from her hair and shook her head. The breeze felt wonderful.

She now felt more like herself, a woman instead of a business entity.

Without saying a word, she joined Matt on Carrie's Hill. The sea was a sparkling blue and the afternoon sun felt wonderful against her face. She had been spending too much time indoors lately.

Five minutes went by before Sierra asked, "What are you thinking?"

"I'm trying to decide if 'horse's ass' is hyphenated or not." Matt knew he had been a horse's ass; he just didn't know where to begin with his apology.

When he had heard her SUV pull up to the lighthouse, he'd realized one very important thing. It was time for him to let go of one dream and reach for another. He would rather have Sierra and Austin in his life than a forty-foot stone-cold lighthouse.

"So Austin and you are moving to Misty Harbor?"

"Yes." Sierra kicked off her navy pumps and started to wiggle her toes in the grass.

"Where are you two going to live?" It was a reasonable question. He couldn't very well ask her to marry him and move into his apartment. He hadn't spoken to her for nine days. Besides, it was a one-bedroom apartment. Austin couldn't very well sleep on the couch every night. "The Alberts are due back in five days."

"I just signed the papers on eighteen acres of land." Sierra didn't look at him; she continued to stare out over the sea. "And I signed a year's rental agreement with Norah's mother for their cottage."

"Next to my parents?"

"One and the same. It fits my needs perfectly for now. Austin is so excited to be moving into a real house, especially one next to Tyler's grandparents."

"I see. So what kind of home will you be building on the land?"

"I don't plan to build on it."

He wished she would turn and look at him. Was that a smile tugging at her mouth? "Why did you buy it, then?"

"I fell in love with the view."

"Where's the property located?" The surrounding area had lots of land with outstanding views, but wouldn't she need a home to appreciate them? "What are you going to do? Park a lawn chair in the middle of it to admire the scenery?"

Sierra waved her arm to the left. "It's right there, and I won't need a lawn chair. I prefer the grass."

Matt blinked and looked left. "Right where?" The village of Misty Harbor was to the left, way left. He didn't know of any property up for sale between the lighthouse and the town.

Sierra picked up a small pebble and tossed it. It landed about ten yards from them. "Right there." She turned and finally looked at him and smiled.

He finally got it. Sierra had bought the lighthouse

and the land. "It's twenty-point-two acres, Sierra, not eighteen." It was a sweet gesture, but he didn't want Sierra to buy his dream. It had been his dream, not hers.

"I didn't buy the lighthouse or the two acres it's sitting on, Matt. Millicent split the property."

"Why didn't you buy it all?" He had done some research into Randall Hotels during the past several days. Sierra Randall-Morley had more money than Millicent, and Millicent was the richest woman he knew.

"I had it on good authority that a local resident has had his eye on the lighthouse for more than twenty years. I couldn't deprive him of that dream."

He might be able to afford his dream now, but it wouldn't be worth a thing if Sierra and Austin didn't share it with him. "How would you like to marry a horse's ass and share his dream?"

Sierra's eyes sparkled with unshed tears. "I was beginning to wonder if you had been calling me the horse's ass, or yourself?"

Matt looked at her as if she was nuts. "You didn't answer the question, Sierra."

"You didn't ask it properly."

"Sierra"—he reached out and brushed a lock of her hair away from her face—"will you marry me?"

"Yes." Sierra threw her arms around his neck and captured his mouth.

Matt allowed himself to be tumbled backward. The feel of her mouth was driving him nuts. "I love you, Sierra."

"I love you too." Sierra's prim and proper skirt was hiked up to midthigh as she straddled his hips.

Matt's hands slid up her thighs. "People are going to think I'm marrying you for the eighteen acres." He didn't like that thought at all. "Maybe you can turn them into a wildlife habitat or something."

Sierra closed her eyes as Matt's fingers went higher. "Can't, the land's not in my name."

Matt's fingers froze. "Whose name is it in?" If she'd bought the property and put it in his name, he was going to be furious. He'd buy his own dreams.

"Austin's. It was part of his trust money that bought the property. I figure he'll thank me in the future."

Part of his trust money? How much money did a four-year-old have in his piggy bank? "Good."

"I was going to buy it, Matt, but I figured the man I fell in love with wouldn't appreciate having the town speculate as to why you were marrying me." Sierra leaned forward and kissed him. "But someone had to buy the property, Matt. When you build our dream home, we won't want the view of the harbor or the town obstructed by an Ed's Beds Motel."

Matt chuckled as he rolled over, bringing Sierra beneath him. "Ed's Beds?"

"There are three of them outside of Seattle. Rumor has it he's looking to expand." Sierra sighed as his mouth trailed down her throat. "Do you realize this is the exact same spot where we first met?"

"Carrie's Hill—how could I forget?" Matt fingers undid her top button. "Where's Austin?"

"With his father and grandfather."

Matt smiled against the rapid pounding of her pulse. "Till when?" There was a chance they might be able to make it back to his place, if they had enough time.

"We have dinner reservations at seven."

Matt glanced at his watch and grinned. "We have three hours?" He stood up and hauled Sierra to her feet.

"Will it be enough time?" she teased as they hurried to his truck.

Matt didn't open the passenger door for her. Instead he pressed her up against it and kissed her like he'd been dying to do for the past nine days.

When they came up for air, he said, "No, Sierra, three hours isn't enough time. I'm going to spend the rest of my life with you, and it still won't be enough."

About the Author

Marcia Evanick lives with her family in Pennsylvania. She is working on her next contemporary romance set in Misty Harbor. Marcia loves to hear from readers, and you may write to her c/o Zebra Books. Please include a self-addressed, stamped envelope if you wish to receive a response.